He reacted violently even before he could identify his assailants. Legs thrashing and arms flailing, he tried to fight off the men who landed on top of him but they showed a remarkable ability to anticipate every move he made.

The odors of rancid fish oil filled his nostrils, and when he saw a copper-colored face, smeared with streaks of vermilion and green paint, looming directly above him, he knew his attackers were Indians. Desperately, in spite of the odds against him, he made an effort to break away, landing several solid punches to the face of the warrior who was trying to catch hold of his right arm.

No man could fight indefinitely against three-to-one odds, and at last the helpless Jonathan lay spread-eagled on the floor. The warriors continued to hold him, and the odor of the fish oil they smeared on their scalp locks was so pungent he wanted to retch. Then a movement from the far side of the room caused him to turn his head.

Looking up, he saw Felicity approach, and beside her was Andrews.

"I regret the need to dispose of you, Lewis," the former innkeeper said. "You and I might have worked well together, and your claim to your relative's estate would have been good enough to save me a great deal of bother. Apparently you still haven't learned that I permit no one to stand in my way when there's something I want. Now you'll never have a chance to learn it."

A HALL OF FAME *Historical Novel* ™

THE SENECA HOSTAGE

CARTER A. VAUGHAN

ace books

A Division of Charter Communications Inc.
A GROSSET & DUNLAP COMPANY
51 Madison Avenue
New York, New York 10010

An ACE Book

Produced by Lyle Engel

Published by arrangement with
Hall of Fame Romantic-Historical Novels, Inc.

Published simultaneously in Canada

2 4 6 8 0 9 7 5 3 1
Manufactured in the United States of America

Other Ace novels of passion, intrigue, and adventure by Carter A. Vaughan:

BRANDED BRIDE
THE CHARLATAN
ROANOKE WARRIOR
SCOUNDREL'S BRIGADE
THE YANKEE BRIG

SENECA HOSTAGE

1

The Awakening

Jonathan Lewis turned over in the feather bed, felt something beside him, and thought he was still at sea. Most nights he had been battered and bruised crashing into the bulkhead beside his bunk, and it was small consolation that, although the spring storms of 1753 were the worst in the memory of merchantmen, he hadn't once become seasick. Then, remembering that the long voyage from London to the New World had ended the previous day, he opened one eye.

On the pillow beside him he saw tousled, blond curls and instinctively reached for the girl. It didn't matter that, for the moment, he couldn't recall her identity. A raw March wind was blowing in through the open window, and, cursing the colonials for their uncivilized love of fresh air, he burrowed closer to his warm, soft-skinned bedmate. But the air helped to clear his head, and bit by bit he remembered.

He had felt both relief and disappointment when, from the deck of the brig, he had caught his first glimpses of Philadelphia. The largest city in the British colonies of North America, with a population of almost twenty thousand, was no more impressive than the sprawling country villages of England. Here and there Jonathan had seen sturdy, handsome buildings of red brick, but most homes, shops, offices, and even churches were made of whitewashed clapboard. And log cabins, which he had associated in his mind with the frontier wilderness, were common. The place looked as dull as the confined quarters of the heaving brig that had been his home for six long weeks.

What he liked best about the colonies was the knowledge that time he would spend here would be limited. He would present himself and the documents he had brought with him from England to Dr. Benjamin Franklin. Then, after completing the necessary formalities, he would dispose of the property located in the far reaches of Pennsylvania that had been left to him by a cousin he had never seen. With luck, he would be on board the *Matthew H.* when the brig returned to England within the week.

The discomforts of travel and of the brief visit to the New World were well worth the trouble. He would go home solvent. A sudden thought struck Jonathan, and he struggled out of bed, shivering as the chilly wind from the mountains of western Pennsylvania played across his bare body.

His wallet was intact, and the documents proving his ownership of the property had not been touched. Similarly, his eleven pounds, eight shillings, and threepence—his total fortune at present—were safe in his drawstring purse. He patted his sword, which rested on the unpainted pine table, then jumped back into bed.

This, he reasoned, was the second floor of the waterfront tavern he had visited immediately after leaving the ship. The dirt roads, which a heavy rain had turned to mud, had discouraged him, and the tavern, with scrubbed pine tables and sawdust-carpeted floor, had looked rather inviting. Certainly the hot, spiced drinks of West Indian rum and the local Pennsylvania ale had been both potent and delicious. Ignoring the slight throbbing of his head, Jonathan told himself that, later in the morning, he would go to the inn to which he had written for a room.

Meantime he again reached for the girl, then paused. His memory was functioning less than perfectly, but he seemed to recall that last night she had been a brunette. In fact, he was positive her hair had been dark. Propping himself on one elbow, he studied his partner and saw that his eyes had not deceived him this morning. She was a blonde, with fair skin, high coloring, and lips of almost cherry pink.

She stirred beneath his gaze, then a pair of long-lashed green eyes were fixed on his. She sighed happily, closed her eyes again, and nestled closer.

Reacting instantly, Jonathan began to caress her. Apparently he had been mistaken, but it really didn't matter. Blondes, brunettes, and redheads were all the same to him, provided they were attractive, and his hands told him this girl's figure was trim. He didn't know her name, but that was the least of his concerns. For the past ten of his twenty-seven years, females had been his principal preoccupation. In fact, women and gaming had cost him his commission as a captain in an elite dragoon regiment, the Second Royal Hussars, but the unexpected New World windfall would put him on his feet again.

And right now there was the girl to enjoy. He kissed her, his tongue probing and exploring, she responded by pressing close against him, and gradually the tempo of their love-making increased. Then, suddenly, a latch rattled and the door to the room creaked open.

Struggling to disentangle himself, Jonathan cursed under his breath. He had neglected to make certain the door was bolted, so he could blame no one but himself.

"What the hell do you think you're doing?" a deep male voice demanded.

Freeing himself from the clutching girl, Jonathan managed to sit up. "That," he said lightly, "should be obvious."

The man, middle-aged and burly, with a graying beard, was not amused. "You'll learn what we do to lechers here!"

Jonathan found himself staring into the muzzles of two heavy, cocked pistols.

His companion, meantime, moaned and burrowed deeper under the quilted coverlet.

"I'll attend to you shortly, miss," the man said.

Jonathan measured the distance from the bed to the table on which his sword rested.

"I wouldn't try that," the man said, then raised his voice. "Felicity!"

A dark-haired girl came into the room.

Jonathan blinked at her and knew his imagination had not been playing tricks on him. This was the wench with whom he had been drinking yesterday, the hussy who had accompanied him to this room. Unfortunately, that was all he could remember; but he certainly couldn't forget her deep green eyes or her hair, so black it had a sheen that was almost blue. Come to think of it, she was wearing the same puff-sleeved dress with the low neckline that had fascinated him.

She had been friendly enough yesterday, but now her eyes appeared hostile and her full, pouting mouth was compressed.

"Is this the rogue, Felicity?"

"Yes, Papa."

So the man was her father, Jonathan thought gloomily.

"What happened?"

"I sat at his table after I brought him his mulled-rum toddies and his ale. He said he'd never seen a colonial house, so I offered to show him through ours." Felicity spoke rapidly in a breathless voice, a quality that Jonathan distinctly recalled. "When we came in here, he said he was sleepy and started to undress, so I ran out."

"I see." The man nodded and tugged at his beard, then turned to the girl in the bed. "What do you say for yourself, Patience?"

"It wasn't my fault, Papa." The blonde spoke in a breathless voice, too.

Jonathan's gloom deepened. The armed man was his bedmate's father, too, and experience had taught him that men rarely appreciated finding their daughters under such circumstances.

"Tell me," the heavy-set man insisted, his pistols still carefully trained on Jonathan.

"The room was dark when I came in, and I couldn't find a lamp. So I undressed, and not until I climbed into bed did I realize anyone was in it." Patience seemed only slightly ill at ease. "That was when he caught hold of me—and threatened to kill me if I didn't stay."

She was lying, Jonathan knew. Never in his life, drunk or sober, had he threatened any female. Not only had it been unnecessary,

14

but he wouldn't demean himself. As for the rest of her excuse, it was lame—and absurd.

"Did he seduce you?"

"He was—trying—just now, Papa," Patience said.

"He won't do it again, I'll promise you." The man raised his voice. "Bailiffs!"

Two burly men in dark green uniforms, trimmed with pewter buttons, that were similar to those of Crown bailiffs in England entered the room and blocked the doorway. "What's your pleasure, Mr. Andrews?"

"As you can see, this fellow has tried to seduce my elder daughter. We got here just in time." The middle-aged man roared and shook his fist.

Jonathan couldn't help thinking that his anger seemed simulated. He was not concerned about Andrews, however; his own predicament absorbed him. Unarmed and naked, he could do little to help himself, particularly when outnumbered by the father of the girls and the bailiffs. Nevertheless he felt he had to try.

Grasping the blond Patience by her shoulders, he twisted her into a position in front of him so he could use her as a shield.

She struggled in an attempt to get away, but he needed her only for a moment, and actually released her before she screamed.

Ignoring his nudity, Jonathan leaped from the bed and made a lunge for his sword.

He moved so rapidly that he caught all three of the men off guard, and his hand shot out for the blade.

Felicity, however, reacted instantly. She was too fast for him and, snatching the scabbard, managed to remove the weapon before his fingers could close over the hilt.

Andrews promptly trained the pistols on Jonathan again, and the two bailiffs started to advance toward him.

Felicity hurried out of the room, still clutching the sword, and Patience followed, wrapping herself in the quilt as she pattered away on bare feet.

Jonathan paid no attention to the departure of the girls. The moment the bailiffs came between him and Andrews' pistols, he threw himself at the smaller of the pair.

The man defended himself with the six-foot pole of seasoned oak that was his badge of office and tried to fend off his attacker.

Jonathan grasped the pole and tried to wrench it from him.

The other bailiff recovered from his surprise and brought his own oak pole crashing down on the back of Jonathan's neck and shoulders.

The pain was stunning, but Jonathan did not loose his grasp on the pole.

The second bailiff, unencumbered, used his own weapon to trip the young Englishman.

Jonathan fell to the floor, still holding the pole, and the smaller bailiff was dragged down with him. Making no attempt to cushion himself, Jonathan concentrated on an attempt to subdue his opponent. Fists flailing, he struck the bailiff repeatedly in the face and stomach, trying to pummel him into sufficient submission to force him to drop the oak pole.

The others, however, did not remain idle. The larger of the bailiffs beat at the Englishman's back with his pole, and Andrews, entering the fray for the first time, brought the butt of a pistol down on the crown of Jonathan's head.

The room swam, and it became impossible for Jonathan to focus. Only by exerting all of his will power was it possible for him to retain consciousness, and, sprawled on the floor, he could neither speak nor move. He felt as though he was bound, hand and foot, and he suffered no pain when the bailiff he had assaulted struggled to his feet and kicked the inert Englishman in the ribs.

"You'll want to take him off to gaol at once," Andrews said.

"Never fear, sir, we'll lose no time," the smaller bailiff declared, gingerly feeling his nose.

"I hope it won't be necessary to bring my family into this matter," Andrews said, delicately clearing his throat. "Since both Felicity and Patience are unmarried maidens, I want to protect them from unwarranted gossip."

Both of the girls were seasoned trollops, the helpless Jonathan told himself bitterly.

Andrews, not waiting for a reply, picked up Jonathan's purse from the table and, opening it, gave each of the bailiffs several clinking coins. Then, absently, as though the money were his, he stuffed the purse into the hip pocket of his breeches.

Jonathan wanted to shout a protest but could make no sound. The purse contained every penny he owned in the world, and he was being forced to watch it disappear. The events of the previous evening and this morning were clear to him, even though the throbbing of his head made it difficult for him to think. Felicity and Patience had tricked him, this morning's dramatic confrontation had been carefully planned, and he had been a willing, stupid victim.

It pained him, too, to think that he was losing his sword as well as his money. The blade had a sentimental value and, as a weapon, would bring at least twenty pounds at the shop of any reputable London armorer.

While he continued to watch through blurred eyes, his anguish mounting, Andrews casually picked up Jonathan's handsome, silver-buttoned coat and draped it over an arm.

"The smallclothes belong to the rogue, as do the shirt, breeches, and boots." Still greedy, Andrews whisked Jonathan's plumed hat from a chair and draped it over a wall peg, as though it were his own. "I don't care whether you make him presentable here or in gaol, but I want all of his belongings removed. I own a respectable tavern, and I don't want my good reputation smudged by one of these waterfront lechers."

All at once Jonathan understood the situation, and wondered how he could have been so blind. He wasn't the first visitor to Philadelphia trapped and bilked by Andrews and his daughters, and undoubtedly wouldn't be the last. Although their haul from him probably was smaller than they sometimes made from other victims, they had no cause for complaint. A physician or lawyer of stature would have to work hard for a fortnight to earn what his sword and coat had cost, and the funds in his purse were a bonus.

"Don't you worry about this, Mr. Andrews," the taller bailiff said. "We'll protect you, all right, the same as always."

Jonathan was outraged when he saw the bailiff close an eye in a broad wink. He should have realized that these colonial law-enforcement officers were in league with the tavern keeper.

"If you'll grant us the use of a sheet, sir, we'll return it to you once we have him safely put away in gaol," the other bailiff said.

"I'll help you," Andrews offered.

All three wrapped the naked Jonathan so tightly in the coarse muslin sheet that, even had he been able to command his body to obey him, it would have been impossible for him to move, much less struggle free.

Andrews collected Jonathan's clothes as the two bailiffs picked up the inert figure. "Not bad boots, these," the tavern keeper said regretfully.

"Don't keep them, sir," one of the bailiffs said, sounding alarmed. "Remember the trouble we nearly had last year when—"

"Yes, of course I remember," Andrews snapped. "Trust me to take care of my end of this matter."

Jonathan's self-contempt was so great that, as they carried him down the stairs, he had no emotions left to despise his captors. It occurred to him that his small sea chest, containing his other clothing, was somewhere in the tavern itself, and that, too, would be confiscated.

A small carriage was drawn up at the entrance to the building, and the Englishman was dumped, without ceremony, on the floor. Then, while one bailiff sat above him, keeping watch, the other mounted to the outside seat. A few moments later they were moving, and every time they struck a bump in the rutted dirt road, Jonathan wondered if his head would drop off.

He must have dozed, for he remembered nothing more until he felt himself being removed from the sheet. The bailiffs dropped him onto a filthy straw pallet, and he realized he was in a cell. Then his remaining clothes fell to the floor beside him, and soon he was alone. A heavy door closed, he heard a bolt grinding into place, and, unable to fight his weariness any longer, he lost consciousness.

2

Gaol

The cell was a miserable hole, nine feet long and eight feet wide, evil-smelling and dark. Apparently it was located near the Philadelphia waterfront: the air was damp, water trickled down the stone walls day and night, and the straw pallet never dried out. The only light came through a window set high in the wall, and as nearly as Jonathan could tell it overlooked an inner courtyard which the sun did not reach. The food consisted of monotonous New World fare, principally parched Indian corn and jerked beef, with an occasional bowl of undercooked, tough venison stew or a dish of bear meat so greasy that someone unaccustomed to a wilderness diet could not eat it.

Neither the living conditions nor the lack of exercise caused Jonathan the most anguish, however. For the time being he had forced himself to accept the fact that he owned only the smallclothes, shirt, breeches, and boots he wore. But he could not tolerate the realization that the papers proving his ownership of the property he had inherited had been stolen from him by the tavern keeper, Andrews. It was bad enough that his purse and sword, his expensive coat, and dashing, plumed hat were gone, but his whole future depended upon his ability to gain possession of the property on the frontier and sell it for a profit.

His jailers would not listen to his story and, looking wise, smirked when he tried to tell them he had been robbed by Andrews and the tavern keeper's daughters. Twice, when Jonathan had explained that he had come to Pennsylvania to see Dr. Benjamin Franklin, who was acting as trustee for the property, the warden of the gaol had laughed aloud. "Dr. Franklin," the warden said loftily, "is the most distinguished man in all America. He doesn't associate with scum like you."

Compounding Jonathan's distress was the knowledge that he was being held indefinitely, without a trial, and that no one had any idea how long he would remain in gaol. "You'll be brought before one of the justices of the Crown Superior Court," the warden told him. "Right now both of them are riding circuit in the colony."

"When are they expected back? In a week? A month?"

"Who can say? But don't set your heart on going into court for at least a year or so!"

"A year? Then there will be no chance to recover my inheritance!"

The warden shrugged. "The justices left only a short time before you were brought here, and they're often away for at least six months at a time when they're riding the circuit, often longer. When they come home you can bet your last farthing the dockets will be crowded, so they're going to hear important cases before they get around to dealing with lecherous bankrupts. Be glad you have a roof over your head and food to keep you from starving. I know your kind. If you were set free you'd just get into mischief again, and would be back here, in my care, before sunset on the day I set you free!"

Jonathan was not permitted to send Dr. Franklin a letter, either, the warden refusing to annoy a man of his standing with a message from a penniless opportunist. So Jonathan languished in his cell and kept count of the days by means of a crude calendar he chalked on the wall with a pebble.

Then, late one afternoon almost seven weeks after he had been imprisoned, the monotony was broken. The bolt was moved, the door opened for an instant, and bailiffs shoved another figure into the cell. Before Jonathan could see the newcomer in the light of the corridor, the door crashed shut again and was locked.

In the deceptive half-light it was possible, at first, only to make out a few general characteristics. The new arrival was tall, husky, and appeared to be dressed in leather shirt and trousers. He was barefooted, the top of his head appeared to be bald, but a tail of long hair snaked down his back to his shoulder blades and, presumably, was held in place by an eelskin, which so many colonists used.

"Welcome," Jonathan said. "The gaol must be crowded if they've put someone else in a hole this size."

The newcomer made no reply.

Peering at him in the gathering dusk, Jonathan saw his high checkbones, became aware of his exceptionally black hair, and, when he finally made out the shade of the man's coppery-colored skin, realized he was an Indian.

Without warning the Indian sprang at him, both hands clutching at the astonished Jonathan's throat. They crashed to the stone floor together.

"Are you mad?" Jonathan demanded, trying to ward off his assailant.

The Indian replied by driving a knee into his groin, doubling him over, then clutching at his throat again.

When the first shock of pain began to subside Jonathan found that the breath was being choked out of him by a pair of exceptionally strong hands. The frustration of weeks combined with his surge of anger, and he smashed a fist into the pit of the Indian's stomach, simultaneously catching hold of the man's nose and trying to tear it off.

The Indian's howl sounded like the scream of a wounded animal, his grip relaxing for an instant.

That brief respite was all Jonathan needed. He tore himself loose and again lashed out at his opponent, his left once more finding a target in the Indian's stomach while his right landed a bruising blow on the attacker's checkbone.

The Indian, although hurt, managed to rally quickly, and both men were locked in a deadly embrace. They rolled over and over, punching and kicking, occasionally landing against the hard wall, but so preoccupied with their struggle that they did not know it.

A pungent odor that assailed Jonathan's nostrils when their faces were only a few inches apart explained the assault. The Indian had

21

been drinking large quantities of potent whisky, and the smell seemed to permeate the cell. He was too far gone in his cups to reason with him, however, and Jonathan was so aroused that he had no desire to calm the savage.

Furiously, almost indifferent to the punishment he himself received, he systematically gave the Indian a severe drubbing. His fists landed repeatedly on every part of the man's face and torso, and although it became an agony to lift his arms and strike again, Jonathan knew his opponent was weakening, too.

Then the Indian's legs caught him across the middle in a viselike grip. Unable to free himself, Jonathan knew he could not tolerate the agony for more than a very short time. Calling on his last reserves of strength, he put all of his body, all of his mental anguish into his final blows. The Indian rocked backward, his head bobbing, and his legs relaxed their grip as he rolled over and sprawled face down on the pallet.

Jonathan wondered if he had killed the man, but the sound of his breathing was reassuring. It was, at best, a small satisfaction, however, to know that he had knocked his assailant unconscious.

Sitting up, Jonathan leaned wearily against the damp stone wall until he caught his breath. He felt too weak to pull the Indian from the only pallet in the cell, so he left him there. An hour later, when the turnkey brought their evening meal, Jonathan enjoyed the spoils of his victory. He ate both portions of the stringy venison stew before stretching out on the hard floor and dropping off to sleep.

The dirty gray light of morning came in through the window, awakening Jonathan, and for a moment he could not remember why his throat and body felt so sore. Then his cell mate stirred and the Englishman sat upright, ready to renew the battle.

The Indian was in no mood for combat, however. He groaned, hauled himself to a sitting position, and slowly drew an exploring hand over his battered face. For some minutes he gave no indication of recognition, but suddenly he spoke.

"For eight winters and nine summers," he said, "Li-solu was the strongest warrior of his people. Many tried to take the feathers of the eagle from his headdress, but none could do it." He raised a hand to his shaved scalp lock and grimaced. "Now he can wear the feathers of the eagle no more."

The remnants of Jonathan's anger vanished. "You'd been drinking," he said generously. "I doubt if I can beat you when you're sober."

The Indian made a curt gesture. "Whisky does not rob Li-solu of his eagle's strength. When he leaves this place, he will give the man of Pennsylvania his eagle's feathers."

Jonathan hastened to assure him that he was not a Pennsylvanian. Then, starved for companionship, he poured out the whole story of the trickery he had suffered. His cell mate made no comment, however, so Jonathan was uncertain whether the warrior understood him.

After a long silence, Li-solu looked at him. "The enemy of the man of England is the enemy of Li-solu." Speaking slowly, with great solemnity, he told his own tale. He had arrived in Philadelphia with two bales of beaver pelts but had made the mistake of stopping at a tavern before selling them. There he had paid for a drink of whisky with three copper coins and had intended to go on his way.

But the proprietor had insisted on giving him another drink, free of charge, then another. Li-solu couldn't remember how many he had consumed; in fact, many details of his day were hazy. But he vividly recalled that several bailiffs had come into the tavern and had placed him under arrest and had overpowered him in the scuffle that had followed. He had been dragged away, forced to leave his very valuable furs behind.

"It sounds like the same rascal who hoodwinked me, all right," Jonathan said. "Was he a heavy man, with a thick chest and red hair?"

The warrior inclined his head. "Li-solu will scalp him but will not keep the scalp. He will give it to Jo-na-tan."

Their friendship was born at that moment, and their fight of the previous night, if not forgotten, no longer stood between them. Over their breakfast of parched corn and jerked beef, which the Indian relished, they began to talk of escape.

23

Weeks of incarceration gave way to months, but none of their many plans materialized. Spring became summer, but they could develop no concrete plan that might give them their freedom, and when the first hint of autumn drifted into the cell on the breeze from the west, they were still talking, still plotting in vain.

The months were not wasted, however. Li-solu, who was also in his late twenties, was as anxious as Jonathan to keep in good physical condition. So the Englishman taught the warrior how to use his fists in a fight, and Li-solu taught him the fine art of wrestling, Indian style. For want of anything better to do, they gave each other language lessons, too, and by the time September came, Jonathan had acquired a crude but effective working knowledge of his cell mate's tongue.

He also picked up a considerable quantity of information about the savages of the New World. Li-solu was the headman of a village in the country of the Seneca, which, he said, was the proudest of warrior people in all the world. His tribe, he explained, were members of a powerful nation, the Iroquois, and one day they intended to regain all of the territory they had lost to the settlers who, in ever-increasing hordes, had come to rob them of their hunting grounds and planting lands, their rivers and lakes.

Jonathan's one desire was to leave America as rapidly as possible and return to the civilized world he had known in England. Indifferent to the New World's fate, he encouraged his cell mate, and one day, when the warrior asked whether he would be willing to help the tribes of the Iroquois, he replied recklessly. "I'll never fight on any other side," he said.

That declaration not only sealed the bond of their friendship but spurred the Indian to action. "Now," he said grimly, "Jo-na-tan and Li-solu will leave this place."

The same evening they struck, using one of the many questionable plans they had mulled and discussed so frequently. The element of risk was great, they knew, but their boredom and sense of desperation were greater, making them indifferent to the possibility of failure. Their wait for justice was proving interminable, and they might continue to languish in prison for many more months, even years, before being placed on trial. So, even if they failed and were forced to face the consequences, they felt they had nothing to lose.

That night, when their evening meal was brought to them, they went into action. The prison routine was unvarying: the guards came through the cell block in pairs, one carrying bowls of food into the individual cubicles, while the other waited for him beyond the door. Jonathan accepted the bowls from the keeper, and meanwhile Li-solu, who had moved into place behind the man, leaped on him, clamping one hand over his mouth. Jonathan sprang, too, as rapidly as he could put down the food, and between them the pair subdued the guard.

Speed was essential, since the keeper who waited in the corridor would raise an alarm if his partner was gone for more than a few seconds. So, the instant the first guard struck the floor, where Li-solu continued to hold him, Jonathan stepped into the corridor and, catching the other man off balance, hauled him into the cell and tripped him.

The man was young and vigorous and tried to shout as he struck back, but Jonathan's strength was greater, and the talents he had acquired as an Indian wrestler gave him an added advantage. He pressed his foe's face into the floor, muffling the man's shout, then deliberately banged his forehead against the stones in order to knock him unconscious. He had to repeat the grim act twice before he accomplished the goal.

Li-solu had done the same to his opponent, and the two prisoners worked swiftly, tearing strips of cloth from the keepers' shirts to use as gags. Jonathan had planned, initially, to steal the uniforms of the guards, but both men were so much shorter than the prisoners that it was not feasible to follow through with the idea. He and Li-solu had to be content to leave the unconscious men in the cell and hope they could make their way out of the gaol undetected, even though wearing their own filthy, stained clothing.

Bolting the door behind them after discovering, to their disappointment, that neither of the guards had been armed, they walked stealthily down the corridor to their left. Neither was familiar with the geography of the building or knew what to anticipate, but they realized they had to depend upon their physical prowess, heightened by their sense of danger.

The corridor was empty, and they could hear nothing but a few muffled, scraping sounds behind the closed doors of some of the cells. At the end of the corridor they peered around the corner, then turned right. Ahead were other cells lining the left side, but on the right, about five feet from the floor, was a row of windows that faced onto the street.

Rather than risk the unknown that lurked beyond the closed door at the end of the corridor, Jonathan decided it would be best to leave by way of a window. He hoisted himself up onto the ledge, Li-solu giving him a hand when the Indian realized what he was doing. The window was closed, although the night was warm, and had been painted recently, so it could not be budged.

Li-solu had been watching anxiously from below, and when he recognized the difficulty he scrambled up to the ledge, too. Both exerted all their strength, and at last the window loosened and began to move, a fraction of an inch at a time.

The sound of a man's voice broke the silence. "I'll relieve Ned as soon as they've finished feeding the prisoners," a man beyond the closed door at the end of the corridor said.

It was obvious that more than one guard was on the far side of the door, so Jonathan and Li-solu worked frantically, trying to make no sound as they worked the window higher. Little by little they raised it, expecting the door to open at any moment. But they remained undetected by the time they had pried up the window a little more than two feet, and Jonathan gestured sharply, indicating in pantomime that he wanted Li-solu to precede him through the window.

The warrior would have preferred the place of honor, at the rear, but this was not a moment to dispute the matter, so he wriggled through. The instant his head disappeared Jonathan followed and dropped to the dirt road outside the gaol.

After months of imprisonment the pair were free. They hugged the outer wall of the building while they got their bearings, and Jonathan drew a deep breath. The air here was fresh and clean, and he promised himself he would die before he would allow himself to be recaptured and sent back to prison.

The night was dark, but, up a narrow lane directly ahead, he could make out the masts of merchant ships a few town squares away and knew his original estimate had been correct. The prison was located only a short distance from the waterfront. Nodding to Li-solu, he started forward, the Indian keeping pace beside him.

Suddenly, on the far side of the street, they saw someone watching them, openmouthed. Afraid a shout would bring guards hurrying out of the gaol, Jonathan raced across the road. Hoping to intimidate the frightened witness, he reached inside his shirt for an imaginary knife.

Li-solu obviously intended to use more violent tactics, and Jonathan had to restrain him. Colonials, the Englishman guessed, were similar to the citizens of London, who not only raised no outcry but actually were pleased when a prisoner managed to escape from Newgate. But the atmosphere would change sharply if an innocent passer-by was harmed; then a town might become ugly and hundreds would join the bailiffs in a search for the escaped criminals.

The witness, Jonathan saw, was a young boy of about seventeen who, in spite of his fear, grinned broadly as he raised a finger to his lips.

"I won't give you away, I swear it," the boy whispered.

Li-solu frowned, flexing his fingers.

But Jonathan decided to take the chance and clapped the boy on the shoulder. "Thank you kindly," he said. "I hope I can return the favor someday." Not waiting for a reply, he made his way down the narrow lane.

The Seneca, at his heels, was dissatisfied. "Only women," he said, speaking in his own tongue, "are soft. Enemies should die."

"The boy isn't our enemy, and we don't want all Philadelphia to join in the hunt for us."

They walked swiftly, in silence, but the boy kept his word. No alarm was given, and they heard no commotion from the direction of the prison.

Jonathan's mind raced, and he knew they needed baths, a razor, and clean clothes to make themselves less conspicuous. Their disreputable appearance marked them, and it would be difficult, perhaps impossible, for them to leave Philadelphia undetected until they changed. Their lack of money and weapons would make the task complicated, however.

Suddenly a thought struck Jonathan, and a trace of humor appeared in his eyes. "We need clothes, food, all kinds of things."

"Steal them," Li-solu said calmly.

"That shouldn't be necessary. There's somebody in this town who's in our debt, and I think the time has come for him to repay what he owes us."

3

Dr. Franklin

Although the waterfront tavern enjoyed its heaviest trade after sundown, the place seemed deserted. Jonathan, carefully peering in a window, saw only one oil lamp burning at the far end of the main room. The tables were empty, no serving maids were on duty, and, when he tried the front door, he found it locked.

He and Li-solu were not to be denied, however, and went around to the rear of the building. There they found a cellar door unlatched and quietly let themselves into the building. Potatoes were stored in bins, garlands of onions were hanging from the low ceiling, and the cellar was badly cluttered. But the Indian, who led the way, apparently had no trouble seeing in the dark and made his way confidently to an inner staircase.

They mounted it and found themselves in the main kitchen, but it, too, had a deserted air. No fires were burning in any of the three hearths, but through the largest of them, which opened onto the main dining room on the far side, came the glow of the single oil lamp. The feeble light faintly illuminated the kitchen, and Jonathan saw a man, facing the counter, who was carving a slice of ham from a large joint. He stood with his back to the room, unaware of the intruders, and was absorbed in his task.

There was no need for Jonathan to signal Li-solu. Together they advanced and together they leaped, the Seneca wrenching the knife from the carver's grasp while Jonathan bore him to the floor.

The man, although surprised, fought valiantly but was no match for Jonathan and soon was spread-eagled on his back. "If I had any money," he said, sweat glistening on his bald head and round face, "I'd give it to you. Since I don't, kill me—and have done with it."

"We aren't robbers, and we aren't murderers," Jonathan replied. "Where is Andrews?"

"I might have guessed you were friends of his," the man said, and laughed savagely. "I'd like to find him myself!"

Li-solu had recovered the knife and stood a few feet away, ready to use it.

Jonathan released the victim. "Answer my question. Where is he?"

"If I knew, I'd follow him to the ends of the earth to get my money back!"

"He cheated you, too?"

Struggling to a sitting position, the man eyed his tormentors. "Everybody in these parts knows he sold me this tavern—and then left with all the whisky, rum, and other liquor that was included in the price I paid him."

Jonathan laughed, too. "It looks as though we might be on the same side," he said, and helped the tavern keeper to his feet. Quickly, without mentioning their imprisonment, he explained that he and the Seneca had been cheated out of all their earthly possessions by Andrews, too.

The tavern keeper nodded as he struggled to his feet. "You wouldn't hear me complaining if you found him and beat him within an inch of his life. But he and those wenches he called his daughters left Philadelphia more than a month ago, and only the Lord God Almighty in His wisdom knows where they've gone. Just like the Book of Proverbs tells us, 'The wicked flee when no man pursueth.'" He broke off and again studied the intruders. "You lads look as though you wouldn't object to a meal."

"We don't have a penny between us," Jonathan said.

"Who mentioned anything about money? Abel French has never turned away a friend in need, and any foe of Andrews is my friend!" He reached for the knife.

Li-solu quickly stepped back, beyond his reach.

"Give it to him," Jonathan said. "Mr. French will do us no harm."

The Indian reluctantly obeyed.

Abel French cut each of them a generous slice of ham, placed a loaf of fresh bread and a slab of sharp cheese on the counter, and gestured. "Help yourselves, lads."

Jonathan and Li-solu ate ravenously.

While they consumed their meal, the first appetizing food they had seen in months, French told them his story. After spending more than thirty years as a cook, first on board merchant ships and subsequently at inns in New York and New England, he had decided to invest his life savings in a place of his own. So he had come to Philadelphia, the largest and fastest-growing city in the colonies, and when he had debarked from the brig that had brought him here from Boston, his footsteps had led him to this place.

Andrews, always attentive to strangers, had joined him at his table, and when French had confided his goal, his host had immediately offered to sell him the tavern. They had concluded the deal the following day and had celebrated the sale with a jug of what Andrews had called a precious West Indian white rum. French could not remember falling asleep, but did not wake up for almost twenty-four hours, and by then Andrews, his daughters, and the liquor supply had vanished.

"It does no good to open a tavern when you can't sell your customers a drink of whisky or a glass of wine," French said mournfully, "and I don't know a soul in this town, so I can't get a ha'-penny's worth of credit. I've been using the last of my shillings for food to keep myself alive, and when that's gone I suppose I'll have to sell this property, getting what I can for it, and hire myself out as a cook again. Yes, and the lack of spirits isn't all. I can't even hire people to help me. I'm a pauper!"

Jonathan's mind raced. He and Li-solu had planned to leave Philadelphia at once, but it was possible he could stay here until he could rehabilitate himself sufficiently to pay a call on Dr. Benjamin Franklin in the hope that, even without the necessary documents, he might be able to put in a claim for his inheritance. Certainly the provincial bailiffs and constables wouldn't dream of searching for the escaped prisoners within a stone's throw of the gaol.

"My friend and I," he said carefully, "might be willing to help you out for a time. All we'd want would be our room and board."

French chuckled. "I've got me a feeling," he said, "that you lads haven't seen daylight in a long time. But I'm not the sort who'll turn on you, and I'm tired of living here alone, waiting for bankruptcy. With no customers to serve, I have no need for a staff, but you could help me put the place in better shape, and maybe I can wangle a higher price when I sell it."

Jonathan and Li-solu had found a temporary refuge.

Within a half-hour they had drawn a dozen buckets of water from the well at the rear of the tavern. Jonathan shaved with French's razor, and Li-solu scraped the top of his head with it while they waited for tubs of water to boil on the largest hearth. They soaked in hot water, washing away the dirt of months with soft, yellow soap that French had made himself, and then boiled their filthy clothes in suds, too.

Clean at last, Jonathan went to bed that night in the room where catastrophe had struck, and all night he dreamed of Patience and Felicity Andrews, who had been responsible for his undoing.

The following morning he chopped wood and started to work scrubbing the floors and walls of every room. There had been a time when such menial labor would have been beneath him, but his months of imprisonment, combined with his desperate situation, had changed him, and he labored without complaint.

At noon Abel French called him out to the kitchen for more ham, bread, and cheese, and looked at him dolefully. "The Indian," he said, "is gone. He disappeared right after breakfast."

Jonathan was astonished. "I thought he was doing things for you elsewhere in the house."

"I haven't set eyes on the creature and good riddance, I say. I've never seen one of them I trust."

"That isn't like Li-solu," Jonathan said.

"They're all the same."

"Not Li-solu," Jonathan insisted as he returned to work.

That afternoon, as he continued to work, he wondered if he had been mistaken. While it was true that he and the Seneca had shared a cell for months, he could not really claim that he understood the

Indian. The mentality of the savage was not like that of civilized men, and he guessed that Li-solu had been anxious to return to his own people in western New York. Jonathan could not really blame him. Sheer necessity was forcing the Englishman to remain in the colonies, and he heartily wished himself back in England, even if he had to give up his now-remote inheritance, not to mention his chances of retaliating against Felicity, Patience, and their father.

Soon after sundown, however, as he and French prepared their evening meal, his faith in Li-solu proved not to be misplaced. The kitchen door creaked open, and the Seneca came in slowly, staggering under the weight of a burlap sack slung over his shoulder. He placed it on the floor and, his expression impassive, began to remove the contents.

Jonathan and the tavern keeper stared at one another in amazement as Li-solu lined up jugs of whisky, rum, and brandywine on the counter. Then, giving them no chance to question him, he hurried out into the yard again, returning with a burlap-covered wheelbarrow. In it were several jugs of English and Dutch gin and more than a dozen bottles of French and Spanish wines.

"This is a miracle!" Abel French exclaimed.

"I don't believe in them," Jonathan said, and turned to the Indian. "Where did you get these?"

"Friend of Li-solu need whisky. Li-solu get."

"I'm asking no questions," French said hastily.

Jonathan, on reflection, was inclined to agree. The Seneca was already a fugitive from justice, so the charge of stealing liquor, if he should be apprehended, would not add appreciably to his sentence.

The tavern reopened the following day, with French acting as cook and host. Jonathan, a leather apron over his threadbare clothing, worked as the waiter and felt fairly secure in the presence of customers. Only the guards at the prison had known him by sight, and even they were unlikely to recognize him without the beard he had grown in his cell. His hair had been matted and so dirty it had looked almost black, but now, scrubbed clean and tied with an eel-skin, it was its own medium shade of brown again.

Li-solu made no appearances in front of patrons, however. In the event that the city knew of the escape of the fugitives from prison, too many guests might regard the presence of the Seneca at the tavern as other than coincidental. So, even though hating the work of civilized men, Li-solu remained in the kitchen, washing dishes, emptying slops, and removing garbage.

By the second day business had doubled, and at the end of the third French had enough cash in hand to buy some beer, ale, and a greater variety of food than he had on hand in his larder. After the tavern had been operating for a week, French showed a profit of seven pounds, which enabled him to replenish the dwindling liquor supplies.

The tavern keeper's future was assured, and he wanted to show his gratitude to the pair who had helped him in his time of greatest need. "The least I can do," he said, "is to split these profits with you."

"Then you couldn't buy more liquor," Jonathan said, and added sternly as he glanced at the Seneca, "besides, Li-solu might not be so lucky next time, if he tries to get you another batch in his own way."

"But I can't expect you to stay on here indefinitely," French protested.

"I'll stay," Jonathan said, "until you can afford to buy me the gentleman's clothes I'll need. Then I'll go about my own affairs."

That day was a month or two away, he thought, but his experiences in the New World had taught him unaccustomed patience. His chances of regaining his inheritance, much less selling the property, were so remote that he could place almost no hope in the recovery of the land. But, once he looked like a member of the gentry again, he might be able to arrange his return passage to England on credit. That was as far ahead as he allowed himself to look, refusing to dwell on the question of what he might do to support himself once he reached London.

The next day was the busiest the tavern had known since it had reopened. The fame of Abel French as a cook was spreading rapidly, and Philadelphians of quality were beginning to appear at the tavern in the questionable waterfront district to sample his baked oysters and thick soups, his roasts basted in the Continental manner with wines, and the pastries that he prepared on an open hearth in the presence of his patrons.

When the last of the diners finally left the establishment it was midnight, and while French and Li-solu labored in the kitchen, Jonathan cleaned and swept out the dining rooms, then spread fresh sawdust on the floor. His legs were weary, his feet hurt, and he was relieved when French decided they could finish in the morning. Jonathan dragged himself upstairs to bed, thinking again of the treacherous Felicity and Patience as he climbed into it.

Just as he was falling asleep he thought he heard Li-solu leaving the adjoining room. But he knew the Seneca was tired, too, so he thought no more about the matter and drifted off.

A shaft of late September sunlight slanting in through the open window awakened him in the morning, and he luxuriated in bed for a few minutes, thinking of the breakfast he would eat. Perhaps he would start with fresh-caught shad, grilled, or sausage meat made by the German settlers who lived in the countryside west of Philadelphia. In any case he would consume a large steak, topped with fried eggs, and with it would drink a pitcher of ale. When a man was not a prisoner in gaol, he thought happily, the New World could be a tolerable place in which to live.

Rising to shut the window, Jonathan stopped short. Neatly piled on a table and chair were mounds of clothing he had never before seen: a handsome suit of dark green wool, a black bicorn hat with a small feather jauntily tucked into one side, a short cloak, silk-lined, stockings of white silk and a pair of black boots made of unexpectedly soft leather. He inspected the items, one by one, and saw that, although not new, they had been worn only a few times.

His first thought was that Abel French had procured them for him, and he was grateful. But, by the time he was dressed, and found that the clothing fitted him surprisingly well, he made another discovery. Resting on the seat of another chair were a pistol, complete with a horn of gunpowder and a little sack of bullets, and a knife with a sharp, six-inch blade and bone handle. It was unlikely that French would have thought in terms of weapons, so the donor must

35

have been Li-solu. In that event, every scrap of clothing had been stolen, as had the weapons.

Abel French, already in the kitchen when Jonathan came downstairs, raised his eyes to the ceiling when he saw the Englishman dressed in the finery. "The Arabs of Tripoli had a saying," he declared, "and I can think of nothing else. 'Hang a thief when he's young, and he won't steal when he's old.' That Indian will come to no good end. He stole that splendid suit you're wearing."

"I'm afraid so," Jonathan said, fingering the butt of the pistol in his belt. "I found all this in my room—"

"Look what he did for me, will you!" French gestured toward the counter, where jugs of whisky and rum and bottles of wine stood in a long row. "Oh, he had a busy night, I can tell you, and this morning the bailiffs are going to search the whole town for him!"

"I'll tell him," Jonathan said firmly, "that everything he stole must be returned."

"It's too late for that. I assumed you knew."

Jonathan looked blank.

"He's gone."

"Where—"

"I was awake early, as usual," French said, "and I happened to look out my window. There was Li-solu, taking the reins of a gelding from a hitching post, mounting and riding off. He stole the horse, too, you can be sure of that! And if they catch him, they'll hang him."

"Nobody will catch him." Jonathan couldn't help laughing. "I'm going to miss the rascal, but I envy him. He's going home to his own people." He paused for a moment, then said, "And now that I look presentable, it's time I do something about going home, too."

"I've seen this coming, and I can't ask you to stay on with me, much as I'd like you here," French said, genuine regret in his tone.

Later in the morning the tavern keeper went off to hire a barmaid to wait on his patrons and an older woman to help him in the kitchen. When he returned, his mission successful, Jonathan left the establishment for his first visit to William Penn Street, in the city's best residential district. Lawns were spacious and well tended, with shade and pruned fruit trees, and the houses were handsome structures of red brick, many with porticos supported by neoclassical columns. Here, at last, Jonathan felt at home.

The house he sought was more modest than its neighbors. Set back about twenty feet from the road, it was small and conservative, with white shutters setting off the reddish-brown bricks. He hesitated for a moment, but a clutter of strange-looking equipment in the side yard convinced him he had come to the right place. An odd contraption of metal and wood stood on a platform that raised the object about eighteen inches from the ground, and several wires trailed from the machine to a shed at the rear of the house.

Tugging at his stock and brushing specks of invisible lint from his stolen suit, Jonathan felt a trace of nervousness as he walked to the front door. Even in England, Dr. Benjamin Franklin, deputy Crown Postmaster General for the colonies, had won renown.

It was said that few men, anywhere, were his equal. His annual book, *Poor Richard's Almanack*, sold thousands of copies each year and had made him wealthy. He was editor and publisher of the *Pennsylvania Gazette*, the leading newspaper of the New World, which he published himself. Scientists hailed him as an inventor. He was the founder of the American Philosophical Society, an organization which every colonial intellectual of consequence had joined. Unofficially, he was known as "the real Proprietory Governor of Pennsylvania," since he was the leader of the colony's Assembly and the president of Philadelphia's city council. And he was active in so many other fields that it was almost impossible to count them. He had founded the Library Company, the first circulating library in the world. He had organized the Philadelphia fire department and led a campaign to replace the city's many wooden buildings with more substantial structures of brick. He had spurred the formation of the Pennsylvania militia, of which he was honorary colonel, and had founded the Pennsylvania Academy, which he and his friends called the University of Pennsylvania. He had also founded Philadelphia's first hospital, invented a new paving block, and designed a new type of street lamp that was being adopted everywhere in the civilized world.

Jonathan's knock at the door was answered by a balding man of medium height in his late forties, who was wearing an old, ankle-length dressing gown over his faded suit and who shuffled in worn carpet slippers.

"I'm looking for Dr. Franklin," Jonathan said.

"You've found him." Benjamin Franklin peered at his visitor through the upper portion of the bifocal eyeglasses he had invented.

"Captain Jonathan Lewis, sir, formerly of the Royal Hussars."

Franklin's smile faded as he waved his guest into the house. "A trifle late for our appointment, aren't you, Captain?"

"You might say I was detained, sir—for six months."

Benjamin Franklin led the way to his book-lined workroom, a chamber of incredible clutter, with newspapers, documents, and sketches overflowing from tables. In one corner stood a model of the lightning rod that had made its inventor famous, and on the far side of the room was his potbellied iron stove, a heating and cooking device so popular that it had helped make him one of the wealthiest men in the English-speaking world.

"May I ask what made you so late, Captain Lewis?" Franklin waved him to a chair, then removed some books from it so he could sit.

Jonathan debated the matter for a moment. He was still a fugitive from justice, and his host, both officially and personally, was Philadelphia's first citizen. But Franklin reputedly was a fair and honorable man, so the risk of telling him the truth was preferable to making up an involved and circumlocutional lie. Jonathan related everything that had happened to him since his arrival in the New World.

Benjamin Franklin listened intently, drumming his short, unexpectedly pudgy fingers on the top of his desk. "When I was your age," he said after Jonathan had completed his recital, "I found the ladies attractive. I still do. But I've always believed in being circumspect, and I dare say you've learned a lesson, so there's no need to lecture you on the wisdom of moderation, Captain Lewis."

"None, sir," Jonathan said.

"I must commend you on learning an Indian tongue while you were in gaol. I've dabbled a bit in languages myself."

Jonathan couldn't help smiling as he glanced at shelves containing dictionaries and other volumes in French, Spanish, Dutch, Italian, Hebrew, Swedish, and the classical Latin and Greek.

"Before we go on to the heart of the matter that brings you here, Captain, I hope you realize you've put me in a most embarrassing position. As head of the Philadelphia council, it's my duty to call in the constabulary to arrest you."

Jonathan half rose from his chair.

"But as president of the American Philosophical Society, it's my duty to look at the human factors in your situation. Are you telling me the truth? I think so, for reasons I shall explain presently. So I believe I may be able to persuade the authorities to drop the charges against you, provided you'll do something for me in return."

"Of course, Dr. Franklin!"

"Tell no one you escaped from the Philadelphia gaol." Franklin laughed, then removed his spectacles and cleaned them. "I designed the place, and I was certain that no prisoner could escape from it. So you've struck a damaging blow to my vanity, Captain Lewis, although you prove my theory that human ingenuity always begets greater ingenuity."

Jonathan smiled broadly, too. "You can rely on me, sir."

"Now, then. Even if we assume you're free of the law, your position is an unfortunate one. This distresses me, as I was fond of your late cousin, Paul Lewis. We worked together, at one time, designing some paper money. Paper, you know, is certain to replace coins as the principal medium of financial exchange. If you're interested, I'll show you a pamphlet on the subject that Paul and I wrote."

"I'd like to see it, sir, although I never had the privilege of meeting my cousin."

"A fine lad, but restless. I encouraged him when he moved up to Lake Erie, in the territory that both we and New York claim. His property there was very extensive—"

"Ten thousand acres, isn't it?"

"Closer to twelve thousand, and he'd have made himself a very profitable plantation there if he hadn't died unexpectedly. A great pity. As trustee of his estate, I can tell you the property has a great potential value. To someone."

"To me, I hope."

"At the moment," Franklin said, "you stand rather far down the list. At about the time you sailed from England, I received the first of several communications from a woman named Elizabeth Johnson. She owns the property adjoining your cousin's, and she tells me she and Paul were betrothed. She insists he left her the estate and that she has ample proof of her contention. She sent me a copy of what she says is Paul's will, made out shortly before he died. If it proves to be legitimate, she has a strong claim. I'm no lawyer, but I suspect some adjustment can be made with the previous heir."

"I'm that heir, Dr. Franklin."

"You were, but your position has been weakened. A month or more ago, I received a visit from a man named Andrews, who was accompanied by his daughters, exceptionally pretty girls—"

"The rogues I told you about, sir!"

"Precisely. He had your documents of proprietorship—"

"Which he stole from me, as I explained to you!"

"—as well as a letter from you, to him, assigning the property to him in payment of your just debts."

"I neither wrote nor signed any such letter," Jonathan said. "After he found my papers he made up the letter himself, out of whole cloth. It's a forgery, Dr. Franklin!"

"I dare say." Benjamin Franklin sighed. "I'm inclined to accept your version of this whole affair, Captain Lewis, but the final disposition of the matter will be in the hands of the courts. If you care to pursue the question under the most difficult of circumstances. I'm under the distinct impression that Andrews has gone off to Lake Erie to take possession of the property personally."

"I'm not surprised," Jonathan said grimly.

"You must understand that, when he came to me, I had no reason to doubt the legitimacy of his position. So, since he seemed intent on going off to the frontier himself, I advised him to work out a personal accommodation with Mistress Johnson."

"I see what you mean about a difficult situation," Jonathan said. "I'm in Philadelphia. Andrews is digging in at the plantation on Lake Erie, and this woman—Johnson—is there, too."

"There's another factor I haven't mentioned," Franklin said. "A question of sovereignty. France has established military outposts in the area. In fact, she's claiming western lands owned by Pennsylvania and Virginia. We're hoping a war can be avoided, but I'm not so certain it can. You might be wise to forget your claims in the New World, Captain Lewis."

"Quarters on a merchantman are expensive these days." Jonathan refrained from adding that no prospects of earning a living awaited him in London.

"If you're short of funds, I'd gladly advance the price of your passage."

"Thank you, Dr. Franklin, but I'd have no way to repay you." A resolve hardened in Jonathan. "Don't misunderstand me, sir. I've dreamed of going home ever since I arrived in the colonies. I have no ties here, and from the little I've seen, America isn't the Promised Land, no matter what one hears."

Benjamin Franklin listened patiently and did not interrupt.

"But I've been wrong to think of going home." A light came into Jonathan's eyes, and they seemed to turn from hazel to green. "If I left now, without putting up a fight, I couldn't live with myself. Not even if I were rich enough to buy a brig for the sole purpose of carrying me across the Atlantic to England."

Franklin tried to remain impassive but couldn't help chuckling.

"I don't believe in surrendering before I've put my troops into the field, sir. I may not win this battle, but I have a score to settle with Andrews, and I'm going to fight."

"How, Captain Lewis?"

"I'll decide my tactics after I've seen the terrain. The other claimants are waging their war at Lake Erie. Obviously, I'll have to go there, too."

"I admire your courage, but I question your judgment. By your own admission, Captain Lewis, you know nothing of the New World."

"I've gone into the field with my regiment for months at a time!"

"In England, and perhaps on the Continent. You've never been more than a ride of an hour or two from a well-cooked bird and a chilled bottle. The American wilderness is unique, Captain Lewis. You'd travel through primitive country, a land of great dangers—"

"You forget, Dr. Franklin, that I've learned a smattering—more than that—of the Seneca language."

"You may never see the Seneca. Hundreds of our settlers have died at the hands of barbarians who scalped them without waiting to find out what languages they spoke."

"I'm not afraid—"

"Anyone who knows our frontier knows fear, Captain Lewis. It's your very lack of it that makes me apprehensive for you."

His opposition made Jonathan all the more determined. "I'm going to visit the property I've inherited, sir, and I'll drive off any poachers I find there!"

Franklin rose and wandered around the room, shuffling from bookcase to bookcase and aimlessly inspecting the titles of the volumes on the tightly packed shelves. "I feel a sense of responsibility for you, and I can't let an outsider who knows nothing of our interior wander alone into a nest of yellow-bellied hornets. Does the name of Robert Dinwiddie mean anything to you?"

"No, sir."

"He's the Royal Governor of Virginia, and my friend. I received a letter from him recently that may be providential." Franklin returned to his desk, sifted through the mounds of documents, and raised a folded parchment sheet, which he waved in triumph before opening and scanning it. "Are you familiar with our geography, Captain Lewis? Does the name of the forks of the Ohio River mean anything to you?"

"I'm afraid not, Dr. Franklin."

"Three rivers meet in the hills of western Pennsylvania—the Ohio, the Monongahela, which flows from the south, and the Allegheny, which flows from the north. The headwaters of the Allegheny's principal branch, French Creek, are located near Lake Erie, only a march of a day or two from the disputed property we've been discussing. Virginia has an interest in the area, and Governor Din-widdie is sending a courier party to visit the commander of the French troops who—as you've put it—are poaching on our soil. I believe I can arrange matters so you can travel with the couriers."

"I need no escort, Dr. Franklin."

"If you mean that, young man, you're a fool. At least four tribes of Indians, none of them our friends, are roaming through the region. Recently several regiments of French troops—we don't know how many—have moved in, as well. Your life would be in constant jeopardy if you traveled alone."

"Andrews has gone there, presumably with the trollops he calls his daughters. And the Johnson woman actually lives in the district. Surely I'd come to no harm in territory that's safe for females."

"In the first place, it isn't. In the second, they know the wilderness —and you don't. Heed my advice, Captain Lewis, or you may not live long enough to press your claim. I'll give you a letter of introduction. Take it, go to Virginia, and be glad of the opportunity to make the journey with men who know the American wilderness!"

4

The Gentleman from Virginia

Rural America in no way resembled what Jonathan had imagined. Riding the horse Dr. Franklin had given him, his purse heavy with the ten pounds in silver that had been Abel French's unexpected parting gift, he was constantly surprised and, in spite of himself, impressed, as he made his way southward to Virginia. He had expected to see wilderness everywhere, but instead found himself in a remarkably fertile land.

Vegetables and grains too numerous for him to count were being grown, and every farm boasted its cows, pigs, and chickens. Most of the inhabitants lived in large clapboard houses that only the wealthier country dwellers in England could afford, and although the dwellings at which he stopped to buy food or ask for a cup of water were simply furnished, usually with homemade chairs, tables, and even beds, the attitude of the colonials was astonishing.

Unlike the English yeomen, who recognized their inferiority to the gentry, Americans seemed to believe themselves the equals of any man. Jonathan found himself being welcomed everywhere, usually with hospitality that was overwhelming, but even though it was obvious that he came from a different class, his various hosts and their friends treated him with easy familiarity and in no way regarded him as their superior. Even those who had been born in England had acquired a new set of values after migrating to the New World.

The women, although quiet and plainly dressed in shapeless, homespun linsey-woolsey, were as forthright as their husbands and fathers. The children were unusual, too, by English standards. The boys could ride and shoot with skill, which only the sons of aristocrats could do on the far side of the Atlantic, and the girls seemed almost as adept at cooking and keeping house as their mothers. The self-reliance of Americans was startling, and it appeared true that they were developing a new breed.

Jonathan had intended to spend his nights at inns on the road but hastily revised his plans. Farmers insisted he remain overnight as their guest, refusing to accept money for his lodging or food, and finally he began to realize why there were so few commercial hostelries in the New World. There was literally no need for them, since the country dwellers, who led isolated lives, were eager for the company of visitors.

Alexandria, the seaport in northern Virginia that, after little more than a half century of existence was already one of the most important towns in the colonies, appeared to be unique. Physically it resembled many towns in England that Jonathan knew. Solid homes were made of brick or stone, and even those of wood were substantial. Graceful church spires dominated the community, the shops were filled with merchandise from London and Edinburgh, and the streets, unlike those of far larger colonial communities, were completely cobbled. The residents, both men and women, dressed with elegance and a sense of style reminiscent of Bath, England's leading watering spa. But there the resemblances ended.

Jonathan discovered that the other guests at the Crown and Sceptre, the inn at which he stayed, were similar in temperament and manners to the American farmers, regardless of their finery and breeding. American gentlemen put on no airs, spoke without restraint to strangers, and treated menials, including the grooms and other servants, as their equals.

It was not easy to adjust to this approach, but Jonathan began to find, as he acclimated to it, that he enjoyed the informality. It would be even more difficult when he returned to England, he thought, to accept the stiff conventions observed there.

The greatest surprise awaited him in the person of the man Governor Dinwiddie had appointed to lead the expedition to the French forts. Major George Washington, an officer in the Virginia militia, was a planter by vocation and owned an estate near Alexandria. Tall and slender, with an austere manner, Jonathan found, in their first meetings, that he seemed lacking in a sense of humor. He dressed in the latest modes, rode his horse with the natural grace of the born aristocrat, and appeared ever-conscious of his dignity. But it was the contradictions in his nature that made him surprising. He was thoroughly familiar with the wilderness, he indicated, having traveled there extensively as a surveyor. And, in spite of all he had done and the obvious high standing he held in the colony, he was only twenty-one years old.

"I suggest," he said when Jonathan presented Dr. Franklin's letter to him, "that we become acquainted during the next ten days before I set out for the frontier. That will give me the opportunity to judge your character, and I can decide whether you'll fit into my party."

Unaccustomed to such bluntness, Jonathan had no real choice and accepted the terms.

Finally, two days before Major Washington was scheduled to depart, he paid a brief visit to the Englishman at the Crown and Sceptre. "My interpreter speaks the major Indian languages, so I'll have no need of your knowledge of Seneca. You'll be no help to us, Captain Lewis, but I don't see you doing us any real harm, either. Come along, if you wish."

Jonathan thought him highhanded but had to conceal his resentment. "Thank you, Major Washington."

"I trust you don't intend to travel in the clothes you're wearing?" Washington raised a patrician eyebrow.

"I have no others."

"Then get yourself some buckskins!" When Washington gave an order, he spoke crisply, expecting it to be obeyed without question.

But Jonathan looked as blank as he felt. He had seen a number of colonials in faded leather clothing but had no idea where to purchase whatever he might require, nor did he know what he would need for the journey. The leader of the expedition proved far more sensitive than he had thought possible and immediately recognized his dilemma.

"You and I are the same height and more or less the same build," Washington said. "I'll send you some of my spare buckskins, and my cobbler, who'll bring them to you, can make you a pair of wilderness shoes. It's important that they fit you properly."

Jonathan couldn't help feeling grateful but didn't want to be in his debt. "You must allow me to reimburse you."

Washington waved a large hand. "It's a trifle," he said, then realized that the Englishman was uncomfortable. "You're doing this at my request, Captain Lewis, and I'm making an issue for my sake, not yours. You'll hamper us on the trail unless you're dressed for the wilderness, and, as I'm anxious that nothing hinder us on the road, I'll take responsibility." He paused and became thoughtful. "You have a military title, so I haven't asked you to prove that you can handle firearms."

"I'll be happy to demonstrate, Major Washington, at your convenience."

"No, don't bother. I have no time today, and I won't see you again until we leave Alexandria. For your own safety, Lewis, I hope you really do know how to shoot. The life of every man depends on his own prowess in our forests, and the rest of us won't be able to save you if you're incompetent."

Jonathan tried in vain to curb his growing feeling of dislike for this conceited, opinionated colonial.

The party that started out from Alexandria before dawn, in the rain, one morning in early November 1753 was a motley group. Washington, although wearing simple buckskins, traveled in style and was attended by two personal servants, one of whom carried a dozen or more of his master's books in a special saddlebag slung over the pommel of his gelding. Christopher Gist, the Virginian who had been hired as a guide, was a taciturn man of about Jonathan's age and looked as though he had lived in his worn buckskins for at least a year. Not until they had been on the trail for many days did Jonathan learn from him that Gist had gone off to the frontier as a boy and for more than ten years had been earning his living as a scout and guide.

The most incongruous member of the group was Jacob Van Braam, a Dutch fencing master, who wore his buckskins with the air of one attired in velvet and lace. Over his rough frontier clothes he had strapped a long, double-edged sword and carried two others in his luggage. He rode his horse well, but his manners were those of a fop, he ate his meals with a gold knife and fork he carried on his person, wrapped in a flannel cloth, and he seemed out of place in the party.

Jonathan soon discovered that Washington knew what he was doing, however. Van Braam spoke fluent French, in addition to German, Spanish, and his native Dutch, and was familiar with at least ten or twelve Indian dialects. Jonathan tested him in Seneca and found that the fencing master not only understood everything he said, but replied so quickly that it was difficult to follow him.

Two traders who were going north into the wilderness to buy furs from the savages were attached to the group, too. Their names were Brown and Henry, they kept to themselves and rarely spoke to anyone else unless addressed, and, as they planned to strike out on their own as rapidly as possible, the others did not consider them as anything but the most casual of traveling mates.

Food supplies were provided by Major Washington and consisted in the main of bacon, flour, parched corn, and jerked beef. Jonathan winced when he first saw the beef and corn, which he had been fed daily for so many months in the Philadelphia prison, but Van Braam, the only member of the party friendly toward him, explained that they would shoot their own game as soon as they reached the wilderness.

The initial phase of the journey was uneventful, and so few hardships were encountered that Jonathan wondered if colonials exaggerated when they talked about the perils of the frontier. Following the Potomac River, the boundary between Virginia and Maryland, the party rode northwest by easy stages into the foothills of the Appalachian Mountains. Although the year was far advanced, the pine forests remained a deep green, and Jonathan was struck by the beauty of the rolling countryside. But he noted that at no time were they far removed from civilization. From the crests of hills they could see smoke rising from chimneys, and the nearest farm was never farther than a mile or two from the river. And rutted roads cutting through the brush led to small towns and villages.

Gradually, however, the settlements became more sparse, and clapboard farmhouses gave way to log cabins. When Washington halted at one of these dwellings to buy eggs and buttermilk, Jonathan's curiosity led him into the place, and he was appalled by the primitive conditions. The entire family lived and ate in the single, dark room, meals being cooked in a stone pit, outdoors, beyond the far end. The farmer, his wife, and their three youngest children slept in the one room, too, while four older children managed to find space for themselves in a tiny, cramped loft.

Caked mud was used to provide the chinks between logs and prevent outside air from seeping in. The windows were small openings, covered by oiled paper that kept out both light and air. It was astonishing that anyone would be willing to give up the comparative comfort of New World cities and towns for such primitive living.

That night he expressed his thoughts when the party sat around the campfire, eating fried chicken, beans, and onions, all of it purchased from the farmer. Only Washington, who ate apart, tended by his servants, apparently did not hear him.

The others glanced at each other, their faces indicating scorn, pity, or both.

Then Christopher Gist broke his habitual silence. "Hell," he said, "anybody who don't leave the towns is mad. That cabin was warm enough to keep out the cold air, wasn't it? The lady and her youngsters were snug! What more could anybody ask?"

Jonathan started to reply that there was more to life than seeking protection from the elements, but Gist cut him off.

"Those folks," he said, "are free. They grow all their own food and flax for clothes. There's fish aplenty in the river, and there are deer and bear and other game in the woods hereabouts when they have a hankering for meat. The food they don't eat, they either trade for other things they want, or they sell for money, so they can buy new skillets and sewing needles and help pay the wages of their schoolmaster and parson. What more could a man want?"

"Nothing," Van Braam said, and the traders agreed.

Jonathan did not know how to debate the matter with men whose horizons were so limited.

Major Washington, it appeared, had heard the discussion after all and approached from his own fire, a book of mathematical principles under his arm. "People move to the frontier for one reason, above all, Captain Lewis," he said. "They've been indentured servants, perhaps. At the very least they've been debt-ridden wretches, lucky if they can call the rags on their backs their own. Then they come out here, some from our own towns, most of them from England and Scotland. And overnight they become men of property. Their land belongs to them and to no one else on earth. Their edibles come from their own soil. They've cut down their own trees to make their homes. They've stopped pulling off their caps to lords, and they've forgotten how to tug their forelocks. Can you blame them for being satisfied with their way of life?"

Jonathan couldn't resist saying, "Your manor house is as fine as that of any belted earl in the realm, Major Washington! You eat fine foods served on fine china, and I'll wager that the Prince of Wales's fourposter is no softer or cozier than your bed. You don't live the way that farmer does!"

"That," Washington replied with his usual candor, "is because I'm luckier. But that doesn't make me any better!"

"What does set men apart in the New World, then?" Jonathan demanded.

"Their talents—and how they use them. I know of no land in the world, other than these colonies, where there are no peasants, where every citizen stands on the same level as the next." Washington tugged at the inevitable eelskin that held his hair at the nape of his neck. "If I were to lose my estate tomorrow—for whatever the reasons—I wouldn't hesitate to stake out my own claim somewhere in the wilds, much farther from the seacoast towns than we are right now. I wouldn't be ashamed of my standing, either, and you'd never hear me complain. I offer you a challenge, Captain Lewis. Wait until you've spent a few weeks in frontier country, the part we're about to approach, and then tell me you could ever be happy with less."

Jonathan inched closer to the warmth of the fire and glanced up at the dark void in the shadows beyond the pines and hickory trees. He would be wise to reply discreetly, he knew, since his very presence in the expedition was due only to Washington's kindness. But he could not prevent himself from expressing his true feelings. "I don't need to wait," he said. "I can tell you right now that all I want is my life in London, and I'm going home as fast as I can finish my business in this barbaric country!"

The party crossed the Potomac and halted at a tiny Maryland village, Cumberland, the last wilderness outpost. Beyond it were no settlements, and only a few rugged farmers had established homesteads. "Out yonder," Gist said, "is a land of silence."

"But someday," Major Washington added, "you'll see cities and roads and bridges and farms. The future belongs to the Valley of the Ohio."

One of the traders, whose mount was suffering from a sore leg, traded the horse for another gelding. Washington purchased extra supplies of bacon, flour, and tea and, as a precaution, added several horns of gunpowder to the quantities he already carried.

That night, for the first time, he joined the others at their campfire outside Cumberland, a practice he would follow thereafter. "Boys," he said, "I must ask you to follow a few simple rules. We're heading into country where it isn't healthy to make mistakes. You'll take your orders from me and, if anything should happen to me, from Chris Gist. I'll tolerate no disobedience and no feuding. Now, Captain Lewis!"

The ring of authority in his voice prompted Jonathan to reply, "Sir?"

"The pistol you're carrying is a pretty toy to fend off cutpurses in London's streets, but it won't do you much good where we're going. If an enemy comes within pistol range, there are certain to be other warriors close enough to scalp you."

The others laughed as though he had made an exceptionally witty remark.

Jonathan could feel his face burning.

"So," Washington continued, "I'm going to make you the loan of a rifle. Have you ever used one?"

"I've used muskets since I was a boy."

"Rifles, Captain Lewis! I'm not speaking of muskets." Washington held up a slim, ungainly weapon.

"I never saw one until I came to the colonies. It looks to me like a metal pole with a musket butt at one end."

Washington thrust it into his hands. "Try it before we leave in the morning. And be careful. There's no other weapon on earth like it."

Jonathan felt contempt for the warning, and a night's sleep, wrapped in a blanket on a cold hillside, did not change either his opinion or disposition. He was curious, however, and while Gist and Washington's servants fried bacon in pans with fish the guide had caught at dawn, he wandered off to test the rifle.

It deserved its name; when the butt rested on the ground, the barrel soared more than a foot over his head, and Jonathan thought he had never seen a clumsier weapon. But the first of several surprises awaited him when he loaded it and he discovered he could complete the operation in a fraction of the time required to load a musket.

Peering off in the early morning light, he concentrated on the crest of another hill about one hundred and fifty yards to the west. A thirty-foot pine stood at the summit, and a cluster of cones was hanging from a branch near the top. Satisfied with his target, he raised the rifle and peered down the absurdly long barrel, then squeezed the trigger.

The sharp crack of the rifle brought the other members of the party on the run, but Jonathan was unaware of them. The butt had slammed back into his shoulder with such force that it had almost knocked him from his feet, and he was disgusted when he saw that he had succeeded only in breaking a branch about four feet below the cluster of cones.

Reloading, and again marveling at the speed and ease, he took aim again, wishing he had no audience to watch his disgrace. Bracing himself, he fired and was gratified to see that he had come within a foot of his target. Again he reloaded and fired, then again and, finally, a fifth time. The last three shots landed within six to eight inches of the target, but the cluster was untouched.

The others were looking at him, their eyes veiled, and Jonathan felt a twinge of annoyance. When they wished, colonials could appear inscrutable, but he couldn't blame them for hiding their reactions. Never had he made such a poor showing, and it was wrong to blame them for silently mocking him.

"You were right, Major," he said to Washington, wanting to demonstrate that he, too, could speak candidly. "The rifle is a weapon that commands respect. It has great power, more than any musket I've ever handled, and once I become accustomed to it I may be able to persuade it to fire accurately."

A rare grin creased Washington's face.

"No firearm on earth is as accurate as the American long rifle," Gist said. "They make it for us in England—but it's manufactured according to our specifications."

"You wouldn't know it was accurate from my shooting, Chris," Jonathan replied.

Washington eyed him for a moment. "Your target was that bunch of pine cones near the top of the tree, I take it?"

"I'm sorry to say it was, Major."

To Jonathan's surprised chagrin the others broke into loud laughter.

"Not even counting your first shot, when you were getting the feel of the rifle," Washington said slowly, "you put four others within a foot of your target. You call that bad shooting?"

"If I can't knock down those cones in three shots out of five— after a little practice—I'll give up firearms and ask Jacob here to polish my swordplay."

Van Braam bowed low from the waist.

Gist raised a hand to his eyes, squinted, and then unlimbered his own rifle.

"Chris," Washington said, "is the best shot I've ever known."

Jonathan was irritated, seeing no need for them to go out of their way in order to humiliate him.

Three times the guide fired his rifle, and the cone cluster remained intact. "Maybe I tied you, Jonathan," he said. "All my shots landed about six inches, more or less, from the cones."

"That," Washington declared, "is remarkable shooting. Anyone who can do as well as Chris Gist is a first-rate marksman, and I trust you'll forgive my temerity last night in suggesting that you might be less than an expert in handling firearms."

For a moment Jonathan thought he was being ridiculed, but then he realized Washington was sincere.

The others became aware of his confusion. "The purpose of a long rifle," Gist told him, "isn't like that of a short-range pistol. The rifle has so much power you can't pinpoint a shot within a foot, but because of that power there's no need to."

"If you land within a few inches of your aim," Washington said, "you'll dispose of your target, regardless of whether it's human or animal."

"I'm going to feel a heap safer," Gist added, "if you'll ride up front with me, Jonathan."

"I'll feel safer," Jonathan replied, "if I can practice a few more rounds before we leave." For the first time since he had met Washington, he saw the major looking at him approvingly.

5

The Wilderness

The party headed west from Cumberland through a deep gorge
that Gist and the residents of the village called "The Narrows,"
and for the first time Jonathan appreciated the natural beauty of
the American interior. Cliffs, their sides heavy with evergreens, rose
hundreds of feet on both sides of the gorge; the men made their
way slowly down a narrow trail that cut through the bottom, and
the Englishman felt strangely insignificant.

Emerging at the western end of the gorge, the party was surrounded by tree-laden mountains as it moved out of Maryland and
headed toward the northwest through Pennsylvania. Wilderness,
Jonathan soon learned, was an apt word to describe the vast area.
There were no trails here, no sign of civilization, no hint that other
human beings had ever visited the area. Even from the crests of
mountains three thousand feet high he could see nothing but the
endless sea of pine and fir and hemlock, oak and spruce, maple and
beech and birch. Never had he imagined a land so filled with trees,
and his companions told him the forest probably stretched across
the continent to the Pacific Ocean.

At first Jonathan found the silence of the wilderness oppressive.
But Gist, no longer reticent, taught him to listen for sounds that the
city dweller did not hear. On the trail, when the horses crashed
through the brush, it was difficult to make out other sounds. But
when the party paused, or when Gist and Jonathan went ahead on
foot, Washington sometimes accompanying them, to cut a path
through a tangled growth with axes, the forest often came alive.

57

Small animals could be heard scurrying through the underbrush. Occasionally a larger animal made its way through the carpet of dead leaves, usually at a distance. And one morning Gist, not bothering to explain, suddenly raised his rifle and fired, then dashed forward. Jonathan, close behind him, saw that he had killed an animal with fanglike teeth that resembled an evil-looking cat.

"Some folks call these lions, some say they're bobcats," Gist declared. "Me, I only know I don't want them skulking around. You hear them rustle—it's the only sound they make. And there's none bolder in the wilderness. A bear won't bother you if you don't annoy him, but these cats will attack you for the sheer, contrary joy of it. When you hear a steady, rustling sound, always stop. If the sound comes closer, keep a sharp watch and the minute you see one, get him. If you don't, he'll get you."

The party headed toward a river called the Conemaugh by the Indians, a branch of the Allegheny that was located due east of the forks of the Ohio. Major Washington, also less reserved in his attitude toward Jonathan, gave the Englishman a lesson in wilderness travel as they sat together at the campfire one evening, after a supper of bacon, biscuits, and tea, inspecting a rough sketch of the area.

"When you and a river are moving in the same general direction, follow it," the Virginian said. "Always. Even if it takes you out of your way from time to time. There are fewer obstacles, and you'll find your path easier. But, if you're expecting an attack, move away from a stream. The land there is usually flat, and there aren't as many trees as you'll find farther from the banks. So you'll be more exposed."

"If it's a question of courage—"

"False courage," Washington interrupted. "Never forget the first rule of the frontier. It doesn't pay to neglect your safety at any time or under any circumstances."

A few days later Jonathan learned a practical lesson. A late autumn downpour that continued for more than forty-eight hours turned the ground underfoot to mud, and eventually the river began to rise appreciably. When the rain still fell steadily on the third morning, Major Washington summoned the others to a conference beneath a towering white pine that offered partial shelter.

"Gentlemen," he said, "we have two choices. We can wait until the rain ends, the land dries out somewhat, and the floods subside. That might be the most sensible course. But, if we do, we may suffer a long delay. Each day we wait brings winter that much closer, and I don't relish traveling any longer than necessary when there's snow and ice on the ground."

Gist and the traders agreed so emphatically that Jonathan realized the hardships of the wilderness winter must be considerable.

"There are risks entailed in our alternative, although we might be able to minimize them somewhat," Washington continued. "We can use the flood so it works for us rather than against us. I propose that we build some rafts, the sturdier the better, and float ourselves and our mounts toward the Allegheny junction. Provided," he went on, turning to Gist, "we won't encounter any rapids."

"The last time I came down the Conemaugh, there were no rapids in this area," the guide replied. "But landslides crashing down the mountains have been known to change the course of more than one river. So I offer you no guarantees, Major."

Washington scratched the side of his large nose. "Would you say we can hear rapids up ahead, Chris, even above the roar of a river at flood tide?"

"I believe I could," the guide said, smiling faintly, "although I'm not sure of anyone else's hearing."

"Then you'll lead us, and if there's danger we'll head for dry land and make a portage past the rapids."

They spent the morning making two large rafts, first cutting down trees, then lashing them together with vines, found by Gist, which were as strong and pliable as any ropes Jonathan had ever seen. The Englishman was impressed by the speed and efficiency of the colonials as they went about their tasks. Any one of them could fell and trim a tree in a fraction of the time he required, and they seemed to work with effortless ease.

Gist added tillers to both crude craft, then cut down a number of saplings to be used as poles if a raft became mired. After resting briefly over a light meal of jerked beef and parched corn, the party shoved off, with Gist, Van Braam, and the traders on the lead raft, while Major Washington, his servants, and Jonathan, the one neophyte, brought up the rear. The horses were frightened and neighed loudly, but their footing was too insecure for them to attempt bolting, and they stood unmoving, rigid with terror, until they became calmer.

Icy, muddy water swirled around the rafts as they moved downstream, and frequently a wave washed over the logs. But the rafts remained buoyant, and, although they rode erratically, bobbing and heaving, there seemed to be no danger they would capsize. Gist and Washington, who manned the tillers, seemed to know what they were doing and steered first toward one bank, then the other in order to compensate for swells and currents in the swollen, fast-moving stream.

At first Jonathan felt uneasy; half a world from the life he knew, he balanced himself on the raft, bouncing and swaying as he tried, in vain, to prevent his thick moccasins of rawhide from becoming wet. Once he gained confidence in the ungainly craft and in the abilities of Washington to handle it, however, he relaxed and after a time discovered he was enjoying the unusual experience. The rafts were moving downstream far more rapidly than the party could have traveled along the bank, and it was a relief to know they would be arriving at their destination that much sooner.

Only because his entire financial future depended upon his ability to gain possession of his New World inheritance was he making this uncomfortable journey. And every day he spent on the American frontier hardened his resolve to return to England the moment he concluded his business here.

The journey on the rafts, although exciting, was uneventful and continued until late afternoon, when the rainfall became still heavier, necessitating a halt for the night. The forest was so wet it was impossible to light a fire, so the men ate a cold meal before rolling up in their sodden blankets for the night. Shortly before dawn the downpour tapered off and became a drizzle, with a hint in the air that it soon might turn to snow.

The ground remained so muddy, however, that it would have been exceptionally difficult to start the march by land. Washington decided to start the journey on the river, and, rather than take time to kindle and light a fire of damp wood, the party ate a cold breakfast before embarking.

Jonathan, thoroughly at home now on the craft, had no duties to perform and occupied himself by looking at the scenery. The sun rose and broke through a layer of dull, gray clouds, and the forest was transformed. Raindrops still sparkled on the evergreen needles, and all at once the wilderness, losing its somber air, became cheerful.

Washington was conscious of the Englishman's fascination with his surroundings and at one point gestured to him, then pointed toward the left bank of the river.

Six or seven deer, including a tiny fawn, were feeding at a salt lick located at the far end of a rocky inlet. They were unaware of the proximity of humans, and the fawn, sharing the relief of the humans in the improvement in weather, danced around its more sober elders.

The picture of the deer remained in Jonathan's mind for some minutes, and he was totally unprepared for the jolting crash that jarred him and sent one of the horses to its knees.

No sooner did it dawn on him that the raft had struck a submerged rock, almost capsizing, than a thrashing sound called his attention to the stern. Major Washington had been knocked overboard and was making frantic but unsuccessful efforts to catch hold of the raft and hoist himself on board.

The servants, too frightened to move, gaped at their master.

The other raft had already swept around a bend in the river ahead, and Jonathan shouted but had no idea whether his cry had been heeded. Then he raced to the stern, took hold of the tiller, and tried to stem the swift pace of the raft. But the current was too strong, and Washington fell behind.

Jonathan saw that, at best, he was a fair swimmer. He was using only his right arm as he tried to stay afloat, so it was possible that he had injured his left in his tumble overboard. Jonathan knew that the servants and horses would be at the mercy of the elements if he abandoned the craft, so he maneuvered desperately and finally succeeded in taking the raft in the direction of the river's right bank.

The current did the rest, and in a moment the logs were scraping against the mud bottom. Jonathan did not wait. "Haul this thing up onto the shore," he shouted to the servants, meanwhile stripping off his shirt, trousers, and moccasins before jumping into the icy Conemaugh.

The shock numbed him for a moment, but he recovered when he saw Washington being carried downstream toward him, and he regained control instantly, striking out toward the major with long, powerful strokes. As a boy he had spent his summers swimming in the Thames when he had visited his uncle's manor house near Windsor, and although he hadn't swum for a number of years, his skills had not deserted him.

For several agonizing minutes he thought he was making no progress, but, little by little, he began to gain on the floundering colonial. Washington saw him coming and made a determined effort to move closer. But he was weakening and could do little to help himself.

Jonathan shut his mind to his own danger and continued to swim with smooth strokes. Afraid he could not reach the victim in time, he redoubled his efforts but failed to gain until the current itself seemed to pick Washington half out of the water and hurl him at the Englishman. All at once it was absurdly easy for Jonathan to reach out, catch hold of him, and prevent him from being swept away. "Catch hold of my hair, Major, below the eelskin," he commanded.

Washington, gasping for breath, managed to obey.

Jonathan swam toward the bank, conserving his strength as best he could. The water was numbing him again, and he knew the rest of his energy would be drained away within a short time, so he tried to make every stroke count. He found it agonizing to suck in the raw air he needed and twice was afraid he might lose consciousness.

"I think we can stand here." Washington's voice sounded close to Jonathan's ear.

The Englishman cautiously lowered his feet and discovered he was standing in vest-high water. Washington stood, too, and together they dragged themselves toward the shore, slipping and stumbling as they crawled up the bank.

Exhausted, Jonathan threw himself on the ground.

Washington, standing above him, was flexing his left hand and massaging his arm. "We'd better go back upstream to the raft," he said, only a hoarseness in his voice belying his seeming calm. "We'll need to build a fire, or we'll catch the ague and die."

For the first time Jonathan realized that a fine, powdery snow had started to fall and that the sun had vanished beneath a thick cover of black-gray clouds. He struggled to his feet and, still unable to speak, began to make his way slowly toward the grounded raft, which was beached about one hundred yards away.

"When a man's life has been saved," Washington said quietly, "any attempt he might make to express his thanks would be inadequate, and perhaps a trifle absurd. But I'm grateful to you nonetheless, Captain Lewis."

Jonathan finally found his voice, thinking it ironic that the man he had saved was now half supporting him. "The current was responsible. I didn't do much of anything."

"If it weren't for you," Washington replied firmly, "I wouldn't be here now. And I won't forget it."

The servants, seeing them approach, recognized their need and began a search for dry wood. They found enough to start a fire, and at the major's direction they cut down a dead tree that, when chopped into logs, sent flames leaping toward the sky.

Jonathan recovered his aplomb when he thawed, and Washington produced a flask of brandywine, from which both men drank. The injury to the major's arm appeared to be superficial, and he had regained at least a partial use of it by the time the men from the other raft made their way toward them along the shore.

Christopher Gist cupped his hands and shouted, "What's wrong?"

Washington and Jonathan grinned at each other, and the major showed that he was not altogether lacking in a sense of humor. "It's such a lovely day," he called, "that we decided to take a swim."

The journey was resumed by raft, and the junction of the Allegheny was reached without further incident. Then, although the party intended to follow the major river almost due north, the ground had dried sufficiently for them to proceed by land. Neither Jonathan nor Washington felt any regrets when the rafts were abandoned.

But the weather continued to turn colder, and a heavy snowfall that began early one evening and lasted through the night suddenly brought winter to the wilderness. The white coating on the branches of trees transformed the appearance of the forest, and both the men and their mounts suffered intensely. The animals picked their way through deep drifts, and the men were forced to slap themselves to prevent their blood from congealing. Van Braam, who had suffered frostbite several years earlier, frequently rubbed his face with snow, a crude remedy that, the colonials assured Jonathan, was always effective.

The silence of the frontier grew deeper, and Gist explained the phenomenon to the Englishman, who had resumed his place at the head of the column with the guide. "It makes sense, Jonathan," Gist said, "that any animal with a lair that'll keep him warm is going to pull into it and stay there. Most of the small beasts—fox, rabbit, coon, weasel, and such—just vanish. The bears hole up for the cold weather, and don't come out unless they're starving. The brown bear I shot the other afternoon is probably our last. The deer stay in the open, searching for grass under the snow, but the covering muffles sounds so much that they can hear us a long way off, farther than they can any other time of year. So our chances of finding any between now and spring are slim."

"What are the animals we hear howling at night?"

"Wolves. Unless you're starving, don't try to shoot one. Their meat is tough as leather, and the other wolves will tear apart the one you shoot before you can even get near the carcass. Wolves are mean, like the savages, and they won't attack if they know you're going to put up a fight."

"Will the Indians?" Jonathan thought it strange that they had encountered no warriors on the journey.

"That depends on the tribe. The Miami, in the Ohio Valley, farther west, are as wild as the bobcats that roam these mountains. One Miami brave will attack a dozen armed militiamen, even if he's carrying nothing but a stone knife."

"Are they mad?"

"They're all mad," Gist replied.

Jonathan thought of Li-solu, whom he would always regard as a friend. "What about the Seneca?"

"After the Miami, they're the nastiest. They're more cunning, though. Shrewd devils if ever I've seen any. They're the strongest of the Iroquois nation, even though the Mohawk badly outnumber them. We'll soon be moving into territory the Seneca claim, and if they know we're in the neighborhood, you'll see for yourself what I mean. No matter how cold the weather, they're guaranteed to give us a warm reception."

There was no indication of savages in the vicinity, however, so Major Washington continued to order a campfire lighted every night. A hot meal and a mug of tea was preferable to cold food, and the men were grateful for the opportunity to sleep near the coals. But, they discovered one morning, they paid a high price for their comfort.

One of the traders, who went off for additional firewood at dawn, was the first to discover a loss. "The horses are gone!" he shouted.

The others ran to the spot, a small clearing high on the slope where the party was spending the night, and Gist waved everyone back while he went forward alone. He spent some minutes studying tracks and prints in the snow, then turned to Major Washington. "It's my fault," he said. "I knew we were close to Seneca country, and I should have advised you to post sentries every night. Now it's too late."

"They've made off with all the animals." Washington made a flat statement.

Jonathan was not only outraged but felt himself sufficiently a member of the group to enter the council of war. "How do we get them back?"

Gist laughed sourly. "We don't. There were at least a half-dozen braves in the party—"

"Then we outnumber them. And unless they're carrying long rifles—and know how to shoot them—we shouldn't have too much of a problem!"

"I admire your spirit," Washington told him, "but you aren't showing much common sense. This is the American wilderness, Captain Lewis, not the English countryside. By now the savages have traveled as far as we can march in a full day. They're mounted, remember, and we're on foot. Wrap your moccasins in rags, boys, and don't forget to rub your feet with snow whenever they feel numb. We have a long walk ahead."

The rest of the journey north was a march of unremitting suffering. Washington maintained a rapid pace, forcing his companions to cover at least twenty miles each day, and only Gist managed the feat without seeming effort. The presence of one party of Indians in the vicinity meant that others might be nearby, so the major ordered that no more fires be lighted, and the members of the expedition lived exclusively on cold food, augmenting their rations of jerked beef and parched corn with snowberries, which everyone picked from bushes. They had a faintly sour aftertaste, and Jonathan loathed them but, at Washington's insistence, ate his share, since the commander insisted that the berries helped ward off what he called wilderness fever.

At no time was Jonathan warm. He shivered on the march, and at night, when his legs ached after the unaccustomed exercise, he found it impossible to warm himself, even when he wrapped his body snugly in his blanket. He discovered, however, that he was growing stronger and more resilient, in spite of his agony. He could carry a heavy pack without tiring, and after a few days his legs proved more than equal to the strain of the march.

"You're turning into a real wilderness man," Gist told him.

Jonathan rubbed the stubble on his chin and wondered why the observation pleased him.

6

Elizabeth

After leaving the Allegheny at its junction with French Creek, Major Washington's party continued to head north toward Lake Erie. The hills had given way to a faintly rolling terrain, and Gist explained that this was the beginning of the Valley of the Ohio, the area that everyone in the colonies called the Northwest Territory. This strip was claimed by Pennsylvania under the terms of the charter that had been granted to William Penn, but the entire region was in dispute. Although several small clusters of English-speaking settlements were located on Lake Erie, France was claiming the entire Northwest as her own.

"Why is it," Jonathan asked Washington, "that the governor of Virginia should send a messenger to the French? Why hasn't Pennsylvania done it, if she owns this land?"

"The fort on French Creek is just a base of operations," the major replied. "It's a toe hold for the French south of the Great Lakes. Their real aim is to push down from their main colony in Canada and take control of the entire Valley of the Ohio, to the west of us. That's the area that Virginia claims, and we'll fight a war to keep the French out."

After a march of several days up French Creek, Gist called a halt one morning in early December when he saw a wooden palisade in the distance. Above it flew the lily ensign of the French monarchy, and on a platform behind the eight-foot wall they could make out the muzzles of several nine-pounder cannon. Here was the truth they were compelled to face: France had invaded the English colonies and intended to stay.

Major Washington bristled but controlled his temper. Taking a large white handkerchief of the purest linen from his pack of personal belongings, he tied it to his sword. Then, holding the blade high as a flag of truce, he led his companions toward the frontier fort.

When they drew nearer they heard a trumpet sound a call, and a few moments later the roll of drums echoed across the snow-covered plain. There was a flurry of activity inside the fort, and soldiers clad in the gold and white uniforms of French infantry moved into position on the palisade platform.

"At least," Jonathan said to Gist, "they're armed with muskets, not rifles, so we'd give a good account of ourselves in a fight."

"There must be a couple of hundred troops in that fort. Would you attack them?"

"If they attack us first, watch me, Chris!"

"I guess you're an American, all right. Only an idiot—or a wilderness man—would think of fighting a battle against those odds!"

There was no battle, however. The main gates of the little fort opened, and a gold-and-white-clad officer rode out, a flag-bearer and three other soldiers as his mounted escort. Their pomp, in this desolate wilderness, seemed absurd to Jonathan, but the Americans apparently saw nothing amusing in the gesture, and Washington returned the Frenchman's elaborate salute with equal correctness. The Virginian explained that he was bringing a message of great importance to the commandant from Governor Dinwiddie, and the British subjects were invited into the fort.

At the gates a squad of soldiers awaited them, taking up positions on their left and right as they were led across the inner compound. Obviously the French, although extending the courtesies of their hospitality, were taking no chances.

The interior of the fort was more spacious than it appeared on the far side of the pointed palisades, and Jonathan, long familiar with French military organization, was quick to identify various buildings. Two separate barracks housed the enlisted men; a structure with real glass in its windows, a luxury on the frontier, served as the officers' quarters, and the commandant had a small but snug house of his own, made in part of clapboard, in part of untrimmed logs. The arsenal, where gunpowder, ammunition, and spare weapons were kept, was a solid structure, and so was the warehouse where provisions were stored. Although materials from the surrounding forest had been used to construct the fort, it was apparent that the French had not done their work lightly or hastily and had come to the upper reaches of Pennsylvania to stay.

Major Washington and his party were taken to the dining room in the officers' quarters and there were served the best meal they had eaten in weeks. Their breakfast consisted of broiled fish, presumably taken from Lake Erie, which was garnished with bear bacon. There were thin, rolled pancakes, stuffed with snowberries which had been soaked in liqueur, and Jonathan found the dish unexpectedly delicious. Platters of cold roasted duck were placed on the table, and the main course consisted of venison steaks which had been marinated in wine. The bread was made of bleached flour, which was unusual anywhere in the New World, and from its taste had been baked only that morning, which was extraordinary. The guests were given ale, two wines, and tea to drink, and, all in all, the meal was a great success.

Then they were taken to some empty rooms in a wing of the officers' quarters, and soldiers brought them tubs of hot water for the first real baths they had enjoyed since they had started their journey in Alexandria more than a month earlier. The hospitality of their hosts could not be criticized, but it soon became plain that the commandant was in no hurry to receive Washington. Not until noon was the major finally escorted to the French leader's house.

There Colonel Legardeur de St. Pierre received him cordially, listening without comment as the Virginian delivered his carefully worded message.

"All of the royal governors representing His Britannic Majesty in the New World are disturbed by the encroachment of France on North American territory to which the claim of King George II cannot be refuted," the young Virginian declared. "My own superior,

Governor Dinwiddie, is particularly upset. Virginia, in the name of the Crown and in our own right, has already taken possession of the Valley of the Ohio. Yet you have established an outpost here, on the British colonial soil of Pennsylvania, and have been sending scouting parties deep into the Ohio Valley."

Colonel de St. Pierre waved a deprecating hand. "We don't necessarily intend to keep this fort permanently. It is no secret that we plan to build our main base at the forks of the Ohio, which is the gateway to the valley. But our intentions are not hostile to your people. We have not molested the English settlements on Lake Erie a short distance from here, and we will continue to let your people live there in peace. You may tell Governor Dinwiddie that France doesn't make war on peasants and their families."

Washington curbed a desire to retort that Americans did not consider themselves peasants. "Your humanity and that of your government does you credit, Colonel," he replied. "But you evade the principal issue. You have already encroached on Pennsylvania, an English colony. You make no attempt to hide your intention of moving into the Valley of the Ohio, which belongs to the English colony of Virginia. Governor Dinwiddie cannot and will not tolerate this situation, sir! You and I both know that His Majesty's government in London will not tolerate it, either. It is not my place to speak on behalf of that government, which will, I feel sure, communicate directly with His Christian Majesty's government in Paris on the matter. But I do speak unequivocally on behalf of Governor Dinwiddie."

"I regret your governor's perturbance," the French commander said. "My feelings are both official and personal. France wants only to live at peace with her neighbors, both in Europe and on this continent."

"In that case, sir, she must confine her colonization to the territory within her own boundaries!"

Colonel de St. Pierre shrugged. "The government and people of France do not recognize the claim of Virginia, or any other British claim, to the Valley of the Ohio. The area was first discovered by French explorers—"

"We believe it was found by English explorers, and the Virginia charter, issued by the Crown, specifically includes the valley!"

"France cannot be bound, Major, by a charter that an English king once issued to his subjects."

"All civilized nations must consider themselves bound by international law, sir!" Washington declared.

"That law is open to interpretation, Major. We are convinced that the Valley of the Ohio belongs to us, and we are determined to take possession of it. I might even say that France believes it her destiny to occupy that territory!"

"If you persist in that attitude, there will be war between us!" Washington became coldly remote.

Colonel de St. Pierre's manner did not change. "France must act out of conviction in her own best interests. . . . I trust you and your associates will join me at dinner."

"I regret that we must return to Virginia at once, Colonel." Washington, equally polite, did not want to say he thought it inappropriate to sit down at the same table with the man who soon would be his enemy.

"You have had a long journey, and another awaits you. Surely you are entitled to a rest of a few days."

"Not when my duty demands otherwise."

"You are a very stubborn people, you English colonials," the colonel said, ushering his visitor to the door. "I am afraid we may not find it easy to persuade you to drop your claim to the valley."

Washington's expression indicated that nothing would persuade him and his compatriots.

He was taken back to the members of his party, and after telling them of the confrontation, declared they would start their return journey immediately. With war imminent the traders quickly revised their plans and decided that they, too, would return to Virginia. Only Jonathan had no intention of accompanying the group.

"This is where we part company, Major," he said.

"I realize you want to look after your own affairs, Captain Lewis," Washington replied, "but you'd be wise to reconsider."

"You just finished telling us that the British colonial settlements on Lake Erie won't be molested by the French."

"So St. Pierre said, but thinking often changes in time of war. What's more, you came from Virginia with us, so he may be inclined to suspect—if you stay on in the region—that you're a spy."

"But I'm not a colonial. I'm English."

"They may not see the distinction, particularly as you served the Crown as a military officer."

Jonathan refused to be dissuaded, however. Neither the threat of war nor the actual start of a conflict could deter him, now that he was so close to his goal. His parting with Washington and the other members of the party was warm, and after the whole group had left the fort, he set out for Lake Erie, about twenty miles away.

On his own now, he applied the principles of wilderness travel to his own march, and although he started in the early afternoon, he covered approximately ten miles before night forced him to halt. Aware of the French in the vicinity, he slept lightly, then forced himself to eat some of his supplies of parched corn and jerked beef before resuming his journey.

At noon, breaking out of the cover of trees, he found himself on the shore of Lake Erie and halted abruptly. Nothing had prepared him for the experience, and he stared at the blue waters of the huge inland sea, awed by its size. The cold waters stretched out ahead toward the horizon, and for a moment he couldn't help wondering whether he had stumbled onto a hitherto undiscovered ocean. If Lake Erie was one of the smallest of the Great Lakes, as he seemed to recall Christopher Gist telling him, the size of the inland waterways staggered the imagination. Never had he dreamed that the New World was so enormous, and he could begin to understand now why the colonials so often thought and spoke in terms of sweeping concepts. The British Isles occupied a territory smaller than the area through which he had traveled since coming to America, and he had seen only a small part of the land claimed by the colonies.

Close to his goal at last, he increased his pace as he headed westward along the shore of the lake. Anxious to reach his destination, he did not halt to eat another meal of the food he disliked but pressed on, and in midafternoon he was rewarded by the sight of a column of smoke rising in the distance.

Aware of the possibility that he might be approaching an Indian campfire, he proceeded more cautiously, moving inland from the rock-littered beach so the trees would screen him. After a walk of the better part of an hour, he saw a clearing ahead, and at the far side, near the lake, stood a two-story clapboard house, painted white, with smoke rising from a brick chimney.

At best he had expected to find log cabins in the vicinity and was startled. But a movement near the water caught his eye, and he momentarily forgot the house when he saw a young boy in linsey-woolsey breeches and a sailor's pea jacket carrying a bucket of water from the lake to the house. Moving into the open, Jonathan noted that the boy's blond hair was tied with an eelskin and couldn't help wondering if the colonials knew of any other style. Waiting until he was no more than twenty feet from the youngster, he called, "You there, lad! I'm looking for the Lewis property!"

The boy stopped short, put the bucket on the ground, and turned.

Jonathan found himself staring into the muzzle of a cocked pistol.

"Drop your rifle!" a clear soprano voice ordered.

He blinked in astonishment and saw a pair of long-lashed eyes which were the same hue as the waters of Lake Erie, and as icy.

"Do as I tell you, or you'll discover I not only know how to use this pistol but won't hesitate to fire it." The speaker was a young woman in her early twenties.

Jonathan couldn't help laughing as he obeyed and studied her with insolent care. Beneath her open pea jacket she wore a shirt of thin wool, open at the throat, that revealed more than it concealed of her firm, high breasts. Her waist, encircled by a man's belt of thick leather, was so tiny he felt he could encircle it with his hands. Her hips were slender, and he appreciated her long, shapely legs, even though they were encased in stockings of homespun wool.

The girl approached him slowly, snatched the pistol from his belt and returned his stare, her eyes stormy as she became aware of his

75

personal interest. "Keep your hands over your head and go into the house!" she commanded, keeping her own pistol trained on him as she followed, carrying his weapons.

Cushions adorned several chairs of maple, a heavy hooked rug covered the better part of the parlor floor, and dimity curtains, together with a spinning wheel in the far corner, gave the chamber an aura of cozy feminine domesticity.

"Turn around!" the girl directed, and there was nothing feminine in her curt tone.

Again Jonathan obeyed, still grinning. "I enjoy your fire," he said. "I've been a little chilled lately."

She ignored the pleasantry. "What's your business at the Lewis place?"

"Is this the property?"

She shook her head.

"In that case," Jonathan said easily, "it's none of your concern."

"Oh, but it is!" she retorted. "I happen to own it."

"Ah. Mistress Elizabeth Johnson. Your servant." He bowed mockingly.

The girl looked perplexed, then angry.

"The issue of proprietorship is in some question," Jonathan began. "It so happens—"

"It so happens that you thieves—all of you—think you can defraud a defenseless woman! Keep your hands over your head."

"I find it very difficult to hold an intelligent conversation in that position." He leaped forward, snatched the pistol from her, and, before she could retrieve it, gently uncocked it.

Elizabeth Johnson hurled herself at him, clawing and kicking.

The fingers of her right hand raked the side of his face before he could disengage himself and hold her, still struggling, at arm's length. "To think," Jonathan said, "that you wilderness people like to pretend you're so hospitable. That reputation is a myth."

The girl started toward an iron shovel that rested at the side of the hearth.

He dropped her pistol onto a table near his own weapons and

raced her to the hearth, arriving just in time to snatch the shovel before she could pick it up.

She looked over his shoulder, estimating her chances of reaching the pistols and rifle before he could stop her.

"Mistress Johnson," he said, "I intend you no bodily harm, provided you stop behaving like a bobcat. I haven't come here to kill, maim, or rape you."

"Like the others, you just want to cheat me!" Suddenly she crumpled and appeared on the verge of tears.

A woman was at her most dangerous when she wept, so Jonathan continued to eye her warily. "Permit me to introduce myself. I am the rightful heir to the estate of my late cousin, Paul. I am Captain Jonathan Lewis of London."

"Another one?" she demanded.

"I'm not surprised to learn that an impostor has preceded me here. He was accompanied, I suppose, by two young women, one dark and the other fair."

"Only one, with dark hair."

"His real name is Andrews, and he's a scoundrel who also cheated me—and stole all my money and papers." Jonathan's smile was ingratiating. "I don't ask you to accept—on faith—my identity or the story of my unhappy adventures. Benjamin Franklin, the executor of my late cousin's will, promised me he'd write to you and—"

"I received Dr. Franklin's letter last week, when the winter supply train was here."

"In that case, you know me."

"I know an improbable tale." Again she eyed the weapons.

Jonathan lost patience. "Madam," he said, "I could have cut your heart out the moment you thought you had disarmed me. When you take someone's means of self-defense, make sure you get all of them. It so happens you neglected the knife I usually carry in my boot top. When I'm using these accursed wilderness shoes, however, I wear the sheath strapped to my arm." He jerked his right forearm in a sharp, downward motion, and his knife dropped into his hand.

Elizabeth Johnson gasped.

77

Every movement a flourish, Jonathan pulled up the sleeve of his buckskin shirt and replaced the knife in its sheath. Then he crossed the room, gathered up the firearms, and sat down in the nearest chair, holding the rifle and pistols in his lap. "Now I suggest we enjoy a quiet, civilized chat."

"I—I left my bucket outdoors, and the water in it will freeze."

"Permit me to get it for you." He jumped to his feet, still holding the weapons, and went to the entrance, where he paused. "Don't try to lock me out, Mistress Johnson. I'd hate to waste ammunition and powder shooting your door off its hinges."

For the first time she relented slightly and giggled.

Sure that he had read her intentions, Jonathan did not look in her direction as he went into the yard for the bucket. The door remained ajar when he returned with it. "You were right," he said to the girl, who had gone back into the parlor, "this is frozen almost solid already." Not waiting for a reply, he placed the wooden bucket near the hearth.

Elizabeth turned, a second pistol in her hand. "When you disarm me," she said, "make certain you take all of my firearms, sir." Laughing at his startled expression, she voluntarily placed the weapon on the table. "There. I declare a truce."

Jonathan refused to be denied his own gesture and put her other pistol on the table, too. But he carefully replaced his own in his belt and leaned the rifle against the arm of his chair as he resumed his seat. "Madam, your kindness overwhelms me."

"A woman who lives alone in this part of the world must know how to protect herself." There was no hint of apology in her voice; she was stating a simple fact, and her attitude indicated that she didn't care whether he accepted or rejected it.

Jonathan glanced around the room before he spoke again. "I've been looking forward to this meeting for some time."

"I didn't know of your existence until I heard from Dr. Franklin," she replied. "I thought the first person who used your name was Jonathan Lewis."

"You still can't be positive of my identity."

"But I can, sir. Dr. Franklin drew a sketch of you, and the moment you told me your name, I knew you."

"I'm even deeper in Dr. Franklin's debt," he murmured.

"I just regret, mostly for your sake, that you came so far, particularly at this season, when it will avail you nothing." Looking at him defiantly, Elizabeth removed the eelskin at the nape of her neck, and when she shook her head, her pale blond hair tumbled around her shoulders.

"We appear to be in dispute," Jonathan said, finding her exceptionally attractive. "Has an attorney given you an opinion regarding your claim?"

"I don't believe I need a lawyer. My claim is solid!"

"I feel the same way. Since we're at odds, however, some sort of arbitration is going to be necessary. Provided, of course, the property in question has any real worth."

"There's no estate in the Fort Presque Isle area that can match it."

"That's a French name."

"Early this year the French built a small blockhouse near the village, but we refused to have anything to do with them, so they put up their bigger fort, inland, and abandoned Presque Isle."

"When may I see the property?"

"The other Jonathan Lewis used the same approach, sir," she said.

"Andrews."

"Whoever he may be. I took him there, hoping we could deal together reasonably and sensibly, and the next thing I knew, he and his daughter moved in and claimed possession."

"I'm not surprised," Jonathan said. "That sounds like him."

"They wouldn't move out until some friends and I used our own means to—persuade him." Elizabeth's blue eyes flickered for an instant in the direction of her pistols. "He and that hussy didn't go far. They've established themselves in the abandoned French blockhouse, and I know they're just waiting for a chance to snatch Paul's estate again."

"I shall very much enjoy meeting Mr. Andrews once more, and

I trust he'll remember me," Jonathan said grimly. "If not, I'll find ways to jog his memory."

The girl tried to look indifferent but laughed.

"I'm far more anxious, however, to inspect the property on which my entire future depends."

"Your future, sir, obviously isn't secure," she said acidly, and paused. "How do I know you won't try to take possession of it, just like the other—just like this Andrews person and his daughter did?"

"You don't know any such thing," Jonathan replied bluntly. "In fact, put yourself in my position for a moment. "You've traveled halfway around the world to claim your inheritance. You've been robbed, jailed without cause and left to rot in prison for months. Then you've marched for weeks through this—this nightmare—that you colonials call your wilderness—"

"We love these forests!"

"I shall bequeath them to you, madam. Let me continue. At last you reach your destination at the far ends of the world. You're surrounded by trees and a large lake, in the dead of winter. You find a house on your property—" He broke off. "I assume there's a house?"

"It's a mansion. Paul said he'd build one, and he did!"

"So much the better. It has fireplaces, and you can chop wood in the forest. Presumably it even has a bed in one of the chambers. Would you sleep in that mansion, madam? Would you light fires in the hearths to keep out the winter cold? Or would you spend your nights in the open, trying to ward off the ague with nothing but a thin blanket between you and the night air? What would you do?"

"That's an unfair question!"

"I find it not only fair but eminently realistic. To be honest, I can't blame Andrews—and the wench they call Felicity—for moving in. No, Mistress Johnson, I can make you no promise that I won't do the same. I've spent enough nights on the trail to appreciate a warm fire, a roof over my head, and a soft bed."

"I shall do everything in my power to prevent you from moving into my future home." She stood, ladled some water from the bucket into a kettle, and suspended the latter from a hook set in the side of the hearth.

Jonathan noticed that she had removed the pea jacket at some point in their conversation and, critically observing her figure, saw that she was even more willowy and more graceful than he had thought. "I'm open to any sensible alternative. Is there an inn located somewhere near the village?"

"Hardly! We thought we were lucky when Papa and Paul persuaded Billy Trimble to open a general store and Indian trading post."

"Then I have no choice, do I?"

"If it weren't for Dr. Franklin's letter, I'd send you packing, Captain Lewis. But it isn't your fault you've been superseded, and you know nothing of the background of Paul's estate."

"I know nothing about my cousin."

"He and my father were partners in a fur trapping and trading company."

"Then Paul was older?"

"He was Papa's age." Elizabeth's tone indicated she had no desire to dwell on that subject. "They became wealthy but instead of going back to Philadelphia, they decided to settle here, in territory they loved. They persuaded others to move here, and they built their houses on adjoining property, houses that are unique in all the wilderness."

"Well," Jonathan admitted, "I thought I was in Philadelphia or Alexandria when I saw this place."

"Of course. Papa and Paul believed that we'll have our own city here, at the gateway to the Valley of the Ohio, and I'm staying on to help make their vision a reality. I won't let anything interfere. That's why I'll fight you—or anyone else—who tries to gain control of Paul's property."

"If the courts award the property to me, Mistress Johnson, I'd be delighted to sell it to you—for the right price. I have no intention of living in a colonial frontier infested with savages and only a short day's march from French troops who'll soon be at war with us."

Elizabeth took a carved ivory box from the mantel, measured tea from it, and let it steep in the kettle. "I have no money, Captain Lewis. Papa and Paul put all their money into land, their lovely houses, and furnishings. You have no idea how much it costs to bring rugs and beds and chairs and bric-a-brac all the way out here from England."

"They were mad!"

"Then I am, too," she declared, her eyes bright. Suddenly, before Jonathan could speak again, she poured two cups of steaming tea and handed him one. "You'll stay for supper, too."

"I can't take advantage of your larder."

"My cellars and larder are full, sir. I may not have much money, but we grow all our own food here, and we have all we want to eat. No one starves in the Erie country, including a stranger who seems determined to fight me in the courts."

"I'm determined to reach a friendly settlement with you."

She sipped her tea, studying him over the rim of her cup. "We learn to judge character out here, Captain Lewis. We have little choice. And Dr. Franklin assures me you're an honest man. Frankly, I don't know what kind of an arrangement we might work out. But I'm encouraged by your lack of desire to settle here yourself."

"It's the farthest thing from my mind." He accepted more honey to sweeten his tea.

After they finished their tea he accompanied her to the cellar bins, where she selected a wild goose from a meat supply, then took onions, corn, and potatoes to the hearth. Jonathan was astonished when she revealed she had shot the goose the previous day, bringing it down when it had tardily been making its way south.

"If a woman can't handle firearms," she said simply, "she can't survive here."

While she prepared their meal Jonathan questioned her and gradually learned how she happened to be living alone on the frontier. She had been born in Philadelphia, and, when she was ten, her mother had died. Her father, off on a fur-trading expedition, had returned to the city and taken her with him to the wilderness, where he and Paul had educated her, forcing her to spend hours every day at studies ranging from mathematics to grammar to Latin.

She had learned even more about the wilderness, spending six years in constant travel with her father and his partner and keeping house for them thereafter, when they built their homes. Her father had been dead for three years, she said, and Paul had become her guardian. Then, two years past, on her twentieth birthday, he, too, had died. Since that time she had lived alone but found nothing unusual in her situation.

"I can take care of myself," she said. "I know as much about these forests—and the lakes—as any man in the Erie country."

Jonathan discovered that she was an excellent cook and ate ravenously. The roasted goose was superb, and he had to admit she made a stew of the onions, corn, and potatoes superior to anything that the members of Major Washington's party had prepared on the march. They drank a wine she had made herself from wild strawberries, too, and by the time they finished their meal Jonathan was completely relaxed.

"It's late," he said, "so I'd better go along to the village. Perhaps you can give me the name of some people who might take me in."

Elizabeth shook her head. "No one in Presque Isle has adequate quarters. I've been taking it for granted that you'd stay here."

The surprised Jonathan indicated his pleasure.

"Everybody hereabouts is hospitable to law-abiding people," she said. "With enemies all around us, we treat strangers as friends, until they prove otherwise. You claim you aren't intending to cheat me, and I'll take you at your word. If I find you're lying, you'll have cause to regret it."

He saw she meant it and knew she would be as dangerous a foe as any strong man, in spite of her femininity. At the least, he would sleep indoors during his stay on the shores of Lake Erie, and although he had no idea how he might resolve his dispute with her over the ownership of his cousin's property, it was far better to be on good terms while they worked out their differences.

Elizabeth's invitation made him more expansive, and soon he found himself telling her about his own past. Elizabeth proved to be adept at drawing him out, and before he quite realized what was happening he found himself talking about the preoccupation with

83

attractive females that had disrupted his military career and had been such a heavy drain on his purse that, foolishly, he had resigned his commission in order to acquire a fortune as a civilian.

"But you haven't made what you thought you'd earn?"

"I'm a near pauper," he confessed cheerfully. "All the belongings I own in the world are in my pack. Andrews stole my papers and clothes, and it was only a few days ago that Indian thieves took my horse. All that stands between me and a sure sentence to a debtor's prison after I go back home is my estate here."

"I sympathize with you," Elizabeth said, "but you aren't going to get it. I promised my father and Paul that their two properties would be joined together for all time, and I'll let nothing stop me from keeping my pledge to them."

Jonathan began to understand something that had perplexed him. "It seemed odd to me that you'd plan to marry someone so much older, who helped bring you up. The reason you and Paul became betrothed after your father died was to keep the estates under one ownership."

Color rose to Elizabeth's face. "It's a common reason for people to marry."

"Love is another."

"My first and only love is the wilderness!"

"That could be changed fast enough. You haven't known any young men." He went to her, intending to take her in his arms.

She rose swiftly and backed away from him. "I'm not one of your London trollops!"

"No, you're an unusually pretty young lady who has never learned the meaning of love."

"I don't want you as a teacher, sir!"

Jonathan continued to edge closer. "It will do no harm to anyone, and I can guarantee you'll enjoy it."

The parlor wall halted her retreat.

Gently, but with unremitting pressure, Jonathan took her into his arms and kissed her.

For a moment she returned his embrace, her hands grasping the back of his head. Then, when he persisted, she struggled to free herself.

He paid no attention, however, and his kiss became more demanding.

The girl seemed to lose her will to resist him and went limp in his arms.

Convinced she was weakening, he began to caress her. Suddenly, however, he felt a pain in his side and it quickly grew more intense. Releasing Elizabeth, he took a step backward.

A poniard glinted in her hand. "You aren't the only one who can hide a knife. And you aren't the only one who knows how to use one."

He stared at her angrily. "You'd have cut me open!"

"If you hadn't stopped, I'd have killed you!"

"You're worse than a bobcat!"

"If you want me to act like a lady, behave like a gentleman!"

"I am a gentleman!" he said, his rage still mounting.

"Then I want to be preserved from the breed." Still gripping the knife, Elizabeth eyed him coldly. "It's time you and I reach an understanding. Until Paul changed his will, you were his legitimate heir. Granted you didn't know about the change, so you've had a right to be upset. I'm prepared to treat with you fairly and honorably, but I warn you—stay away from me."

"Never fear, madam." Jonathan bowed. "You'll be safe in my presence, I assure you. I don't enjoy the feeling of a knife in my ribs, and I wouldn't touch you if you were the only woman in the whole of the New World!"

7

Felicity

Jonathan spent the night in a comfortable bed, the first he had enjoyed since leaving Alexandria. But he slept fitfully, awakening again and again to find himself thinking of Elizabeth, sometimes in anger, sometimes with a feeling of amused frustration. He did not see her when he came downstairs, so he went outside to chop wood for her and carry two buckets of water from the lake to the house.

When he completed his chores he found her in the kitchen, finishing preparing a breakfast of broiled lake whitefish and an Indian corn and venison sausage pudding. She thanked him for his assistance, and he replied that he felt the need to earn his keep. Thereafter both were restrained and ate their meal in almost complete silence. Both of the dishes were delicious, unlike anything Jonathan had ever before tasted, and his good humor was somewhat restored.

Elizabeth became more companionable, too, and they chatted about inconsequentials as she led him down the beach toward the Lewis estate. The weather was bitterly cold, and a sharp wind from the northwest made whitecaps on Lake Erie, but the sun was shining in an almost cloudless sky and Jonathan was inclined to forget that he was strolling deep in the wilds of a primitive continent with a young woman who, no matter how attractive, became a savage when crossed.

"There's the blockhouse the French abandoned," Elizabeth said, pointing far down the beach.

He shaded his eyes and peered at the structure. It was small, surrounded by a palisade, and seemed sturdy enough to withstand a siege. "You say Andrews and his daughter are living there?"

She nodded. "They moved in when my friends and I—ah—persuaded them to evacuate Paul's house. The Fort Presque Isle doesn't actually belong to anyone, so we can't drive them out."

"Maybe you can't," Jonathan replied, his tone hardening, "but I can—and will."

"At this season they'd starve, or freeze to death, before they could reach the seaboard towns."

"That will be their worry. They came here under false pretenses, with Andrews using my name. I'm rather particular about that name."

Elizabeth tilted her head to one side as she looked at him. "In some ways you remind me of Paul."

"I never knew him."

"He was proud of his name, too."

"A family trait, no doubt."

She turned in toward a patch of woods and led him through it. "My father and Paul each staked out five thousand acres, but they built their houses close together, near the inner boundaries of their adjoining properties."

Jonathan stopped short when they emerged from the screen of trees. He had discounted her description of his cousin's house as a mansion, but she had exaggerated less than he had imagined. The building of stone, logs, and clapboard stood three stories high and looked vaguely familiar. Georgian pillars stood at either side of the entrance, and the place had been constructed to last for centuries.

"How could anyone build a place like that in the middle of nowhere?" he demanded.

"Paul worked very hard, and so did Papa. I did quite a bit, too. And three Tuscarora braves who had lived at Fort Albany spent almost a year here. Paul fed them and paid them wages."

Jonathan continued to stare at the building, and suddenly slapped his thigh. "I have it!" he exclaimed. "The logs used above the stonework on the ground floor fooled me. This is a replica of a manor house an uncle of mine owned near Windsor."

"Now I know you're a Lewis. I realized Andrews was an impostor when he hadn't even heard of the manor house in England. But Paul said it was owned by a cousin, not an uncle."

"That's right, a mutual cousin. My uncle—and his—was still alive when I was a boy. But the title and manor house were inherited by the present Lord Lewis, our cousin. That was about ten years ago."

"I'm glad you aren't an impostor, too," Elizabeth said as they started across the snow-littered yard toward the house.

"Why is that?"

"Because it might be more difficult to get rid of you than it was to oust the Andrews person." She paused to pick up a number of logs from a pile of firewood at the side of the house.

He took them from her. "When I'm fighting for something, I can be stubborn," he admitted lightly.

"I burn fires in some of the hearths here two or three days a week, all winter." She took a key from a chain at her waist and turned the metal lock in the door. "There are so many valuable things here that I don't want them hurt by the cold."

Jonathan followed her into an anteroom, beyond which stood the main parlor, and stopped short. Cabinets, chairs, and tables were of excellent craftsmanship, obviously made in England. On the parlor floor was a rug, similar to one at the Windsor manor house, that came from Turkey. And a number of oil portraits decorated the walls.

"No wonder Cousin Paul had no money. He must have paid a royal ransom to bring these things from England."

"I've stored the bric-a-brac in my own attic," Elizabeth told him. "The Indians don't come here to steal anything because the furniture and rugs are of no use to them, but they'd sell or trade carved ivory animals and snuffboxes."

"So that's how you prevent anyone from breaking in."

"The Indians have no reason, and all the settlers in the area are honest."

Jonathan wandered around the parlor, looking at the portraits. "That's my uncle." He paused to inspect some miniatures clustered together on one wall and fell silent.

Elizabeth joined him and saw he was staring at a small portrait of a handsome woman with blond hair.

"My mother," he said, his voice barely audible.

"I can see the resemblance. It's very strong." On sudden impulse she took the miniature from the wall and handed it to him.

"Not now, thank you," he replied, surprised by the huskiness he heard in his voice. "It might be ruined in my pack. I'll leave it here until I find some way to protect it on the trail when I leave for civilization."

"As you will. You'll find other family portraits in Paul's bedroom upstairs, too. I don't know any of them, of course, but I'm sure you'll recognize some. You may want to spend the whole morning looking around."

"I'm sure I will."

"I wish I could take the time, but I want to finish putting in a new cellar bin before the ground freezes. Suppose I leave you here for the morning—"

"Well, madam. You trust me."

"I'm trying to be fair," she said. "I appreciate your position, sir."

"I'll return to your house at noon," Jonathan told her. "And I give you my solemn pledge that I won't steal the furniture or dismantle any of the rooms," he added with a laugh.

She smiled, too. "I'll give you the key so you can lock up when you leave."

"That's real trust!"

"Yes, but it isn't as much as you might think. If you tried any tricks, I'd have no problem ousting you."

"Really?"

"There's no food in the place, so you'd have to come out sooner or later. And people from the village would be standing guard day and night, waiting to drive you off when you did." She handed him the key, still smiling, and started toward the door. "I'll ask you to build fires in the hearths here and in Paul's room," she said, and left the house.

Before beginning his inspection, Jonathan took some kindling from a basket at the side of the hearth and started a fire with a tinderbox and flint he found on the mantel, adding logs as the blaze began to grow. It was amazing, he thought, that Elizabeth kept the house in readiness for occupancy; he, or someone, could move in and feel completely at home.

Elizabeth was herself so amazing, he thought, that nothing she did should be surprising. Never had he known any woman as self-reliant, as sure of herself—or as ready and willing to use lethal weapons against anyone who crossed her. She would be a dangerous, unpredictable foe, and he hoped he could reach some sort of accommodation with her. He had never feuded with a woman, and didn't want to start now, when so much was at stake.

He had to admit that she was going out of her way to be honorable and to treat him with kindness. She was proving exceptionally generous in taking him into her home, although he realized she was motivated by more than a sense of frontier generosity. While he was living under her roof she could keep watch on him and in that way could better protect her own interests.

The basic problem, as he saw it, was her own lack of funds. If she had no money it would be difficult for her to pay him a substantial sum in return for his claim to this property, which she wanted so desperately and for which he himself had no use. On the other hand, if she wanted it badly enough, she could obtain a loan from a seaboard merchant or, through Dr. Franklin, from a London banker.

She would protest, of course, and might even use force to frighten him away. Obviously she was accustomed to violence. When nothing else worked, she might fall back on her femininity, and the prospect intrigued him. Dressed like a lady, her allure would be irresistible.

Last night, of course, she had behaved like a Puritan prude, but he couldn't quite believe she had been serious in her protestations. He had known so few virgins he discounted the possibility that she really might be one. Her eyes indicated a wisdom in worldly matters that belied her words. The nagging suspicion struck him, as it had during the night when he had awakened so frequently, that she might have objected on the grounds that she didn't find him appealing. That, however, was absurd. In spite of the blow to his vanity, he told himself he had never yet encountered a young woman who didn't respond to him.

Once again putting Elizabeth out of his mind, he made his inspection of the house. The ground floor was spacious, boasting two auxiliary parlors as well as the main living room and, at the rear, a dining room and book-lined library. It amused him that Elizabeth had not deemed it necessary to pack away the leather-bound books that filled the shelves; apparently the Indians who stole bric-a-brac and other small objects had no use for books.

The kitchen, a separate outbuilding made completely of stone, was connected to the house by a roofed, open-sided passageway. It, of all the rooms on the ground floor, least resembled the manor house in England. Instead of wood or coal stoves there was a single large hearth and, opposite it, a stone-lined pit large enough to roast a whole side of venison or beef.

The bedchambers on the second floor were laid out in the pattern of his uncle's mansion, and in the master bedroom he found, among the miniature paintings, portraits of both his parents, made when they had been young. The third floor, with three more bedchambers and a large storeroom, was also similar to the Windsor manor house, and Jonathan marveled at the hard labor his cousin had put into the place. Only a man with the strongest sense of family loyalty could have done so much in this remote place to reproduce the family seat. In a sense it would be a shame to give up his claim to it, Jonathan reflected, but he had to be sensible.

Walking to the window of the room that was a duplicate of that in which he had spent his summers at Windsor, he stared out at the spreading countryside below him. Five thousand acres of this endless terrain were his, and for a moment the very concept numbed him. Cousin Paul had cleared no more than fifty or sixty acres, he saw. In other words, there was enough open land to plant sufficient crops for the support of a small family. The rest was still virgin forest, and the stands of oak, in particular, would be worth a huge sum in England.

Perhaps he could discuss with Elizabeth the possibility that she might sell that wood in order to buy him out. There was an eager market in England for American timber, he knew, although he was unfamiliar with details of the business. It struck him that it might prove very difficult to transport timber from this place in the North American interior to a seaport. But, perhaps, logs could be floated eastward on Lake Erie and then carried in some manner to a river that flowed to the Atlantic Ocean. His knowledge of New World geography was vague, but the notion was worthy of exploration.

In any event, the view was breath-taking. All of the property he could see belonged to him, Elizabeth Johnson's claims to the contrary notwithstanding. He would do his best to work out an agreement with her, but, if she balked, he would fight her to the end in every colonial and English court. New World territory might be cheap, but a property like this, already developed, would be worth a fortune anywhere.

Building a fire in the master bedroom, on the second floor, Jonathan warmed himself at the hearth for a time, then again amused himself by going to the window to admire this room. This chamber looked out on Lake Erie, about two hundred yards away. The pine woods through which he and Elizabeth had walked stood between the house and the beach, and he wondered why Cousin Paul had elected to build inland when he could have erected the house on the water's edge. The waves that rolled in, agitated by the high wind, provided at least part of the answer, he thought. A house screened from the beach was better protected from the elements.

Someone emerged from the woods, and Jonathan, wishing he hadn't left his rifle at Elizabeth's house, instinctively reached for the pistol in his belt. Then, peering harder, he made out the figure of a woman in an ankle-length cape, fur-lined. She had long, flowing hair, and when she moved across the yard he saw it was very dark. Glancing at the fire in the hearth to make sure he hadn't built too big a blaze, he hurried down to the ground floor and took up a position at the wall behind the front door.

He wasn't in the least surprised when the visitor tried the latch, then opened the door, and stepped inside.

"We meet in unexpected places, Mistress Andrews," he said, his voice bleak.

Felicity turned toward him, surprised by neither his greeting nor the pistol he aimed at her. "Jonathan, my dear!" She might have been speaking to an old friend or a former lover.

He kicked the door shut and bolted it from the inside. "If your father and sister—or whoever they may be—are out there in the woods, waiting for you to clear the way, I'll put an obstacle or two in their path."

"Oh, Papa is in the little French fort. He hates this weather and goes out only to catch fish and dig up roots in the vegetable garden the French left. I don't mind telling you I'm sick of fish and vegetable roots."

"Some people ought to stay in the cities, where they belong. The frontier is no place for delicate appetites." The treacherous wench, he told himself, had no right to look so enticing.

Aware of the effect she was creating, Felicity opened her cloak and revealed herself in a low-cut gown of lilac satin.

"They ought to dress in a manner befitting rough country, too," Jonathan added dryly.

She smiled, her full lips parting. Then, paying no attention to the pistol pointed at her, she wandered into the parlor and stood near the hearth, extending her slender hands toward it.

In spite of her elegance, Jonathan noted, her hands had been roughened by the hard work entailed in making at least a temporary home in an abandoned blockhouse.

"If you're wondering how I knew you were here," Felicity said, "Papa and I saw you earlier this morning when you walked over here with that dreadful Johnson girl. She had us evicted from this charming house, you know."

"So I heard." He waited, then said heavily, "Perhaps you thought you were still living here. You didn't bother to knock at the door."

"I thought you might not let me in," she replied candidly.

"Well, you've had the satisfaction of getting in. Now you can leave."

"I've come to talk to you." Her violet eyes were devastating as she unleashed their full power on him.

"You have great courage," Jonathan told her.

"Papa and I are terribly sorry about the—misunderstanding with you."

"There was no misunderstanding." His voice became harsh. "It was all very clear."

"Please try to be charitable." Tears appeared in Felicity's eyes. "I realize it isn't easy after the terrible things that happened to you. But it was all Patience's fault."

"Ah, yes. Your sister." His memory of his months in prison and the loss of his belongings made it easy for him to refrain from laughing at the wench's cleverness.

"Oh, didn't you know? She isn't really my sister. We aren't related at all. It was convenient to call her my sister when she came to work for Papa at the inn. We thought she was a decent person, and it took us a long time to discover she's really a trollop."

"Fascinating," he murmured.

The girl removed her cloak, dropping it over the nearest chair, and then turned back to him so he could miss none of her glory. He had to admit her figure was spectacular and that the snug-fitting gown did it justice. But her high-heeled sandals had been soaked by the snow, and her stockings were wet, too, blunting the impact she was trying to create.

"Papa thought he was doing the right thing when he had you arrested. After all, he was trying to protect Patience, as much as if she really were his own daughter. It wasn't until later that we discovered she willingly slept with any man. By then, when we got rid of her, we were no longer in Philadelphia, but Papa sent letters to the chief bailiff and the warden of the prison. So he was responsible for your release, you see."

"I see a great deal." The boldness of her lies was astonishing, he thought. "I suppose you can also explain why your father came out here—with my papers—and pretended to be me."

"That's a very involved story, and Papa wants to tell it to you himself. I'm sure this is hard to believe, but his motives were honest. They still are."

Both father and daughter, Jonathan reflected, must think him an utter fool. It would be worth hearing Andrews' ingenious tale before making it impossible for the man to rob or cheat anyone else, ever, but Jonathan was afraid he would lose his temper before listening to much of the gibberish.

"Your father," he said, "can save his breath." He saw no reason to reveal what Abel French had told him about Andrews' plan to claim an inheritance on the frontier, much less mention what he knew about the scoundrel's visit to Dr. Franklin.

"I suppose the Johnson woman has been talking about us." When Felicity pouted her mouth looked particularly sensual.

"There was no need for her to say anything."

"She's a very cruel person. We might have been killed when she turned the settlers of this neighborhood against us. At the very least we'd have been homeless if Papa hadn't remembered Presque Isle and moved into the little fort."

"Your father, if that's who he is, has a knack for survival."

"I swear he's my father. And I swear that every word I'm saying is the truth." There was a tremor in Felicity's husky voice.

"Why have you come to me?" Jonathan demanded, tiring of the shabby game.

"Because we know why you're here. You want this house and the land that goes with it. But the Johnson woman won't let you have them, and if you insist, you'll be treated as we were."

"Does Andrews think I'll be grateful for this warning?" he demanded scornfully.

"He hopes you'll give him the opportunity to explain his side of an unfortunate situation that led to even more unfortunate consequences. He hopes you won't condemn him until you've heard what he has to say."

"Why should he care what I think?"

Felicity's violet eyes seemed to grow larger. "He believes he can help you. I think so, too."

"In my experience," Jonathan said, "the Andrews family hasn't been noted for its charity. No matter how seductively you blink your eyelashes at me, I can't accept such nonsense. You people want something for yourselves."

"Of course we do." Again there was a tremor in the girl's voice.

"Papa has been familiar with the wilderness for many years, but he isn't comfortable here. And I despise this country."

At least they had that much in common, Jonathan told himself.

"We're stranded in this desolate place, hundreds of miles from civilization. No companies of traders and hunters will come through Presque Isle until spring, and we'd be mad if we tried to go home by ourselves through Indian territory, especially at this season. So we're marooned here all winter in a drafty, uncomfortable block-house." She looked longingly around the handsomely appointed parlor.

Jonathan felt certain he understood the offer but wanted the girl to spell it out. "Just exactly what are you proposing?"

"Papa can help you gain control of this property. In return, he hopes you'll give us a home for the winter and that you'll show him some financial token of gratitude that will help us pay the expenses of our return to the seaboard when the warmer weather comes."

Her innocence could have fooled almost anyone, and he reminded himself that she was Beelzebub's daughter. He had no intention of accepting the partnership offer, of course, but wanted to learn what was in Andrews' wily mind. Delaying tactics seemed the best approach. "Why didn't your father come to me himself?"

Felicity became defensive. "He was afraid you might become violent."

Jonathan pressed his advantage. "So he sent you instead, hoping I wouldn't beat or kill you."

She regained her poise and struck a provocative pose. "I know you wouldn't. Besides, Papa didn't send me. I wanted to come."

"Why?"

"That should be obvious." She flirted with him even more blatantly.

"Ever since I've come to the New World," Jonathan countered, "I've discovered that nothing is obvious. Life here is very complicated."

"You're making something very simple appear complicated. Surely you know why I wanted to see you." She took a step toward him, her violet eyes shining.

Slowly, deliberately, he unloaded his pistol, rendering it harmless, and placed it on the mantel over the hearth. "I'm listening."

"I've never been drawn to any man as I have to you."

"That isn't the way you acted in Philadelphia, the last time we met," he replied dryly.

"Oh, dear. You don't understand girls, do you, Jonathan?" Her sigh was light, delicate. "I found you attractive the moment you walked into the inn. We spent a pleasant evening together, one of the happiest I've ever known. Then, the next morning, I discovered you in bed with that slut, Patience. How do you suppose I felt? I was jealous! And when a woman feels that way, she wants revenge!"

Silently congratulating her on the cleverness of her explanation, he decided she must be Andrews' daughter. Their brand of sharp, quick thinking had to be inherited and couldn't be taught.

"Now you know." She advanced another step, her full lips parted.

Jonathan immediately decided to play her game. Not only might it be easier for him to learn what he wanted to know, but he could obtain more than information and it had been a long time since he had enjoyed a woman.

Felicity needed no invitation other than the expression in his eyes. Her arms curled around his neck, and, her lips still parted, she raised her face for his kiss.

The immediate intensity of her passion stunned Jonathan. Regardless of whether it was simulated or real, it was overwhelming. Felicity pressed hard against him, her ripe body undulating slightly beneath the rustling silk of her gown, and her proximity was a further reminder of his long abstinence.

His grip tightened, and she responded with an abandon that made it difficult for him to think clearly. Then, without warning, she disengaged herself, took a backward step, and, silently reaching around to the back of her dress, began to unhook it.

Her brazen lack of modesty, although not surprising when he thought about it, nevertheless bemused him, and Jonathan watched her in fascination.

The gown dropped to the floor, and she stood before him bare to the waist, her petticoats swaying as she approached him again.

Even more provocative than her nudity itself was her lack of reticence, but there was nothing blatant in her attitude. She knew her full, high breasts were alluring, and, proud of them, she offered them to him without artifice.

He cupped a breast in his hand as he embraced and kissed her again. Fondling it, he felt the nipple harden, and his mind stopped functioning. Their kisses became more demanding, their caresses more insistent, and Jonathan's patience vanished. He quickly undressed, then removed the rest of Felicity's clothing.

There was no sound in the room but the hissing and crackling of the fire as he took her, on the Turkish rug in front of the hearth.

They stretched out, side by side, lazily caressing each other again, and Jonathan had to remind himself that this woman had been a party to the perfidy that had robbed him of his belongings and sent him, without justification, to prison for so many months.

Eventually they donned their clothes again, still saying very little, and when Jonathan glanced out of the window and saw the sun almost directly overhead, he remembered he had promised Elizabeth he would return to her house by noon.

Retrieving his pistol, he reloaded it and slid it beneath his belt. Then, smiling, he took Felicity's cloak and draped it around her shoulders. "It's time to leave now," he said. "I've got to lock up this place."

"You'll come with me to see Papa." She was confident of her power over him, and there was no hint of doubt in her flat statement.

Jonathan shook his head.

"He's very eager to tell you how he intends to be rid of the Johnson woman."

So that was it. If they disposed of Elizabeth in some way, Jonathan's claim to the property of his cousin would be uncontested. He had suspected something of the sort, but definite knowledge that such a scheme was being planned still came as a shock.

"You might remind Andrews," he said harshly, "that he's vulnerable himself. He'd be wise not to try playing any of his tricks."

The abrupt change in his attitude bewildered Felicity, and her wide-eyed expression was not feigned.

"It won't pay for you, either," he continued, propelling her toward the door.

Before she could reply they were out in the cold, and Jonathan had locked the door of the Lewis house behind them.

"Thank you," he said, "for paying a debt you've owed me."

For an instant he thought Felicity intended to strike him. Instead she stood very still, sheer hatred in her eyes, before turning and hurrying off across the lawn and through the trees.

Jonathan relished the sweet taste of vengeance, but her cold fury was a warning that he had not seen the last of Felicity Andrews.

8

Treachery

Jonathan told Elizabeth Johnson about Felicity Andrews' threat, relating in detail the full story of the other girl's visit, except, of course, any mention of the intimacy he had enjoyed with her. "That pair learned nothing when you and your friends threw them out," he said, "and they've been sitting in the French blockhouse, plotting."

Elizabeth was unconcerned and laughed.

He paced the length of her kitchen, frowning. "They have no conscience, and they don't care what happens to people who stand in their way, as I found out. If they lived in England they'd have been sent to Newgate long ago. Only in this barbaric land are they allowed to wander freely. They're a menace, and something needs to be done to clip their claws."

She was still amused. "What do you suggest?"

"Round up your friends, Elizabeth, and drive them away!"

"But that would be condemning them to certain suffering, perhaps death."

"It's what they deserve."

"Do you set yourself up as their judge, Jonathan?"

"Of course."

"Because of the harm they did you."

"No," he said, "because they're scheming against you, and their brand of mischief is vicious."

"I appreciate your concern," Elizabeth said, "but that isn't the way we administer justice in America. We don't condemn—or punish—on the basis of talk. We act only when a wrong has been committed."

"Would you wait until they hurt you?"

"Let's say," Elizabeth replied, "until they try. If they really do try, and aren't just trying to frighten you, or me, or both of us."

"It wasn't so long ago," Jonathan said, "that I would have told you nothing could frighten me. But that would be a lie now. I don't mind admitting that it makes me uneasy to know unscrupulous people are scheming. Against both of us."

"Why should they care about you at this point? I hold the Lewis property. You don't."

He couldn't tell her Felicity wouldn't be satisfied until she evened the score for his insult to her this morning. But there was an equally compelling reason. "They see me standing next in line to you, and I know too much about them. My refusal to join forces with them makes me your ally."

"They don't know you're as anxious as they are to get hold of the estate."

"More anxious. But I'm going about it in an honorable way." He paused. "If you won't sound the alarm and call in your neighbors to help, that gives me the full burden of responsibility."

Although Elizabeth didn't really know him, she could see his mind was made up. "What will you do?"

"Why, I'll order them out of the area, naturally, and if they don't obey, I'll have a perfect opportunity to sharpen my marksmanship with a rifle. I've had very little practice since I acquired it."

"Has it occurred to you that you'll be a splendid target yourself, outside the blockhouse?"

Jonathan grinned at her. "You forget I'm a soldier by profession, my dear Elizabeth, and I'm not in the habit of exposing myself to danger unnecessarily. Andrews and Felicity can't maintain a watch outside the blockhouse twenty-four hours a day."

"No," Elizabeth replied impatiently. "But they can bolt the palisade gate and lock the inside door. They have no need to keep watch."

"I've been active in three major sieges," Jonathan said, unable to help sounding a trifle smug, "and I've stormed forts far stronger and better manned than a puny New World blockhouse. I'll borrow a length of rope from you, and that will solve the problem of Andrews and his daughter. Tonight, when it's dark, I'll scale the palisade and climb into the blockhouse itself. I believe I can give you a flat guarantee they'll be on their way within the hour."

Elizabeth looked unhappy. "You'll be lowering yourself to Andrews' level."

"I'm not asking for your approval, much less your participation." Jonathan felt a twinge of annoyance. "I consider my stake as great as yours, so I intend to rid us of this menace as I see fit."

It was useless to argue with him, at least for the present, so she dropped the subject.

He did not refer to it again, either. They ate a light meal of whitefish and fried turnips, and then Jonathan finished making the new bin she had started in her cellar. An hour or two of daylight remained, so he went into the side yard to chop more wood for her. Perhaps it was a little ridiculous to be performing domestic chores for his avowed opponent, but he was a guest under her roof, eating her food, and the performance of a few services was the least he could offer in return. Besides, she was a decent and honest foe, and he found it difficult to bear her a grudge.

Felicity and her father presented a far different problem. Their avarice and cunning, their willingness to go to any lengths to achieve their ends made them the most dangerous of enemies. He was willing to admit to himself, somewhat reluctantly, that he had been wrong to make love to Felicity before rejecting her. She had already been committed to his undoing, but now she would be even more implacable in her determination to avenge the humiliation he had inflicted on her.

The commander who hoped to win his battle always tried to take his enemy by surprise. That was an axiom Jonathan had learned when, as a youth, he had been granted his initial commission as a third lieutenant of Hussars. But he had ignored the rule today, and now Andrews would be on his guard. Therefore, since the man expected an attack, he had to move quickly, before the scoundrel had time to improve his defenses.

Deep in thought as his ax cut into the logs he was chopping, Jonathan was so preoccupied that he didn't realize someone had come onto the property until the newcomer had crossed the better part of the yard and was approaching the front door. Snatching up the rifle that rested on the cordwood beside him, he hurried around the corner of the house, arriving just in time to see Elizabeth admitting a young woman with dark hair, wearing a fur-lined cloak.

The mere fact that Felicity Andrews had chosen to come here, and so soon, was a cause for alarm, and he sprinted to the door.

"There he is!" Felicity dramatically pointed a slender forefinger at him.

"All I told you," Elizabeth replied mildly, "was that I didn't know just where he was at the moment."

"It was no use trying to hide him." Felicity seemed intent on making a scene of some sort. "I'd have searched the house from attic to cellar until I found him."

Jonathan had no idea what new trick she had in mind but wanted to be rid of her at once. "What do you want here?" he demanded roughly.

Felicity ignored him and addressed herself exclusively to the other girl. "Release him to me. Please. I hope he hasn't hurt you too much, but what he's done to me is far worse. I can't tell you how often he's done something like this."

"What in the devil are you talking about?" Jonathan shouted.

Still facing Elizabeth, Felicity raised both arms in a theatrical gesture. "He's my husband!"

Elizabeth was too stunned and bewildered by the totally unexpected accusation to reply.

Jonathan was tempted to laugh at the outrageous remark but knew there was something behind it and felt, even more urgently, that she was a menace as long as she remained here. "That's a damned lie," he said brusquely. "Now get out."

Felicity continued to pay no attention to him. "Did he tell you we saw each other this morning—at the place he calls his house?"

Elizabeth regained her composure. "Of course," she replied calmly.

Jonathan admired her poise but felt this was a situation he alone could handle and put a hand on Felicity's shoulder.

She shook him off. "I don't suppose he told you we planned this meeting long ago, in Philadelphia. But he's broken his word to me. He swore he'd have only business dealings with you, Mistress Johnson. I'd had no idea he'd stay here, as your guest. And I warn you, if he hasn't already tried, he'll make love to you. He'll do anything to persuade you to give up that property."

The remark struck home, and for a moment Elizabeth was thrown off balance, but the attempt to stir up trouble was so obvious that she finally smiled. "Captain Lewis has behaved like a perfect gentleman," she said.

"You have no need to defend yourself," Jonathan told her. "This slut has no claim on me!"

Felicity glanced at him sorrowfully, then turned back to the other girl again. "I'll never understand why he's so deceitful. Just this morning he swore I was the only woman in his life. That was when he made love to me, in front of the hearth, at the Lewis house."

Jonathan felt the blood rush to his face.

"Deny it, if you can!" Felicity played the role of the injured wife to perfection.

Elizabeth glanced at Jonathan, and the guilt in his face confirmed the charge.

Before he could reply, Felicity threw herself at him, her arms around his neck. "I don't know what I've done to offend you, but I beg you, dear, come back to me!"

Jonathan tried to disengage himself, but she clung to him with surprising tenacity.

Elizabeth made no attempt to intervene, but suddenly her expression of disgust changed to one of alarm and she screamed.

Jonathan threw off Felicity, but by then it was too late for him to turn. Someone crashed into his back, sending him staggering forward; at almost the same instant someone else knocked his legs from under him and he fell.

He reacted violently even before he could identify his assailants. Legs thrashing and arms flailing, he tried to fight off the pair who landed on top of him, and he remembered that Li-solu had taught him the secret of hand-to-hand encounter was balance. If he could throw his attackers off balance he might be able to cope with both of them.

But they showed a remarkable ability to anticipate every move he made, and soon he felt his legs being pinned to the floor. Then one of the assailants immobilized his left arm, and he realized, belatedly, that three men rather than the two he had imagined were attacking him.

The odors of rancid fish oil filled his nostrils, and when he saw a copper-colored face, smeared with streaks of vermilion and green paint, looming directly above him, he knew his attackers were Indians. Desperately, in spite of the odds against him, he made an effort to break away, landing several solid punches to the face of the warrior who was trying to catch hold of his right arm.

In the background he heard Elizabeth scream again, and the sounds of a brief scuffle he could not see told him that she, too, was the victim of the braves.

No man could fight indefinitely against three-to-one odds, and at last the helpless Jonathan lay spread-eagled on the floor. The warriors continued to hold him, and the odor of the fish oil they smeared on their scalp locks was so pungent he wanted to retch. Then a movement from the far side of the room caused him to turn his head.

Looking up, he saw Felicity approach, and beside her was Andrews.

"I regret the need to dispose of you, Lewis," the former innkeeper said. "You and I might have worked well together, and your claim to your relative's estate would have been good enough to save me a great deal of bother. If you had cooperated, the girl would have vanished, and we could have shared this property as well as the neighboring one. But you wouldn't act reasonably, so you gave me no choice. Apparently you still haven't learned that I permit no one to stand in my way when there's something I want. Now you'll never have a chance to learn it."

Felicity impatiently pushed her father aside, and there was venom in her eyes as she stared down at Jonathan. "Humiliate me, would you?" She spat in his face. "You damned swine!"

Jonathan felt the pointed toe of her slipper striking him repeatedly in the ribs and realized she was kicking him.

Andrews drew her away. "There's no need for personal vengeance, child. Our friends are taking care of the matter for us."

A faint moan on Jonathan's other side attracted his attention, and he craned his neck in that direction. Elizabeth, her eyes wide with terror, was stretched out on the floor near him, her wrists and ankles bound with thongs, a torn piece of her shirttail stuffed in her mouth as a gag.

Jonathan understood the whole plot now. Andrews had bribed or otherwise persuaded the savages to remove, permanently, both claimants to the Lewis property. Then he himself would take possession not only of the larger estate but of Elizabeth's house and lands, too. Deep in the wilderness, hundreds of miles from seaboard justice, he could act with impunity. No magistrates or law-enforcement officers ever came this far from the seacoast, and it would be easy enough for him to forge documents or resort to some other trickery in order to persuade the Presque Isle villagers that he had acquired both estates by legitimate means.

Furious, Jonathan made a supreme effort to free himself. His sudden movement was so unexpected that he threw off the brave who had immobilized his legs, and when the savage, snarling like a wounded animal, came at him again, a well-placed kick in the pit of the stomach sent him reeling against the far wall.

Jonathan thought he had at least a chance now and struggled even harder. He felt his left arm coming free and drove the warrior backward with a sharp thrust of his elbow and forearm.

But his valiant surge was in vain. He failed to realize there were still more warriors in the room, and one of them, racing forward to help his comrades, struck the Englishman on the head with the flat side of a stone ax.

Jonathan felt a scaring pain that spread from his head through his entire body. A thick, black curtain seemed to envelop him, and he drifted into unconsciousness.

The nightmare was endless. Jonathan's arms and legs felt as though they were being torn from their sockets, his head ached dully, and a heavy, dead weight seemed to be pulling at the base of his spine. Repeatedly awakening, then lapsing into unconsciousness again, he had no idea what was happening to him and knew only that, when the pain was so intense he could not refrain from moaning, someone struck him a sharp blow across the face.

Gradually his periods of awareness grew longer, clearer, and finally the truth of his situation dawned on him. His ankles and wrists were bound by rawhide thongs, a pole had been passed through them, and he was being carried by warriors at opposite ends of the pole. Dangling like a slaughtered deer from the pole, he was helpless as his captors marched through the endless forest. He did not know what had become of Elizabeth, and although he occasionally heard the savages speaking to one another, their voices were both distant and indistinct.

One day seemed like the next, but when Jonathan woke up one morning there was no pain in arms or legs, and, although he was still trussed, he realized he was lying on the frozen ground. A campfire was burning nearby, and although he was too far from it to enjoy its full benefits, he nevertheless appreciated the waves of warm air that drifted toward him.

"Jonathan." A whisper sounded only a few inches from his ear.

He detected a note of urgent caution in the single word and, twisting his head, saw Elizabeth on the ground beside him. Her clothes were ripped and filthy, and there were jagged welts on her face and throat. Her hands were bound tightly behind her, and a long leash, tied around her throat, trailed off toward the fire, where the Indians were sitting in a semicircle, eating.

"Thank God you're fully conscious again," Elizabeth murmured. "I can see it in your eyes."

"What have they done to you?" His whisper was a hoarse croak, and he realized his throat was painfully dry.

108

"They—make me march."

He saw that her ankles were no longer bound; her shoes were falling apart, and her feet looked raw and swollen. "Your face," he muttered. "Are they beating you?"

"Not too badly. Only when I fall."

"Those marks—"

"From bushes and other underbrush."

"Are they feeding you?"

"Scraps. When they've finished." Elizabeth fell silent, a warning in her eyes.

Jonathan realized a warrior was approaching, a gourd in his hand. He placed it on the ground, and Elizabeth, hands still tightly bound, hauled herself to her knees and ate from it, like a dog.

The Indian saw that Jonathan was conscious, watching the scene. Not speaking, the brave returned to the fire and said something in a low tone to his companions. A husky warrior stood and, with effortless grace, walked to the prone Englishman.

Staring up at him, Jonathan saw a broad-checked man, hair stiff with fish oil, his face heavily daubed with green and vermilion paint. He was clad only in a loincloth, moccasins, and a rawhide shirt but seemed impervious to the cold.

Returning the stare, the brave bent down and with a knife cut the thongs that held Jonathan's ankles, then hauled him upright.

His legs and knees refused to support his weight, and Jonathan buckled, then pitched forward onto the ground.

The brave laughed, as did others at the fire.

Someone brought the captive a gourd, and he followed Elizabeth's example, his sense of humiliation becoming of secondary importance when he realized he was ravenous. His meal consisted of scraps of cooked whitefish and bits of meat, apparently the remains of some small animal. Jonathan soon lost his appetite but forced himself to consume the entire contents of the gourd. He had no idea when he might eat again, and, equally important, he knew it was vital that he regain his strength as quickly as possible.

Then his ankles were trussed again, his captors evidently realizing he was too weak to walk. Not until the pole was inserted through the loops made by his wrists and ankles and he was hoisted onto the shoulders of two braves did it occur to him that the crude method of transportation had rubbed away his skin and that the thongs bit deeply into his flesh.

The agony, although intense, was less painful than the jerking at his sockets had been. They felt numb now, however, and he reasoned that his arms and legs had become accustomed to the strain.

Occasionally he caught a glimpse of Elizabeth in the column, a brave holding the leash fastened around her neck as she stumbled, scrambled to her feet, and plodded forward again. A feeling of anger overwhelmed the Englishman, but he forced himself to curb it. Now, of all times in his life, he needed to think clearly.

As nearly as he could judge, the savages were not planning to kill their captives. Had that been their intention, they would have disposed of both long before now, rather than bother with either on the wilderness trail. All the same, it was impossible to guess what fate might be in store.

The day passed interminably. The braves maintained a rapid pace, Jonathan's bearers showing no signs of fatigue in spite of their burden. It was evident, however, that the long march was a torture for Elizabeth. By afternoon she fell to the ground more often, and Jonathan could hear the brave guarding her slap her repeatedly as he forced her to her feet again.

When the party halted about an hour before sundown, however, she made no complaint. Throwing herself to the ground near Jonathan, she suffered in silence as she rested. He saw that both her shoes were gone now, and she had worn through her stockings, revealing feet that were cut and bleeding as well as swollen. He marveled at her fortitude.

"The savages endure great hardships," she told him, "and they expect the same of everyone else. I'd weep—if I dared—but I know they'd really mistreat me."

He could think of nothing to say that might comfort her. "What are they intending to do with us?"

"Keep us as slaves, maybe." Her shrug was caused by weariness rather than indifference. "Sell us to others. Or put on a spectacle by torturing us at one of their festivals."

"Is that what they do?"

"So I've been told, but no one has ever survived one of their pagan festivals to pass along the word."

Their plight was even graver than Jonathan had thought. There were eight braves in the party, however, and, with no weapons, suffering from a weakened physical condition, there was little he could do.

One of the warriors shot a deer, and there was so much meat that night that the prisoners were allowed to eat their fill. The Indians relented sufficiently to untie their hands, so they were spared the indignity of being forced to eat like animals. Their captors appeared to be in a good mood and made no objection when the captives conversed.

"You know this part of the country," Jonathan said. "How would you estimate our chances of escape?"

"We have none. I'd faint if I had to run. You probably can't even walk yet." Elizabeth spoke calmly, as though discussing remote acquaintances. "Even if we managed to get away, somehow—and the idea is ludicrous—we'd either starve or freeze to death."

"That might be better than slavery or torture."

"As long as we're still alive," she replied, "we can still hope. My hatred of Andrews and his daughter will keep me going. As long as there's a chance that I can even the score someday, I refuse to die!"

Jonathan, feeling precisely as she did, fell silent.

Gradually it occurred to him that the Indians were discussing the probability of a heavy snowfall later that night and were estimating the approximate time of arrival in their own town. For the first time he heard them clearly, and the sudden realization that he could understand almost every word overwhelmed him.

"Seneca!" he said.

Elizabeth stared at him. "Of course. I thought you knew."

He continued to peer at the braves, hunched around their fire. "Brothers!" he called to them in their own tongue. "Why do those who worship Gu-goc-ro-no, who rises in the sky each morning and goes to his rest each night, treat as a captive one who is their brother?"

Hearing him speak their own language, the warriors gaped at him, then raced toward him.

Jonathan painfully hauled himself to his feet and, with all the dignity he could muster, faced the husky brave who appeared to be the leader of the group. "Gu-goe-ro-no," he said, "will burn to ashes those who mistreat a brother."

Elizabeth could not understand a word he said but was astonished by his seeming self-confidence. He faced the braves as an equal, showing no trace of fear or uneasiness.

The principal warrior was impressed, too, and a gesture caused the others, who were crowding around the captive, to step back a few paces. Still suspicious, however, the principal brave looked at the Englishman through narrowed eyes. "Who is it that calls the mighty Seneca his brothers?"

"Jo-na-tan, the brother of Li-solu, a Seneca eagle who is the sachem of one thousand warriors."

A light of recognition appeared in the Indian's eyes when he heard the name of Li-solu, but he remained unyielding. "When did the dog who is weaker than a woman become the brother of the Seneca eagle?"

Jonathan explained they had been imprisoned together in Philadelphia and that he had been responsible for Li-solu's escape. He knew he was on shaky ground, however: he and Li-solu had never gone through the Seneca ceremony of brotherhood that his friend had described to him, and he did not want to be questioned too closely.

The warrior, however, had heard enough to become unsettled. Turning away abruptly, he returned to the fire, beckoning to the others. Retreating to the far side of the fire, they conferred in tones too low to hear.

Jonathan told Elizabeth what had transpired. "I don't know that it will do us any real good," he said. "But I can't imagine our situation becoming much worse."

9

The Seneca

The braves treated Jonathan with greater respect after learning of his alleged relationship with Li-solu, but his basic situation remained unaltered: he was still a prisoner. He was given a stew of forest roots mixed with corn meal, which improved the taste of his venison, and the warriors looked the other way when he shared the dish with Elizabeth. Later that evening, when the girl's hands again were tied behind her back, no attempt was made to bind Jonathan, and the leader of the group, showing some reluctance, gave him a blanket in which to wrap himself.

Waiting until the savages were asleep near their fire, he covered Elizabeth with the blanket and thought the gesture had not been detected. Then, belatedly, he discovered that a brave who was standing guard had observed the scene and was making no objection. Indeed, the Indian's face registered disgust, his attitude clearly indicating his contempt for anyone foolish enough to sacrifice his own comfort for a mere woman.

Shortly thereafter Jonathan discovered that his freedom was limited. A cold, wet snow began to fall, and he instinctively started to move closer to the fire. But the guard stood, silently, and pointed his ancient musket at the Englishman. The weapon was so decrepit that Jonathan doubted it could be fired accurately, but he knew the sound of a shot would awaken the others, and he decided not to tempt fate. Although chilled to the bone, he was so weary he dropped off to sleep, heartened by the prospect of lenient treatment for Elizabeth as well as for himself.

Large quantities of venison and corn-meal stew were cooked for breakfast, and both prisoners were permitted to eat their fill. The snow, still falling, was already almost knee-deep, but the braves appeared unconcerned. From the little Jonathan overheard, he gleaned there was just a short distance still to travel.

When the march was resumed, his own status was vastly improved. One of the warriors had made him a walking stick out of a sapling, and he found he could manage under his own power with its aid. The snow slowed the party's advance, making it possible for him to keep up the pace, and he was far enough toward the rear of the column that he could walk in the footprints made by the others.

It distressed him, however, that there was no change in Elizabeth's situation. She and the warrior who guarded her still brought up the rear, the girl with the leash around her neck and her hands tied behind her back. She was barefooted, Jonathan knew, so her suffering undoubtedly was intense, and he winced, too, every time he heard the warrior slapping her. But he did not dare protest, sensing that the relative courtesy being shown him was strained to its limits.

Soon after noon, with the snowfall so heavy it was possible to see only a short distance, the leader halted and the others stopped, too. One of the braves cupped his hands and uttered a cry that sounded uncannily like the hooting of an owl. Everyone seemed to be waiting for something, and after a few moments the call was answered.

Both cries were repeated at intervals of a minute or two, with that in the distance constantly drawing closer, and eventually two other braves, both wearing shaggy bearskin cloaks, materialized out of the snowstorm. The leader conferred with them briefly, then the whole group continued forward again at a slower pace.

The braves in the fur cloaks were armed with long rifles, which they handled with familiarity, and Jonathan realized they were sentries. The Seneca, he thought, might be a primitive people, but their technique of guarding their communities was highly developed, and European armies would benefit by emulating them.

Additional sentries, some in fur cloaks, some in heavy buckskins, appeared occasionally, glancing with seeming indifference at the prisoners before vanishing again into the forest. At the crest of a high hill the woods ended abruptly, and here a larger detachment of warriors was stationed. They, too, appeared to take no notice of the captives.

At the bottom of the hill, in a long, narrow valley, stood the Seneca town, and, beyond it, a large lake. Jonathan was quick to appreciate the military cunning of the men who had chosen the site. Surrounded on three sides by hills, the valley was easy to defend, and the lake not only discouraged an attack by water but offered an avenue of escape in the event the defenders were overwhelmed.

The inner slopes of the hills leading down to the valley had been cleared of trees and bushes, and it was apparent that the hillsides were used, at other seasons, for the cultivation of crops. Here, again, the Seneca utilized an advanced system of their own; at intervals, on the slopes, were storage bins with thick, thatched roofs to protect the corn and other grains placed there for safekeeping. These, Jonathan guessed, were used at harvest time to make it easier to store the foodstuffs without carrying them any considerable distances.

The patterns in the town itself, laid out at the base of the valley, were easy to see from above. Four long, single-story buildings of logs were laid out in a rectangle, and, from what the Englishman remembered of Li-solu's description of Seneca living, these were the barracks of the unmarried warriors. The inner portion of the quadrangle was dotted with stone-lined pits which the single braves used for the cooking of their meals.

Closer to the lake were several other long houses, laid out in parallel rows. These, Jonathan guessed, were the dwellings of the unmarried maidens, who were taken there at the same age the boys left their familes, usually when they were seven.

The private dwellings of the married men were laid out in circles stretching across the town. These were building of logs and clay, little more than huts; virtually all were conical in shape, windowless, with openings at the apex of each house to permit the escape of smoke. As nearly as Jonathan could make out, flaps of animal skins covered the entrance to each dwelling.

The huts in one circle, near the shore of the lake, were larger than the other homes, so it was safe to assume that these were the homes of the ruling sachems and elders. One house in particular stood out, and behind it was a building that resembled a miniature long house. Jonathan had no idea what it contained.

Another mystery on the side of the valley farthest from the lake perplexed and intrigued the Englishman, too. Crude platforms about ten feet square were laid out on the tops of poles that stood about fifteen feet above the ground. Several were empty, but two or three contained objects of some sort, which the thick layer of snow obscured and made impossible to identify. Nothing Li-solu had said about his people had contained even a hint of these strange platforms.

In all, Jonathan estimated, the town contained about three or four thousand inhabitants. No more than that lived in any one Seneca community, but the nation's towns were laid out in circles some miles apart in the wilderness. All were close enough to neighbors, Li-solu had indicated, to obtain help from others in the event of an enemy attack. But if one suffered a severe loss, the others might escape unscathed.

The group paused at the crest while the leader conversed in low tones with an older warrior who wore two eagle feathers in his scalp lock. This badge of rank was the same as Li-solu's, and Jonathan wondered if this was his friend's town. If not, he hoped, fervently, that word would be sent to one of the other settlements and that Li-solu would come to his rescue.

A sudden jab of a musket's muzzle in the small of Jonathan's back jarred him into the harsh reality of the present, and a moment later the party descended the slope and approached the town. All at once the community came alive. Women and small children, the former in ankle-length gowns of skins and woven reeds, the latter clad only in loincloths, despite the cold, filled the areas between the rows of houses.

Before Jonathan quite realized what was happening, he and Elizabeth were under attack. The women, screaming and cursing, threw rocks and snowballs at them, while the children, armed with short sticks, beat at the prisoners' legs and jabbed them. Scores

116

of yapping dogs appeared, too, and joined in the torment, nipping at the captives' heels as they stumbled and staggered.

Warriors stood in the entrances to the huts, impassively watching, and the younger braves emerged from the long houses but took no part in the torture. The worst, however, was yet to come. Single women raced out of their long houses, screaming, and hurled themselves at the captives. Jonathan was clawed, scratched, and bitten, and when he fell to the ground the young women trampled on him, kicking him until he was afraid he would lose consciousness.

Twice he was rescued by the braves who were escorting him, but these men, also enjoying the spectacle, intervened only when they felt it was necessary to prevent their charges from being killed. A commotion behind Jonathan told him that Elizabeth was suffering a similar fate, and during a momentary lull he tried to offer her encouragement.

"Don't lose heart!" he shouted hoarsely. "We'll survive this, and anything else they may do!"

Elizabeth was too far gone to reply in words, but he could hear her high-pitched, hysterical laugh.

Groggy after four or five attacks, Jonathan could scarcely move by the time the braves dispersed the women and led him to a small hut. A hand between his shoulder blades sent him sprawling, and he landed on the cold dirt floor just as the flap at the entrance was lowered. He had no idea how long he stretched out on the ground, but gradually he began to recover his senses and was able to sit up.

He found himself in a hovel so small that only in the center could he stand erect. The log walls, chinked with clay, were thick and kept out the snow, and there was no opening in the conical roof, no fire pit in the center. Therefore, although the hut was dry, it was bitterly cold. The interior was completely devoid of furnishings, and the thick flap over the entrance kept out all but a tiny sliver of light.

As Jonathan's eyes became accustomed to the gloom, he realized his own condition was deplorable. He was bleeding from a number of small cuts, his shirt had been torn from him, and his trousers were in rags. One of his moccasins was missing, too, and the chill ate into his bones. He could do nothing but sit or lie on the dirt floor, shivering.

There were no discernible sounds outside the hovel, either, and the silence was as oppressive as the cold. After what felt like an eternity of waiting, the flap opened and a guard armed with a musket thrust a large, steaming gourd inside. Its contents were a mixture of smoked fish, jerked venison, and a number of unidentifiable plant roots, all cooked in coarse corn meal. The odors that rose from the gourd were nauseating, but Jonathan knew he had to eat and dipped his fingers into the container.

After a few bites he felt a little warmer, and by the time he finished the meal he was able to forget his weariness and bruises. Eventually the flap opened again, and the older warrior, two eagle feathers in his scalp lock, filled the entrance. He stared at the prisoner in silence, then threw a blanket into the hovel and dropped something onto the floor at the Englishman's feet. A moment later he was gone.

Jonathan picked up the object and discovered it was a cleverly hollowed elk horn. Removing the top, a stone wrapped in rawhide, he sniffed the contents and almost gagged. The horn was filled with a foul-smelling, thick liquid, a combination of rancid fish oil and sharp herbs. At first he thought the savages were mocking him, but apparently the oil had a purpose, so he replaced the stopper, then decided to wrap himself in the blanket while he pondered.

As he opened the blanket a Seneca loincloth fell out, and he couldn't help smiling. His buckskin trousers were useless, so he donned the new leather garment, then huddled beneath the blanket, which was dirty but warm. It was ironically amusing to realize that the woolen cover had been made in England.

At last the mystery of the elk-horn container was solved. On the march from Presque Isle the lightly clad warriors had covered themselves with a film of oil, and he was being offered the opportunity to do the same. He saw nothing to be gained and intensely disliked the idea of smearing himself with the evil-smelling stuff. But his one hope of survival was to persuade his captors that he was one of them, at least in spirit.

Throwing the blanket aside, he poured a little of the oil into the palm of his hand and began to spread it over his torso. Within moments he discovered that his bruises and cuts miraculously stopped smarting, and even the pain in his wrists and ankles lessened considerably. The herbs in the ointment were responsible, he assumed, so he ignored the odors and covered his entire face and body.

Then he wanted to laugh aloud as it occurred to him that he was no longer chilled. The oil provided him with a covering that prevented the cold from penetrating, and all at once he knew why the warriors had been able to withstand the rigors of a wilderness winter so easily.

Warm and fairly comfortable at last, he rolled up in the blanket, and, in spite of his concern for Elizabeth and his worry about his own situation, he dropped off to sleep.

For five days and nights Jonathan remained in the hovel. Four times each day his captors brought him food, and although he found the strange tastes unappetizing, he certainly could not complain of hunger. Late in the third day of his captivity another flask of oil was brought to him, and this time he unhesitatingly smeared it on his face and body. His cuts were healed now, he was warm, and, in spite of his cramped quarters, he felt his strength returning.

At last, on the fifth day, the leader who wore two eagle feathers as a badge of his rank returned. Again he stood impassively in the entrance, but this time he raised his left hand, palm forward, to the level of his face. "Mi-la-ine," he said solemnly, "greets Jo-na-tan."

Jonathan's heart pounded. He was being addressed by name, and hope flared within him, but he took care to imitate the other's wooden expression. "Jo-na-tan," he replied in the traditional Seneca manner, "greets Mi-la-ine."

The warrior continued to regard him unblinkingly. "Mi-la-ine," he said, "sent a message on the bark of the birch tree to his brother, Li-solu. Now Li-solu has sent to his brother a message on the bark of a birch tree. Jo-na-tan will come."

Wrapping himself in the blanket, Jonathan followed him into the open. The snow lay more than four feet deep on the ground, but the oil on his bare feet and legs protected him, and he walked without difficulty through the drifts. The guard stationed outside the hovel raised his musket high in a salute to Mi-la-ine and then strolled away. Apparently the hut would no longer be used as a prison.

Here and there women looked out of their houses at the leader and the English captive, but there was no commotion. Not one squaw raced out to attack the stranger, and the children as well as the dogs remained out of sight, too. It was evident that Jonathan's status had changed, thanks to the exchange of messages with Li-solu.

Mi-la-ine halted at the front of a large hut and pointed. "Jo-na-tan will go. There he will stay until Li-solu comes."

"When will Jo-na-tan's brother come?"

"The sachem of the town of the red maple will send a message to the sachem of the town of the yellow maple. Then he will come."

Jonathan had to be content with the evasive reply, but there was something else he wanted to know just as urgently. "What is the fate of the maiden with the hair of pale honey color?" he asked.

Mi-la-ine gave no sign he had heard and pointed again at the entrance flap.

"She is protected by Gu-goe-ro-no, who will grant the people of this town all they wish if she is treated with kindness." Jonathan realized he was pushing his luck to its limits but, for Elizabeth's sake, took the risk. Her welfare, perhaps her life, was at stake.

Again Mi-la-ine pointed toward the large hut.

Jonathan had no choice and, pushing aside the flap, walked in.

To his astonishment, three Indian women were waiting for him, one a squaw of middle years, the others young women with the headbands of white and yellow beads that marked them as maidens.

The older woman indicated with a gesture that Jonathan was expected to remove his loincloth.

When he hesitated in embarrassment they crowded around him, and he was afraid they might try to take it from him by force. Rather than suffer the indignity, he removed it himself.

At the direction of the squaw the maidens smeared him with a tarlike substance that had a mild pine odor and then began to scrub him so vigorously with birch twigs that his body became raw. The treatment was totally unexpected, but, realizing they were cleaning him, he submitted without protest to their energetic ministrations.

When they were finished they sloshed him with cold water, and the younger women giggled when he winced but immediately sobered when the older squaw glowered at them.

Jonathan was permitted to don the loincloth again and then was required to sit cross-legged on the floor. The squaw approached him, a sharp knife in her hand, and he braced himself, ready to grapple with her if she tried to plunge the blade into him.

She became aware of his reaction and, for the first time since he had come into the hut, favored him with a toothless grin. Then she indicated her intentions in pantomime, and he offered no resistance when she cut away the five-day stubble of beard on his face. To his surprise she was not yet finished, however, and shaved off the hair on both sides of his head, leaving only a scalp lock that extended from his forehead to the nape of his neck.

The younger women smeared him with oil, and the squaw handed him a new pair of moccasins and a loose-fitting rawhide shirt of the sort the warriors wore in winter. Before they departed the trio built a fire in the stone pit located in the center of the hut, and when they finally withdrew, Jonathan realized this was his new home.

Gingerly feeling his scalp lock, he discovered it was stiff and even greasier than his body. Looking down at his attire, he realized he must closely resemble a Seneca brave now and started to laugh. It was hard to believe he actually felt relief and gratitude for his rise in the world to the status of a savage. His friends in London wouldn't believe him when he told them the tale of his adventures.

The improvement in Jonathan's lot was as dramatic as the change in his appearance. His meals were prepared for him in his new hut by squaws, and he was given liberal portions of food. He slept on a bed of young evergreen boughs, and although the day was not far past when he would have protested, he now considered the accommodations a luxury.

The Seneca permitted him to wander where he pleased through parts of the town, principally the section where the married warriors lived with their families. But sentries halted him when he tried to wander in the direction of either the braves' or women's long houses, and he was directed to return to the valley on the two occasions he started up a hillside toward the forest. The fact that he was permitted to carry no weapons emphasized an inescapable conclusion: although he was living in far greater comfort, he was still a prisoner.

It soon became evident that the residents of the town were under instructions to have no intercourse with him. The squaws looked through him, and the children ran when they saw him walking around the town. The warriors literally pretended he did not exist, and even the women who came to his hut to prepare his meals made no reply when he addressed them.

Deeply concerned about the fate of Elizabeth Johnson, he repeatedly requested an interview with Mi-la-ine, but the squaws gave no indication that they even passed along the demand, and neither did the warriors he accosted at random in the snow-littered paths between the Seneca huts.

Had he been completely alone, Jonathan would have been tempted to escape, even though the odds were against him. But he could not allow himself to contemplate the idea while Elizabeth was still being held in bondage of some sort. To the best of his knowledge no ceremonies or festivals had been held, so it was unlikely that she had been offered as a sacrifice to the Seneca gods or had provided the savages with a day of entertainment. Consequently it was safe to assume that she was still in the town or, at the worst, had been moved to another of the tribe's communities. In any event, he had no intention of leaving without her. She was headstrong, self-willed and stubborn, and had too high an opinion of herself for his liking, but she was a civilized woman, and he refused to leave her behind when he returned to Presque Isle for a final settling of scores with Felicity Andrews and her father.

For almost two weeks there was no change in Jonathan's new situation. He regained his health and energy, and the restricted life he led made him increasingly restless, but he tried to wait patiently for whatever might lie ahead. Even if the rescue of Elizabeth were not an inhibiting factor, he knew it would be foolhardy to try to escape in the dead of winter, without arms or provisions, from a town that was guarded far better than any English or European military base he had ever known.

Late one morning, as he was returning to his hut from a long, aimless stroll, he saw a warrior with the two eagle feathers of a sachem in his scalp lock approach the building from the opposite side. Thinking his visitor was Mi-la-ine, he increased his pace.

The warrior was enveloped in a bearskin cloak, his face was daubed with yellow and orange paint, and not until he spoke did Jonathan recognize him.

"Li-solu greets his friend!"

Forgetting that Indians maintained their dignity at all times and under all situations, Jonathan pumped his hand after the manner of civilized men and enthusiastically pounded him on the back.

Li-solu allowed himself to be pummeled, and then they went into the hut, where two squaws were finishing their preparations of Jonathan's meal. But the young sachem wanted privacy, and when he clapped his hands together sharply, the women scurried away, leaving food cooking over the fire.

"For nearly a moon Li-solu could not come to his friend. Many strange alliances are being made, and Li-solu was needed by his own people to prepare the defense of his town."

Jonathan thanked him for the improvement in his own lot and immediately inquired about Elizabeth.

Expression vanished from Li-solu's face. Removing his cloak, he went to the fire, removed the food, and ladled the hare and corn-meal stew into two gourds.

Jonathan accepted his food and sat crossed-legged opposite the man with whom he had shared a cell for so many months. "Li-solu knows," he said severely, "that one's heart grows heavy when one who has done no wrong is held as a prisoner."

The sachem concentrated on his food and would not meet the Englishman's steady gaze.

Jonathan's patience snapped. "Damnation!" he said, reverting to English. "You know you have no right to hold her! She's done no harm to you or your people!"

The Indian, obviously growing more uncomfortable, replied in the same tongue. "The warriors who brought her-with-hair-like-wheat to the land of the Seneca want reward. Two rewards were promised. Now Jo-na-tan has been taken from them. They want reward of squaw-girl."

It was necessary for Jonathan to remind himself that he had to curb his temper. His friend was a barbarian who was incapable of thinking in civilized terms. "What in the devil do you mean, they want her as a reward?"

"Sell squaw-girl. Get rifle, maybe. Get new blanket. Get many new things."

"Who wants to—to buy her?" Jonathan almost choked on the words.

"Many warriors want for squaw." Li-solu's tone indicated he was dealing with the obvious.

The very idea that Elizabeth would be forced to remain with the Seneca for the rest of her days as the wife of a warrior and the mother of his children was infuriating. "That's against every law!"

The sachem shook his head, and the eagle feathers bobbed. "Not Seneca law," he replied reasonably.

"I won't stand for it!" Jonathan shouted, momentarily indifferent to his own precarious, undetermined future.

"Jo-na-tan want for squaw?"

"Certainly not!" Jonathan was so indignant that he couldn't imagine how to explain that marriage to Elizabeth—or anyone else—was farthest from his mind.

"Many warriors want." Li-solu remained matter-of-fact. "Mi-la-ine want for slave."

"No!" Jonathan's fist pounded on the dirt floor of the hut.

"Squaw of Mi-la-ine no want. Mi-la-ine no get."

"Look here," Jonathan said. "The girl and I were minding our own business when we were kidnaped and brought here. And we were damned badly mistreated on the trail, too. Is that fair or honorable or just? Give me a straight answer!"

Li-solu continued to eat his meal, completely unruffled. "Not fair when men of Fi-la-del-fee-ah put Li-solu in prison."

"I wonder if you know that it was our old enemy, Andrews, who made the arrangements with your warriors to kidnap the girl and me. He and that brunette harlot, his daughter, are responsible for the whole thing."

Li-solu blinked but otherwise did not show his surprise. He remained silent for a long time, the food in his gourd forgotten, and finally he murmured the name of Andrews, speaking it as though it were a curse.

"Then you didn't know!"

Again the sachem was lost in thought. "An-ru wicked man. An-ru squaw-girl wicked. Warriors of Seneca big fool to make treaty with An-ru."

Jonthan felt solid hope for the first time. "What can be done about it?"

Li-solu reverted to his own tongue. "Gu-goe-ro-no sees what all Seneca do. Li-solu will go to the altar of Gu-goe-ro-no. There he will make sacrifice. The god will tell him what to do. Li-solu also seeks the blood and scalp of An-ru." The hard, icy gleam in his eyes did not indicate that he had ever been exposed to the supposed benefits of civilization.

It was highly possible, Jonathan told himself, that he and Elizabeth would be set free in the immediate future and, in addition, that Li-solu would take an active part in the administration of justice. Andrews and his daughter were living in Presque Isle on borrowed time.

But the sachem promptly dashed his daydreams. "Jo-na-tan will become the true brother of Li-solu," he said. "He must pass the test of the Seneca. Then he will be a warrior. Then Jo-na-tan and Li-solu will go to the altar of the gods and become brothers."

Wanting only to leave the Indian town and attend to his own affairs, Jonathan gestured impatiently.

Before he could speak, however, his friend raised a hand. "Li-solu," he said in English, his voice surprisingly gentle, "know how Jo-na-tan feel. But Li-solu not the chief sachem of all the Seneca. Ten sachem of two eagle feather. Five sachem of three eagle feather. Leader of five thousand. One grand sachem of five eagle feather.

Sachem of all Seneca. All sachem have council. Gods tell sachem Jo-na-tan become warrior of Seneca. This Jo-na-tan do."

The apology, if it could be called that, was matter-of-fact. Jonathan realized his friend was telling him there was no choice, that the decision made by the leaders of the Seneca nation could not be altered. And it was impossible to argue, since Li-solu had indicated that his own hands were tied.

"What must I do?"

"Many test. Start now." Li-solu finished his meal, wiped his mouth with the back of his hand, and, standing, threw his gourd into the fire.

Jonathan, who had never before seen the gesture, followed his example.

"Seneca warrior," Li-solu said, "very strong. Seneca warrior know how kill. Seneca warrior have courage. Not weep like squaw. Jo-na-tan be strong, know how kill. Jo-na-tan have courage. Then Jo-na-tan be Seneca warrior."

Apprehension and a sense of challenge mingled in Jonathan as he and Li-solu left the hut, walked rapidly through the town, and headed up the far slope beyond the valley. He had no idea what trials might await him but knew that for Elizabeth's sake, as well as his own, he could not afford to fail.

10

The Warrior

A sachem, middle-aged and grizzled, with three eagle feathers in his scalp lock, stood unmoving at the far end of the clearing set deep in the pine forest. On his left, equally impassive, was Mi-la-ine, and Li-solu, not looking at Jonathan, joined the other leaders. Behind them were grouped at least twoscore senior warriors, burly men who proudly carried the scars of combat on their faces, arms, and bodies. All were armed with muskets, pistols, or long knives, and all were silently grave, their attitude one of tense anxiety.

Their feeling communicated itself to Jonathan, who stopped short and surveyed them. Unwilling to reveal his nervousness, he managed to keep his features composed, and his military training was a help to him as he instinctively approached the senior sachem and raised his right hand in a stiff Royal Army salute.

The warriors murmured their approval, several looking surprised, and he realized he had done the right thing.

A warrior stepped out of the front rank and approached the Englishman, and Jonathan saw that he carried a number of bone-handled knives suspended from a thick belt that was looped outside his shirt. "He who would become a Seneca will prove his worth," the brave intoned. Taking a knife from his belt, he handed it to the neophyte and pointed to the trunk of a slender birch at the far side of the clearing.

A gash had been marked in the tree at shoulder height, and Jonathan wanted to ask if that gash was his target. But the understanding of the savages he had acquired caused him to remain silent. They would tell him what they wanted him to know and would volunteer no more than they believed necessary. Therefore it was his responsibility to exercise as much initiative as he could.

He balanced the knife in the palm of his hand, then twice flipped it into the air and caught it by the handle when it descended. He had no doubts regarding his prowess with a knife, having learned the art of throwing during a six-month tour of duty in Spain as a liaison officer. But the blade in his hand had been fashioned by a savage, not a master craftsman, and the weight of the weapon was unevenly distributed.

Testing it again, he realized it was heavier in the center than it should have been, so he compensated for the difference by grasping it low on the hilt. Sighting his target, he let fly, and the warriors grunted in approval when the blade grazed the tree only a few inches from the target, taking off some slivers of bark.

Jonathan was dissatisfied but had an immediate opportunity to do better. He was given a second knife and went through the same balancing procedure. This time the blade cut deep into the tree less than an inch below the gash and remained there, quivering.

The grunts of approval were louder, Li-solu grinned, and Mi-la-ine looked pleased, too. Only the older sachem failed to respond.

His attitude annoyed Jonathan. "You frozen-faced bastard," he said in English, "I'll show you how to throw a knife!"

Snatching another blade from the warrior's hand before it was offered to him, he weighed it quickly, then released it with a snap of his wrist. It dug into the tree so close to the other blade that he thought he could hear metal shaft grating against metal shaft.

Several of the warriors stamped their feet, raised their muskets above their heads, and howled their approval. Li-solu was delighted by his protégé's prowess and nodded enthusiastically when Mi-la-ine said something to him.

But the senior sachem was not yet satisfied. Beckoning, he reached under his wolfskin cloak and took out a tomahawk, which he handed to the Englishman.

Jonathan's sense of accomplishment disappeared. Never in his life had he handled such a weapon and had no idea how to use it. Ex-

amining it with care, he saw that it was not the usual Indian tomahawk with a metal or stone blade. This weapon was a small English
ax, its handle having been chopped off to the savages' customary
eight- or nine-inch length.

The balance, Jonathan discovered, was true, so he decided not
to change his throwing technique for one that would require great
practice before he could perfect it. He would need to use greater
force, he knew, because the ax was far heavier than a knife. Resisting the temptation to lob the heavy weapon at the target, he hurled
it with all of his might.

There was a clatter as it struck the knives embedded in the tree,
knocking them to the ground and falling beside them. Even the
principal sachem's reserve vanished, and he joined in the cheers of
his subordinates.

The knife-throwing test was at an end, but that which followed
was far more difficult. Jonathan was required to retreat as far he
could across the clearing and from that distance throw javelins at the
same target. These light, stone-tipped shafts of wood were new to
him, and he quickly found that his knife-throwing technique was of
no help. Missing the tree with his first two javelins, he adjusted his
stance and tried four more. Each effort came closer than that which
preceded it, but he missed his target with all four and felt disgusted
with himself.

To his astonishment the Seneca cheered him again when he finished, and at first he thought they were mocking him. But their
expressions indicated the sincerity of their applause, and he finally
realized they were pleased because he had improved steadily with
each throw. So, it appeared, they appreciated the difficulty he encountered in handling an unfamiliar weapon.

The next test was one that required both strength and skill.
Jonathan was directed to strip to his loincloth, and a warrior, simi-
larly attired, came forward into the clearing to wrestle with him.
The lessons Jonathan had received in the Philadelphia prison from
Li-solu stood him in good stead, and, although his heavy-set oppo-
nent outweighed him by at least twenty pounds, Jonathan won the

match after a short, vicious struggle, pinning his foe's shoulders to the cold ground.

A second warrior promptly stepped forward to challenge the Englishman, and again Jonathan won, although he needed more time. His victory won him no applause, however. On the contrary, the braves stared at him glumly, all three of the sachems scowled, and it took a moment before he realized they were disturbed because an outsider had beaten two of their senior warriors.

Then, suddenly, Mi-la-ine stepped forward to retrieve the honor of his tribe. Shedding his cloak, shirt, and moccasins, he lunged at the Englishman, bearing him to the ground so quickly that Jonathan had almost no opportunity to defend himself, much less mount a counteroffensive.

Mi-la-ine was far superior to either of the braves, and Jonathan realized from the outset that he was fighting a real champion. The sachem knew precisely what he was doing and caught his opponent in holds from which there was no escape. Showing surprising grace for someone of his bulk, he writhed and squirmed at the right moments to avoid being caught himself, and the match ended as abruptly as it had started, with Jonathan spread helplessly on his back.

The braves cheered their leader, and Jonathan was encouraged, after they regained their feet, when Mi-la-ine clasped his forearm in the traditional Indian gesture of friendship. It appeared that, in spite of his defeat, the Englishman had not lost favor.

There was no opportunity for Jonathan to don his shirt and moccasins. A brave came into the clearing with a rifle and thrust it into his hands, along with a pouch of ammunition and a powder horn. Turning the weapon over in his hands, Jonathan recognized the weapon as his own.

The ranks of the warriors parted, and he caught his breath when he saw Elizabeth being dragged into the open. She was attired only in the woven reed breastband and ankle-length skirt, slit at the sides, that were worn by slave women. Her hair was matted and there were streaks of dirt on her face and arms, but Jonathan could see no bruise marks or other signs that she had been physically mistreated.

Her captor hauled her to the birch tree, lashed her to it with her hands tied behind her back, and then made a fresh slash in the trunk less than a foot above her head.

The entire assemblage was laughing, and Jonathan realized his courage was being tested to the utmost. He wanted to communicate with Elizabeth but was afraid to address her in English, knowing that Li-solu could understand them.

"Do you speak French?" he called.

She nodded almost imperceptibly.

Quickly he outlined his own situation, told her of Li-solu's help, and indicated his belief that the sachem, who also had cause to carry a grudge against Andrews, would be of even greater assistance. "So," he concluded, "don't lose hope."

"I haven't—and I won't," she replied.

The senior sachem clapped his hands together, indicating there had been enough talk.

Jonathan knew what was expected of him and examined his rifle with infinite care, then loaded it. It was outrageous to fire a high-powered weapon at such short range, and he understood, far better than did the savages, that the slightest error might well result in Elizabeth's death.

He was tempted to fire wide of the mark, taking no chances, but that would not satisfy the Seneca, who would brand him as a coward. His temper soaring, he wanted to put his bullet between the eyes of the senior sachem, but that would be a senseless gesture, a guarantee that neither he nor Elizabeth would leave the clearing alive. Waiting until he became calmer, he concentrated on the deadly, delicate business at hand. In spite of the coating of grease that covered his body he felt a chill and lowered the rifle until he stopped shivering. Then, raising it again, he called, "Have faith in me! I won't hit you!"

"I'm sure you won't!" Elizabeth's courage matched his.

Steadying the rifle, he sighted the gash above her head and, bracing himself, squeezed the trigger. There was a loud report, and when the smoke cleared away he saw that Elizabeth was still standing, a faint smile on her lips. The shot had burrowed deep into the narrow birch trunk about two feet above her head.

Again he was required to shoot, and this time he lowered his sight a trifle, reducing the margin above her head to slightly less than eighteen inches. His marksmanship was superior to any the Indians had ever seen, and, aroused by the possibility that an instant's carelessness could result in the death of the squaw slave, they clamored for more.

The senior sachem indulged them, and Jonathan was ordered to fire again and yet again. In all he fired ten rounds before the savages were satisfied, and when at last he was done he saw that five of the ten shots had penetrated the tree trunk. Elizabeth had escaped unscathed, but by now her smile was forced.

When her bonds were untied she collapsed at the foot of the tree, giving in suddenly to the strain.

The brave who had been guarding her came forward and, grasping her wrists, started to pull her across the rough, snow-strewn ground, but Jonathan could tolerate no more. Throwing aside the rifle so the Seneca would not think he was intending to attack the man, he ran across the clearing.

Picking up the unconscious girl, he held her in his arms. "E-liz-bet," he said loudly, so all could hear, "has the heart of a brave. Let her be carried to the town by a brave." Not waiting for a reply, he thrust her into the arms of the guard.

For an instant the Seneca debated whether to drop her onto the ground. But Jonathan remained unyielding, and the warrior turned away and headed toward the valley, carrying the girl.

Only then did Jonathan wonder if he would pay for his temerity.

But the senior sachem broke the tense silence. "Li-solu," he said, "tells it true. Jo-na-tan will wear the feather of the eagle." He clapped his hands above his head in a gesture of ultimate approval.

The warriors cheered, and Li-solu looked particularly pleased.

Jonathan assumed that his trial was at an end, but he was mistaken. As he soon learned, his tribulations were just beginning. He was given a knife and, clad only in his loincloth, was ordered to go deeper into the forest. There he would remain for two suns. If he still lived at the end of that time he would be directed back to the town by the owl calls of the sentries.

This new situation, the Englishman realized, was the most perilous he had yet faced. The weather was bitterly cold, and the grease on his body offered him too little protection against it. Without food, shelter, or firearms his chances were dim. But he had no opportunity to contemplate the predicament. He was told to leave at once, and the warriors watched him in silence as he trudged off through the snow on bare feet.

A sense of panic swept over him, but he conquered it and, his mind racing, tried to look ahead. An hour or more of daylight remained, so he would utilize that time by trying to find a place to rest and, if possible, some food. He was sufficiently familiar with the wilderness to know that his chances would be reduced if he spent much time wandering around after dark.

It proved surprisingly easy to find food. Remembering the plants that Christopher Gist had declared edible, and recalling what he had seen his Seneca captors do on the march from Presque Isle, he used his knife to dig up roots of plants that he recognized, even if he did not know their name. These he tied together with a vine and, slinging the odd contraption around his neck, continued through the deep woods.

Resisting the temptation to hurry, he moved very slowly and cautiously, examining everything he saw. It was a trifle warmer in a semiclearing beneath some giant white pines, and when he saw some snowberry bushes near the edge of the clearing he wanted to laugh aloud. Tasting the fruit, he found the berries a bit tart but palatable and knew that, with the roots he had already obtained, he had enough food for two meals.

He had spent more time in his search than he had realized, however, and again a surge of panic overwhelmed him when he saw that night had fallen. But he could see surprisingly well in the dark and reasoned that he should stay in the stand of white pines until morning. The ground was littered with needles, so he worked for another hour, gathering them and piling them into a high mound. Then, eating some of the roots and his fill of snowberries, he saw that his estimate had been correct. He had food left for his breakfast.

Burrowing deep into the mound of pine needles, he eventually became fairly comfortable, if not warm. He was still rather hungry but consoled himself with the thought that the edge had been taken off his appetite, and he resisted the urge to eat the rest of his meager supplies. His bed not only warded off the worst of the chill but was surprisingly comfortable, and soon he drifted off to sleep, his slumber disturbed only by dreams of Elizabeth standing against the birch tree while he fired shots directly over her head.

Daybreak awakened Jonathan, and after eating the rest of the food he had gathered, he took stock of his situation. He had traveled only a few miles from the Seneca village and guessed he might even be within hailing distance of the Indian sentries. But he saw no reason to wander farther from the base than was necessary. Above all, he wanted to sleep in the same spot the following night, although he had eaten most of the berries.

Carefully marking a path for himself by gashing the trunks of trees as he continued through the forest, he kept a sharp watch for more food but found no more edible roots and wondered if he had been lucky. After marching for several hours he discovered he was growing weary and found himself a dry patch of ground where he could rest for a time.

He dozed, felt somewhat refreshed when he roused himself, and suddenly realized he heard the sound of running water in the distance. He followed the sound until he came to a small but deep brook, partly frozen on the top. He broke through the ice to drink and while quenching his thirst realized the water was so clear he could see the bottom.

A large fish swam past, close to the pebbles and stones that lined the bed of the river, and Jonathan plunged his hand into the icy stream, but the fish easily escaped. Necessity made him inventive. He cut down an oak branch to use as a fishing pole, made a line of a length of stout vine, and fashioned a hook from the largest barb he could find on a prickly bush. Bait was a problem, but he solved it by lightly fastening a tiny pine cone to the hook.

Lowering his line into the water, he began to fish. For the better part of an hour he enjoyed no luck whatever and became so numbed by cold that he knew he soon would be forced to abandon the enterprise. Then, just as he was about to retire from the riverbank, his line grew taut and he saw a fish had taken both bait and hook.

Hauling gently but firmly, he landed the fish and discovered that he was ravenous. Removing the head, tail, and bones with his knife, he scaled it and ate it raw. On many occasions in London he had sent a dish back to the kitchen, complaining that it was underdone, but the knowledge that he was eating uncooked fish did not bother him in the least, and when he finished it he told himself it had been delicious.

For a half-hour he moved briskly up and down the riverbank to warm himself, then returned to his fishing. But he had to wait for a long time before he brought up his next catch, and not until late afternoon did he snare three more, two at least eight inches long.

Aware that night was coming, he hurried back to his bed of pines before eating his evening repast. Then, with enough to assuage his appetite, he ate all but the largest of the fish. He buried the remains to discourage prowling animals during the night, packed the whole fish in snow, and placed it as high as he could reach in the branches of a white pine.

Again he enjoyed a good night's sleep, and in the morning he ate his last fish, finishing off the meal with the snowberries that still clung to the bushes. Soon his ordeal would be over, he thought, and he could live through the rest of the day without eating again. So he climbed back into his pine bed and remained there until he finally heard the owl call.

Hurrying toward the spot from which the sound had emanated, he forgot his weariness, the cold, and his hunger. There had been a time when he would have decried the feat he had just performed, but he felt proud of his accomplishment and knew he would cherish the memory for the rest of his days. He had met the wilderness on its own terms, under the most difficult of circumstances, and had survived. It was an extraordinary achievement, and his step was light.

11

The Warpath

The ceremony was interminable. Jonathan sat cross-legged on the dirt floor of Mi-la-ine's long house, his face and body streaked with foul-smelling paint, his arms folded across his bare chest. For hours senior warriors danced around him, chanting, and when some seemed ready to collapse, their places were taken by younger braves. The savages were celebrating the acceptance into the Seneca nation of a new warrior, and through it all Jonathan, following Li-solu's instructions, remained unmoving and impassive.

At one climactic moment he was required to drain the contents of a gourd, and the liquid was so bitter and rancid that he gagged and thought he would become ill. But the feeling soon passed, and thereafter he felt curiously lightheaded, so that time passed more quickly. He had another brief crisis when he was given a chunk of raw, sinewy meat to eat and did not think he could chew it, much less swallow it. But he realized that a failure to observe the barbaric amenities might compromise all that he had suffered to achieve, so he forced himself to complete the ritual and struggled to preserve his façade of equanimity.

The ceremony lasted for the better part of a day, but finally it came to an end, and the warriors adjourned to the inner quadrangle formed by the long houses. There fires were glowing in cooking pits, and several elderly squaws were supervising the roasting of a variety of meats. The actual preparation of the food was being handled by a motley group of half-naked warriors and squaws, and Jonathan quickly realized these miserable creatures were prisoners of the Seneca. They were beaten with sticks and leather whips when they did not perform to the satisfaction of the old squaws in charge of the operation, and occasionally a particularly clumsy wretch was kicked and sent sprawling on the hard ground. But the prisoners, like their captors, were Indians, and their faces remained wooden. They had learned from earliest childhood to accept captivity without complaint, if that lot should be inflicted on them. But not one was willing to be disgraced by crying out in pain or mortification.

Jonathan, whose age and skills set him apart from the young, unmarried braves, sat at the bottom end of the long line of senior warriors, accepted by them yet not one of them. As he tried to conceal the indignation he felt over the treatment of the captives, he suddenly stiffened and caught his breath. He caught a glimpse of Elizabeth Johnson's blond hair, in wild disarray, and seethed when he saw an old squaw strike her repeatedly for her lack of agility in throwing more wood on a fire near the place where the elders and sachems were gathered.

She endured her misery in silence and did not flinch when lashed mercilessly across the shoulders and back. She continued to gather wood from a pile beyond the fire and throw it into the flames, her face as drained of expression as those of her fellow captives. Once she stumbled, but recovered in time to avoid a vicious kick that would have propelled her dangerously close to the fire over which a side of venison was roasting.

Jonathan churned but used all of his will power to prevent himself from acting rashly. Even though he had just been accepted by the Seneca as one of their number, he recognized his inability to help Elizabeth, at least at the moment. If he used force, he would be subdued, and not only would all he had gained be lost again, but Elizabeth would be subjected to even more cruel treatment, too, as punishment for his temerity.

He could not complain aloud, either, since no warrior ever protested the rulings and acts of his superiors. Such conduct would have been considered unmanly, and he would be subjected to public disgrace for it, perhaps losing his status.

Looking at the sachems, who were already eating venison, bear meat, and buffalo steaks, Jonathan became aware of a complicating factor. Mi-la-ine was conscious of Elizabeth, too, and the Englishman could see that the principal sachem coveted her. So it would be doing her no service to call still more attention to her and, perhaps, impel Mi-la-ine to take her into his own household as a slave in spite of the objections of his senior squaw.

For the present, Jonathan concluded, he would be wise to do nothing, and he decided to wait until he could speak privately to Li-solu. Although no Indian considered a woman very important, it was at least possible, Jonathan told himself, that he might be able to persuade his mentor to find some way to alleviate the girl's situation. Meanwhile he would follow the example that Elizabeth herself was setting. It was unlikely that she had failed to see him in the line of warriors, yet she gave no sign of recognition and made no move toward him. In a sense, he knew, she was showing her trust in him, relying on him to find some way to help her overcome her predicament within the rigid framework of the savage society in which they had been thrust. He would not betray her faith, he promised himself.

The feast was the most gargantuan meal Jonathan had eaten since coming to the American wilderness. He consumed smoking, greasy chunks of venison and bear meat as well as buffalo chops and roasted portions of smaller animals that, he suspected, might be foxes and porcupines. There was dried, whole-kernel corn which had been boiled in the juice of a sweet-tasting plant, which made the kernels plump again. The men ate large quantities of fish, too, some of it smoked, some fried in iron pans of obvious English or European manufacture, and everyone helped himself to one or two small, roasted wild fowl. Jonathan did his best to keep up, although he made no attempt to emulate the warriors when they chewed even the bones of the birds.

The final dish consisted of gourds filled with a gray paste, and although the scent was of still more fish, the Englishman found the taste surprisingly good and ate with relish. Later he learned that the delicacy consisted of the inner bark of elm trees, wild raspberries, and raw lake fish, which had been pounded for hours to make the paste. The mere thought of such a dish was revolting to a civilized man, but Jonathan could not remember when he had found any food more to his liking. Perhaps, he thought uneasily, he was being transformed into a savage.

The squaws and prisoners had departed after the meal had been cooked, and the warriors were alone as they ate, the younger braves going to the fires to hack off more meat for those who wanted it. Then, when appetites were sated, the braves edged closer to the fires, curled up, and promptly went off to sleep. They were being sensible, Jonathan had to admit, and needed no urging to follow their example.

A commotion shortly before dawn awakened him. The younger braves were feeding the fires to dispel the bitter cold, and some were already eating meat that had not been consumed at the feast. But the attention of everyone was centered on the sachem of three eagle feathers, Li-solu and Mi-la-ine, who had moved apart from the others and were conferring in low tones with a runner who had just arrived in the town. Judging from his appearance, this young brave had traveled a considerable distance; his moccasins were worn thin, his rawhide shirt was badly stained, and he was eating ravenously as he talked, which made it likely that he had not paused in his journey to eat more than the provisions he carried with him.

When Mi-la-ine turned to face the assemblage and raised his hand for silence, the gesture proved unnecessary. Every senior warrior and younger brave was waiting to hear what he had to say.

His remarks were curt, lacking the rhetorical flourishes that the Indians liked to use when they addressed an audience. "The Algonkin who live in the land of green trees and rocks march to the land of the Seneca," he said. "The Seneca will not ask their brothers of the Iroquois to help them kill their foes. The Mohawk and the Tuscarora have many warriors who know great greed. They would steal the fire sticks and sharp sticks of the Seneca after the Algonkin are killed. The Seneca will go on the warpath alone."

The warriors responded with shrill, high-pitched shouts so intense, so full of venom that Jonathan felt a slow chill move up his spine. Never in his experience as a soldier had he heard fighting men express such cold-blooded yet ferocious lust for battle.

The braves had brought their rifles, muskets, and knives with them to the ceremony and feast, but hurried off to their huts and long houses for the additional equipment and supplies they would need. Jonathan, who had none, was given an English blanket, powder and ammunition for his rifle, and a large, empty rawhide pouch. He quickly discovered its purpose.

The warriors, returning to the quadrangle, lined up before several elders who had gone into the storehouses for food supplies. Each brave's pouch was stuffed with the inevitable parched corn and jerked beef and, in addition, slabs of a dark brown substance that looked like leather. Oil was distributed for the anointing of bodies, and the warriors daubed themselves and each other with smears of black and yellow paint, the colors they wore when they went to war.

In little more than a quarter of an hour after Mi-la-ine had made his announcement, the Seneca were ready to march. Li-solu had already departed, and Jonathan guessed he had gone to alert the fighting men of his own town. It was contrary to custom to ask questions, however, and when the braves formed in loose ranks behind Mi-la-ine, Jonathan realized that any attempt he might make to help Elizabeth would have to wait until the campaign ended. Taking his own place behind the senior braves, but ahead of the younger men, he could only hope he would survive the savage conflict.

The column straggled to the largest of the strange platforms that Jonathan had noted when he had first arrived in the Seneca community as a prisoner, and there, with the braves gathered around it, the sachem of three eagle feathers, who was not accompanying his men, intoned a prayer to Gu-goe-ro-no, the sun god, asking for help in annihilating the nation's enemies. Jonathan, prostrating himself on the ground in imitation of the savages, suddenly realized the purpose of the high platforms. There the bodies of dead warriors were placed, so wolves and other animals could not sneak down out of the forest at night and devour them. The Englishman shuddered, then reflected that the burial customs of the Indians were merely different from those of more civilized people and that he was wrong to think of them as more barbaric.

Few residents of the town came out to see the fighting men depart. The squaws of a number of senior warriors appeared at the entrances to their huts and watched the procession, unmoving. But the unmarried maidens and the elders absented themselves, as did the children and even the dogs. This, it appeared, was a solemn occasion that the savages chose to mark without any sentimental gestures.

Jonathan, holding his place in the line, hoped until the last that he might catch at least a glimpse of Elizabeth so he could call encouragement to her. But he had to give up the idea as the braves climbed the hill on the north side of the town and, plunging into the wilderness, started toward the northeast.

The sentries stationed in the forest remained at their posts, so it was evident that a force of some strength was being retained to protect the town in the event of attack. Jonathan wished he had been left behind, and thought rather wistfully that, with most of the men gone, it might have been easier to escape with Elizabeth.

Soon, however, he found it necessary to abandon his daydreams and concentrate on the formidable march. The warriors moved at a trot, wasting no motions and never conversing, and they maintained the same even, unbroken pace for hours. The Englishman was grateful for his sound physical condition and the stamina he had started to acquire from the time he had set out from Alexandria with Major Washington. Not even the most experienced regiments of infantry, he knew, were a match for the tireless savages.

Not until sundown did Mi-la-ine call a halt, and when the exhausted Jonathan sank to the frozen ground and stretched his aching legs, he discovered that the Seneca were no less tired. Warriors massaged their feet, kneaded the calves of their legs to prevent cramps in their muscles, and reluctantly went off in small groups to a nearby stream to drink water. It was comforting to know that, in spite of their remarkable stamina and strength, they were as vulnerable as were more civilized men to fatigue.

Following their example, Jonathan ate only a very small quantity of his parched corn and jerked beef, guessing that the food supplies might have to be stretched out for many days. Several of the braves, he saw, were chewing on the leatherlike substance they had been issued, so he took an experimental bite. The food was a smoked meat of some kind, without taste at first, which gained in flavor the longer it was chewed. Jonathan found that by the time he was able to swallow the single bite, his appetite had disappeared. So, like the senior warriors, he saved these provisions, aware of how much more he would prize them if supplies became short.

Since the Seneca were on the warpath, no campfires were lighted. The braves spread out in the forest, each man seeking and finding individual cover, and then rolled in their blankets to sleep. Knowing the demands their type of march made on their bodies, they utilized every available moment for rest and, unlike more civilized men, had no need for companionship. Each brave seemed to be self-sufficient, able to live in the field with his companions while feeling no need for conversation.

The relieved Jonathan dropped off to sleep, too, and not until morning, when the braves quietly began to stir, did he discover that at some time during the night Li-solu had joined the column with reinforcements from his own town. Neither then nor later in the day was it possible for him to seek a word with his friend, however. Li-solu held an early morning council with Mi-la-ine and several warriors who wore single eagle feathers in their scalp locks, and immediately thereafter, when the column spread out over a large area, he disappeared.

The day's long march was as rigorous as that which had preceded it, but Jonathan found himself a trifle less tired when nightfall approached. He was growing accustomed to the grueling routine and was gratified by the realization that he was holding his own with men who had spent their entire lives in the wilderness. Again he ate sparingly, and then, even though a desire to sleep almost overpowered him, he sought out Li-solu.

Others directed him through the far-flung encampment, and eventually he found his friend. Li-solu ranked as deputy commander of the expedition but enjoyed no special privileges and when Jonathan approached him was already settling down for the night in a thread-bare blanket.

Jonathan realized that other braves were within earshot and therefore spoke in English, hoping Li-solu might be willing to speak more freely in a tongue his followers did not understand. "Where are we going?"

"To the wilderness of the land that the foreigners call Massachusetts Bay."

"Is that where we'll meet the Algonkin?"

"The Algonkin," Li-solu said, "cannot march with the speed of the Seneca, but that is where the two will meet."

"Why are they intending to attack you—us?"

The sachem shrugged. "Why is the eagle wise?" he asked in his own tongue. "Why is there no wisdom in the spirit of the wolf, only greed?" Apparently he did not know the reasons for the unexpected hostility of the Algonkin, a large tribe that had spread southward from its original home in French Canada into the Maine District of Massachusetts Bay.

"Are we strong enough to beat them?" Jonathan wanted to know.

"The Seneca," Li-solu replied proudly, "eat the heart of the bear and have the strength of the bear. The Seneca are as many as stalks of corn in a field."

Jonathan raised an eyebrow. "In a small field," he said, "there might be only fifty stalks. But on the estate that's been stolen from me, thousands upon thousands could grow."

Li-solu grinned, knowing he wanted specific information. "Seneca," he said in English, "have two thousand warrior."

"And the Algonkin?"

Again the sachem shrugged. "Soon find out."

His phlegmatic reply, Jonathan gathered, meant that the column was marching against an enemy of undetermined strength. If the Seneca were badly outnumbered, and consequently were defeated, there would be only a slim chance that any surviving members of the force could find their way back to their own land, located in the western part of the colony of New York. This was especially true when a formal war was being waged, since Indians of all nations disliked taking prisoners in such conflicts and habitually neither gave nor asked quarter.

Although willing to take his own risks, Jonathan became increasingly apprehensive when he realized that, if he should be killed, Elizabeth might remain the captive of the Seneca for the rest of her life. "What will become of the colonial girl?" he demanded.

Li-solu glanced at him with sleepy indifference, then yawned. "Work hard. Good slave. If warrior want," he continued, his broad gesture seemingly including every brave in the camp, "make girl Seneca squaw."

It was useless to remind him again that he had felt righteously indignant about his own unfair imprisonment in Philadelphia. There was no connection, in his mind, between the treatment a proud and honorable warrior received and that accorded a mere woman.

Before Jonathan could think of a suitably persuasive reply, Li-solu had pulled his blanket around him and immediately fallen asleep. His former cell mate knew the futility of trying to awaken him for a sensible discussion, so there was nothing for Jonathan to do but return to his own bivouac area, try to put Elizabeth out of his mind, and gain as much rest as he could.

At the end of the third day's march a pleasant surprise awaited the column. The advance guard had found a school of fish in a large lake, and, borrowing nets from the residents of a small village of Oneida, their Iroquois allies, they caught vast numbers. Each brave was given two fish for his evening meal.

Jonathan quickly realized that, the making of fires being forbidden, he was expected to eat his meal without benefit of cooking. Unable to follow the example of the warriors near him, he cut off the heads and tails, which he gave to his comrades. But he knew he could not afford to pass up the opportunity to augment his meager rations and forced himself to taste the raw meat. Perhaps he was hungrier than he realized; in any event, he did not find the flavor objectionable and by the time he started his second fish was actually enjoying his meal.

The next day a heavy snow fell, but did not slow the column appreciably, although the bitter cold made the march a torment. Everyone anointed himself with a thick coating of oil to ward off the chill, and that night Jonathan was surprised to see the braves burrowing into the snow when they went to sleep. He did the same, and found he was much warmer. Then, while eating his frugal breakfast the following morning, he was given a two-inch length of a withered root that one of his companions had just dug from the frozen ground. It looked like a dead bit of wood, useless and unappetizing, but the warrior urged him to eat it and the reluctant Jonathan complied. Again the Englishman enjoyed a pleasant surprise: for a short time the inside of his mouth felt raw, and then, gradually, a new warmth crept through his body. He did not suffer again from the cold that day.

Late the following morning a signal was passed from brave to brave, and the usual quiet of the march deepened. The Seneca moved through the forest like silent ghosts, and Jonathan sensed that a time for action was drawing near. His belief was strengthened when the column halted, and for more than two hours the braves waited in the biting cold, without explanation.

Then, at last, a warrior wearing one eagle feather moved from group to group. The Algonkin were approaching through the forest, he said, and had no idea their foes were directly ahead. As nearly as Jonathan could gather, the Algonkin force consisted of about fifteen hundred men. Had he been in command he would have favored a direct confrontation, partly because the Seneca outnumbered their enemies, in part because they were supposedly endowed with superior qualities as fighting men.

But he was given no voice in the decision and was expected to obey orders without question. So he kept his misgivings to himself and, with his comrades, moved out into a thin, semicircular line. The Algonkin would move into this net, the warriors were told, and the trap would be closed.

Taking up his position about ten yards from the warrior on his left and even farther from the brave on his right, Jonathan became increasingly convinced that Mi-la-ine and Li-solu were making a serious mistake. Like all Indians they were enamored of the element of surprise, but were giving away a number of natural advantages in return for it. By spreading out so much they were dissipating their greater strength, and, surprisingly, they were taking up their battle line at the position in which they happened to find themselves, rather than seeking an advantage in the rolling hill country.

The Seneca did not have long to wait. The advance guard of the Algonkin appeared, advancing cautiously but confidently through the sparse forest, and from the little that Jonathan could see, he was forced to admire the Seneca technique. No firearms were used, as they would have given an alarm to the main body of the Algonkin. Instead the most accomplished of the spear and tomahawk throwers went into action at short range, and within a matter of a few moments the entire advance guard of the Algonkin was cut down. So accurate were the tomahawk wielders and spearmen that the advancing savages died without making a sound. Even more impressive, the Seneca discipline was so strong that not one brave left his place of semiconcealment to obtain the prized scalp of his victim.

The main Algonkin force unwittingly entered the trap, and the echoing report of a sachem's rifle gave the Seneca the eagerly awaited signal to open their general attack. Everywhere on the long line braves fired their rifles, muskets, and pistols at will. The trap had been closed, and the Algonkin were under fire directly ahead and on both flanks.

But the savages from the north reacted with cool aplomb. Recovering quickly from their initial surprise, they either threw themselves to the ground or sought cover behind the nearest trees. Neither retreating nor becoming panicky, they stood their ground.

Jonathan, firing and reloading his rifle methodically, soon realized there was a purpose behind the Algonkin stance. They were waiting for their foes to identify themselves by the flash of their firearms, and whenever a Seneca gave away his position, an Algonkin immediately opened a return fire. The northern braves, ferocious-looking in thick white and blue war paint, were proving to be no less courageous than the proud Seneca.

Several bullets screamed high over Jonathan's head, and when another passed far to his right, it belatedly dawned on him that the Algonkin were notoriously poor shots. Surveying what he could of the forest battlefield, it occurred to him that the Seneca were no better. Although the Indians achieved a deadly accuracy with their own primitive weapons, firearms were too new to them to be completely effective and most shots went wild.

But the Algonkin possessed one distinct advantage. Their fighting men were formed in a single, relatively cohesive unit, and the massed firepower of their warriors managed to blast holes in the too-thin Seneca line in spite of the inaccurate fire. Jonathan was disgusted, then felt a growing anger when the sachem of one eagle feather who commanded his sector ordered a retreat. He, like his comrades, had no choice and fled far in advance of the slowly moving Algonkin.

The retreat continued for more than an hour, the Seneca hurrying through a wooded valley, crossing a high hill, and finally pausing in deep pine woods behind the crest of another. There the leaders gathered for a hasty consultation, knowing the pursuing Algonkin were not far behind. The sachems were stunned by what had happened; the Seneca were unaccustomed to the taste of defeat. Most wanted to halt, make a stand, and repeat their original battle tactics. It was unthinkable that the Seneca could be driven from the field, and no leader wanted to survive such a disgrace.

While they were discussing their problem an angry Jonathan interrupted their conference. Too aroused to care about his grave breach of protocol, he brandished his rifle at them and was so furious he addressed them in English rather than their own language. "You damned, thickheaded idiots!" he shouted. "You're doing everything all wrong!"

The leaders could not understand his words, but his hostile tone needed no interpretation, and several reached for their knives.

But Li-solu halted them. "What would Jo-na-tan do?" he demanded.

"Give me all our best marksmen. Warriors who really know how to use rifles and muskets. We'll make a small spread in the center—right where the thrust of the enemy advance will come. Let us halt the Algonkin—and we will, if your lads can shoot! Then, but only

148

then, move in on both flanks and give them a heavy shower of spears and tomahawks. Yes, even pistols at close range!"

Li-solu quickly translated, and Mi-la-ine gave his subordinates no opportunity to discuss the proposal. "It will be done," he said.

The new plan was translated into action with remarkable speed. Jonathan soon found himself with about one hundred and seventy-five braves who, he noted, handled their muskets and rifles as though they understood the weapons. Mi-la-ine took command of one wing, giving the other to Li-solu, and they moved off, leaving Jonathan and his supposed marksmen in the direct line of the enemy advance.

This was no time to let himself be overwhelmed by misgivings, Jonathan knew. He was afraid he had spoken out of turn and heartily wished he had kept his mouth shut. By no stretch of the imagination were the savages equal to English troops or, for that matter, colonial militia of Major Washington's and Christopher Gist's caliber. But he would have to do his best with the material at hand.

Some of the braves assigned to him were sachems of one eagle feather, and their sullen stares made it evident that they resented him, that they felt degraded because they were forced to serve under an outsider who, only a few days earlier, had been accepted as a member of the Seneca.

There was no time to deal with them diplomatically, however. If they wanted to live and recover their honor, Jonathan told them bluntly, they would do what they were told. Then he stationed his entire unit in a long, double line, with lateral distances of about four feet between the warriors, and the second rank stationed about five feet behind the first.

The success of the maneuver, he told the braves, depended on both surprise and the accuracy of their fire. He wanted them to wait until he himself opened fire before they did the same, and, hopefully, he wanted them to fire in volleys. The warriors were intrigued by his insistence on surprise, and, as he had no time to drill them in the tactics, he could only pray they would follow instructions.

It became very still in the forest as the Seneca awaited their enemies. Jonathan, who had stationed himself behind a thick pine tree in the center of the line, dropped to one knee and peered off through the branches. He could hear what would have been inaudible to him before he had come to the New World: the faint but distinct sound of many feet thudding on the hard-packed snow. He smiled wryly as he congratulated himself.

He, who had commanded some of King George II's finest horse-men in battle against distinguished foes, was mired in a dense wilderness, thousands of miles from home. Half naked, smeared with fish oil and daubed with war paint, he and a motley group of savages were awaiting an assault by another band of primitive barbarians. It was absurd that any professional military man could have sunk so low.

The thudding footsteps became more insistent, and Jonathan put everything but the immediate present from his mind. In spite of his self-disgust over the situation in which he found himself, he was growing more tense as the climactic moment approached. He alone was responsible for what would happen, and he could blame no one but himself if he failed.

Suddenly the first line of Algonkin appeared, their blue and white war paint looking almost luminous in the late afternoon light. They were moving with the caution of men who respected their foes, but when they came closer Jonathan could see the contempt on their faces. They had already beaten the Seneca in one skirmish today, the fresh scalps of dead enemies were hanging from their belts, and they believed they had destroyed the myth of Seneca invincibility. It was difficult to blame them for their scorn.

The Seneca sharpshooters made no move, and not one betrayed his presence behind the pines. But the tension was becoming un-bearable as the Algonkin edged still closer, and Jonathan did not know how much longer his braves could maintain their self-disci-plined silence. It was better, he decided, to risk opening fire before the enemy came as close as he would have wished, rather than allow a warrior's premature shot to give away the surprise.

Surveying the approaching warriors, Jonathan took careful aim at a husky Algonkin who wore a necklace of animal teeth, apparently a symbol of his rank. Steadying the rifle, Jonathan sighted the brave down the long barrel, then squeezed the trigger.

The Algonkin dropped to the ground, screaming as he died, and his fall marked the opening of the new stage of battle. The Seneca warriors fired a ragged volley and, following Jonathan's instructions, began to reload swiftly without waiting to assess the damage.

Jonathan, studying the field ahead even as he himself reloaded, estimated that ten or fifteen Algonkin had been either killed or wounded by the first salvo. The volley had been disgracefully imprecise, but he could not really complain. The marksmanship of the Seneca warriors was at least adequate, and if they did not falter, there was at least a chance his scheme would succeed.

Again he fired and again hit his target. The Seneca were firing, too, each warrior finding a target as quickly as he reloaded, and no further attempt was made to fire in volleys.

Suddenly Jonathan laughed aloud. He had made a vital miscalculation in his thinking and would have been ashamed of himself had he not found his situation radically improved. He had wanted his men to fire in volleys because he had assumed that the enemy would press its drive forward regardless of what their foes did. But the Algonkin were not trained British or French troops and halted when they saw comrades dropping. Eventually they reorganized and started to move forward again, but their lines were as ragged as the Seneca fire, and the faults of one side were equalized by those of the other.

Seneca marksmanship was fairly accurate, and the braves knew their rifles and muskets sufficiently well to reload quickly, so the rate of fire was steady. It soon became apparent that the Algonkin had been halted, and Jonathan had to shout and curse to prevent his braves from breaking their lines and dashing forward to engage their enemies in hand-to-hand combat. At his insistence the steady fire from behind the screen of evergreens was maintained, and at last the Algonkin leaders became convinced that their thrust had been halted.

Mi-la-ine and Li-solu possessed sufficiently well-developed senses of generalship to realize, instinctively, that the moment had come to take part in the battle. They promptly committed their own forces on the flanks, and a shower of arrows and spears descended on the Algonkin from both sides. Those who wanted to fight their way out of the trap soon discovered their error: when they approached the flanks, flying tomahawks cut them down.

There was only one way open to the braves from the north, and they began to retreat, their panic increasing as their foes pursued them. Jonathan released his own warriors, and they raced after the enemy, too, every Seneca determined to take as many scalps as he could. The victory was complete, and Jonathan slowly climbed to the crest of the hill in order to see what he could, through the trees, of the Algonkin retreat.

When he had first come to the New World he would have thought it ludicrous that he could take pride in the triumph he had just won. But his feeling of exaltation was fierce, all consuming, and his shouts of joy were as loud as those of any Seneca warrior.

12

The Slave

The Seneca collected more than two hundred scalps, and the survivors of the Algonkin force fled the area and made their way northward to their own villages. The immediate threat of invasion was dissipated, but the cautious Seneca did not celebrate their triumph immediately. Instead they maintained the same rigorous secrecy on the march as they started toward home, and not until two days later, when they reached territory controlled by the Oneida and the Mohawk, their Iroquois allies, did they relax.

Then, for the first time, they sent out hunting parties to find fresh meat, a difficult endeavor in midwinter, and other groups went fishing in the rivers and lakes. They built huge campfires, and Jonathan, who had thought himself acclimated to the cold, thoroughly enjoyed the rare warmth.

His own sense of accomplishment had become clouded by bewilderment and doubt on the start of the homeward journey, and he found the attitude of the Seneca perplexing. Not one of the leaders had offered him thanks or congratulations on his major contribution to the victory, and the senior warriors seemed equally indifferent. Only the younger braves, less phlegmatic than their elders, seemed to be treating him with a slightly increased measure of respect. So he concluded that savages of the New World, unlike civilized men, did not recognize an individual's extraordinary efforts.

Trying to accustom himself to this strange approach, he found there were consolations. The campfire he shared with a score of braves dispelled the numbing cold, and his fish, cooked in an English frying pan, was the most delicious meal he had ever eaten. He consumed two and was working on a third when a solemn senior warrior interrupted him to announce that his immediate presence was desired by the sachems, who were holding a council.

Jonathan followed the man to a fire at the far side of the bivouac, and there saw Mi-la-ine, Li-solu, and more than thirty sachems of one eagle feather seated cross-legged in a circle around the fire. No one looked up as the Englishman approached, and his first thought was that he was in trouble of some sort. The leaders, it seemed, were sitting in judgment on him.

Jonathan knew enough of Seneca ways to show no sign of impatience. He moved closer to the fire, folded his arms over his chest, and stood erect, staring into the flames as though he found the strange silence unnatural.

At last two sachems of one eagle feather stirred. Rising to their feet, they joined him before the fire, and before he quite realized what was happening, one of them cut a small but deep gash in his left arm with a knife.

Thinking they were attacking him, he drew his own knife, intending to defend himself, but quickly discovered he was mistaken. The man with the knife cut his own arm and that of his companion, then pressed several drops from each of the three wounds into a gourd he carried in his other hand.

While Jonathan watched in astonishment, the warrior moved slowly around the circle, inflicting a cut on the arm of each of the other leaders in turn, and then adding a little of their blood to that in the gourd. When he was done, he handed the gourd to Mi-la-ine.

The senior leader reached behind him, and Jonathan had to curb a desire to laugh when he saw a large earthenware jug of obvious English make. It was the sort in which Londoners carried alcoholic spirits, but to the Seneca it had acquired a ritualistic significance. Mi-la-ine filled the gourd with a dark liquid from the jug, then took a small sip and handed the container to Li-solu.

Each of the Seneca drank in turn from the gourd, and finally it was passed to Jonathan. No one had spoken a word during the ceremony, but now the sachem who had drawn his blood indicated in pantomime that he was expected to drain the cup.

The gourd was still more than half filled, Jonathan saw, each of the others having taken no more than a token sip, and the noxious odor of the brew made his nostrils twitch and his eyes water. It was evident that the jug contained a savage concoction of some kind rather than English liquor. Taking a deep breath, he downed the contents in a single gulp, then wished, fervently, that he had been more cautious. His insides felt as though they were on fire, and he gasped, struggled for breath, and hoped he would not disgrace himself by becoming sick.

Before he could recover, the two escorts took him before Mi-la-ine and Li-solu, and he was required to kneel in front of them. The senior leader, still silent, proceeded to shave away the regrowth of stubble on either side of scalp lock, and then Jonathan felt someone pulling at his hair. Not until Li-solu indicated with a gesture that he was expected to rise did it occur to him that something had been fastened to his scalp lock, and all at once he realized what had happened.

He had been awarded an eagle feather and was promoted to the rank of sachem.

The ceremony concluded, the Indians at last became convivial. The jug was passed, as were two more like it, and Jonathan, forced to join the others in drinking repeatedly, gathered that the brew had been made from a number of herbs and roots. It made him feel a little giddy but, he noted, had a less intoxicating effect than the alcoholic beverages made by civilized men.

The others freely expressed their admiration of his efforts in the battle, and each of his fellow sachems made a point of seeking him out. It was good to know that the Seneca, like the English, rewarded merit.

But Jonathan was kept so busy that the evening's celebration was coming to an end before he had an opportunity to take Li-solu aside for a private word. "Now Jo-na-tan wears the eagle feather of a sachem," he said gravely, "but his heart is still heavy."

Li-solu looked at him in surprise.

"The maiden-with-pale-hair did no harm to the gods. But she is still the prisoner of the Seneca."

His friend continued to stare at him for a moment, then broke into wild, almost childish laughter, which he could not or would not explain.

There were no farewells when Li-solu and his braves parted company with the rest of the force. One morning the warriors, awakening beside their fires, saw that their comrades had gone. Jonathan, still hoping to glean some hint of Elizabeth Johnson's future fate, felt severely frustrated but decided to demonstrate continuing patience rather than question Mi-la-ine. The savages, as he had learned, were expert in revealing no more than they wished.

Two days later the returning warriors reached their own town, and the entire population came out to greet them. A messenger had arrived earlier with the news of their triumph, and the community was prepared for a celebration. Yet, as the warriors moved down into the valley and marched through the town, no one cheered or called out to them; that was not the Indian way, and only the broad grins on the faces of the elders and squaws indicated their pleasure.

Jonathan, marching with the other sachems of one eagle feather, soon realized he was a center of attention. Everyone in the town was aware of his new status: the elders whispered to one another as he passed, squaws stared at him with new respect, and the unmarried maidens, who were the most demonstrative, giggled and flirted shyly with him.

The sachem of three eagle feathers, Olu-a-su, whose name Jonathan had not known previously, awaited his victorious braves in his long house, surrounded by his squaws and young sons. He exchanged greetings with each of the returning warriors as they filed past him, a ceremony that seemed endless, and occasionally, when he elected to chat with a subordinate, the wait for the others became interminable.

The reception Olu-a-su gave the new sachem of one eagle feather was almost effusive. "Gu-goe-ro-no, sachem of the gods, shines on Jo-na-tan," he said. "Now Jo-na-tan is the son of Olu-a-su."

Reacting in the approved Seneca manner, Jonathan remained wooden-faced.

The principal sachem continued to praise him and suggested that he conduct special training classes to teach expert marksmanship to every warrior in the town.

The idea was sound, and Jonathan indicated his conviction that a corps of marksmen would make the Seneca invincible against all of their Indian foes.

"Jo-na-tan," the pleased Olu-a-su said, "will live in his own house. He will be given all that he wishes."

It was impossible to pass up this unexpected opportunity, and Jonathan quickly replied, "It is the wish of Jo-na-tan that the maiden-with-pale-hair come to his house."

The principal sachem's eyes became expressionless, and he turned to the next warrior in the waiting line.

Jonathan felt rebuffed and could only conclude that some disposition of Elizabeth already had been made. But he could not question the senior leader of the Seneca and decided to bide his time. Since he himself now ranked as a sachem, he thought, it should not be too difficult for him to gain information.

When he emerged from the long house he found two elders waiting to escort him to his new hut. One carried a beaded length of rawhide, a symbol of leadership, and the other held aloft an English-made frying pan, also a symbol, which the delighted Jonathan knew he could put to good use.

His new house, located near those of other sachems, was easily twice as large as the hut in which he had lived previously. A solid structure of logs, it appeared, at least from the outside, to be as well built as the cabins of colonial settlers he had seen in the wilderness. A stone-lined pit outside the entrance, in which a fire was already blazing, was used for cooking, and he guessed, when he saw a hole in the center of the roof, through which smoke was rising, that the interior fire was utilized for warmth. At last, he thought, his living conditions would more nearly approximate those of civilized men.

The elders handed him the strip of beaded leather and the frying pan, and Jonathan, pushing aside the entrance flap, walked into his new dwelling. As he had thought, the fire burning in the center of the room was small, and it was not easy to make out details. A fresh bed of pine boughs stood on one side, and near it, on the bare earth floor, someone had placed his blanket and supply pouch. Dropping the beaded leather strip and frying pan to the ground, he propped his rifle against the wall and went to the nearest window. Raising the animal-skin flap that covered it, he turned to inspect his quarters in daylight.

To his amazement he was not alone. On the far side of the room, her forehead touching the earth in a deep salaam, was a woman. Two thick braids of dark hair fell forward, helping to obscure her face, and he could see only that she was dressed in a breastband and skirt of woven reeds. Her copper-colored skin glistened, and he guessed that she was young.

"The servant of Jo-na-tan greets the sachem," she said, her Seneca marked by a strong accent he could not identify.

He was too startled to reply.

Slowly, hesitantly, she lifted her head.

Something in her appearance puzzled him, striking him as odd, and all at once he realized her eyes were blue. At the same instant he recognized her. "Elizabeth!"

Her eyes were remote, completely impersonal. "The servant of Jo-na-tan," she said, still addressing him in the language of the Seneca, "obeys her master."

Relieved and puzzled, Jonathan found an outlet for his feelings in sudden irritation. "Speak English! And why do you look so different?"

She started to reply in Seneca, but his glare changed her mind. "I rub my skin with a juice of berries, and I soak my hair in a horrid mixture boiled with roots. So I look completely like an Indian woman. And," she added bitterly, "I hope that satisfies you."

Totally unprepared for her outburst, Jonathan could only continue to stare at her.

She reached behind her on the ground and picked up some objects, which she held out to him. "I was ordered to bring these when I came here. Which do you prefer?"

Jonathan identified a birch rod and what looked like a rawhide whip. Perhaps her ordeal had unhinged her mind, he thought, so he spoke gently. "You can't be very comfortable on your knees." Without thinking about his own actions, he sat cross-legged on the ground, Indian-style, and indicated with a gesture that he wanted her to do the same.

She obeyed, the meekness of her attitude infuriating him.

He curbed his temper and managed a faint smile. "I'll appreciate it if you'll tell me the meaning of all this."

"It should be apparent. I've been given to you as—your property. Your slave."

Jonathan was too stunned to reply.

"I was told you asked for me, and for some reason you're such a hero they'll give you anything you want."

He began to understand and laughed.

Again Elizabeth held out the whip and the rod to him.

His amusement gave way to another surge of annoyance. "Don't let me see those damned things again!"

It was her turn to be surprised.

"Thank the Lord for your blessings, as I'm doing!" Jonathan said.

Elizabeth continued to look blank.

"From the time we were first brought here," he said, "I've been trying to learn about your situation, and have been making efforts—feeble efforts, I'm afraid—to help you."

She gasped and tears came to her eyes.

Quickly he told her all that had happened to him, touching lightly on his achievements in the battle with the Algonkin.

"And now you've become a powerful leader of these savages. I found it hard to believe when they first told me about it."

"It's true enough, but they're as fickle as children, and I could be in trouble again if I made one false step. Now, what's happened to you?"

Elizabeth's story was as dreary as it was painful. She had been treated as a slave from the first and had been repeatedly degraded. But, aside from frequent cuffings and kicks, she had suffered no serious physical harm.

"We're fortunate," he told her when she finished her tale. "We've survived, and eventually we'll find our way to freedom, although we'll have to be careful. If we're caught trying to escape, not even my new rank will save us from torture and death. I've learned a great deal about the Seneca mind."

"You've changed," she said, "although I don't know quite how."

Jonathan ignored the irrelevant observation. "For the present we're safe and won't be abused. I've learned to be grateful for such basic things in life. Later, when we've put all this behind us, we can worry about the recovery of your property and mine."

"All of it," Elizabeth said, showing spirit for the first time, "belongs to me."

He grinned at her. "Determination is a commendable trait."

She had the grace to become embarrassed. "I must admit that the question of property ownership isn't a primary concern at the present moment."

"We see the problem in the same way." His levity vanished, and he became lost in thought.

Surreptitiously, but almost unaware of what she was doing, Elizabeth studied him.

"We have no choice," Jonathan said at last. "It's too soon to ask the Seneca to give you your freedom. One of their most prominent leaders has been—interested in you, and I don't want to give him any excuse to take you into his own household."

"You mean Mi-la-ine?"

He felt a stab of jealousy. "Then you know!"

"I'm grateful to his wives—for hating me." She volunteered no additional information.

Jonathan tried to put Mi-la-ine out of his mind. "There's something else. They've put us together, so we're free to talk and plan as we please, without arousing any suspicions. We've both learned it isn't easy to meet in an Indian town, and it would be wrong to reject the opportunities and conveniences they've granted us."

She knew he was leading up to a conclusion and waited.

"So, it seems to me, we must play the roles in which they've placed us. I, by the grace of their gods, have become a very minor chieftain. This gives me unlimited access to my superior, the right to attend war councils, and several other privileges, the most obvious of them being a hut somewhat more comfortable than an impoverished peasant's. And you're required to take the part of my servant, for which I'd apologize if it were any of my doing. The Seneca is even more sensitive to differences in class and station than my former compatriots in England, so I'm afraid we must accept our roles and play them to the best of our ability."

"It hasn't crossed my mind," Elizabeth replied calmly, "that we might do otherwise."

Her flashes of common sense surprised and encouraged him; they were unexpected in one who had been so stubbornly determined to deny him his inheritance.

"In the presence of others," Elizabeth continued, "we must be careful to speak only in their language. And we must let nothing provoke or jar us into forgetting the differences in our positions."

"That may be difficult at times, but you're quite right."

She stood, folded her hands over her breast, and bowed low. "So I must prepare my master's meal and take care with it. If I should be late, or it isn't to his taste, I'm sure he would beat me." Moving to a far corner, where various provisions were piled, she took some food and went out to the pit beyond the entrance.

Many thoughts crowded Jonathan's mind, and one, above all others, took precedence over the rest. Elizabeth's figure was even more enticing than he had remembered it, and he couldn't help wondering if it was her flimsy attire that so forcibly called his attention to her body. He could think of no other reason.

The routines of daily living were established and maintained more easily than Jonathan had thought possible, due, in the main, to Elizabeth's sensible acceptance of the situation in which they found themselves. She prepared his meals and herself ate only what he left, which caused him to make certain that she did not go hungry. When he enjoyed good fortune and shot a buck on a brief hunting trip with several other warriors, Elizabeth struggled alone to butcher and roast the carcass, then take gifts of choice portions to Olu-a-su and Mi-la-ine.

Thereafter she went to work curing the hide, then making him a new shirt and loincloth, and only when he insisted did she consent to fashion herself a breastband, skirt, and moccasins of the leather.

"A Seneca never makes a gift like that to a slave," she said. "A self-respecting warrior would give a hide only to a favorite squaw."

"I'm giving it to you," Jonathan said, "and you'll do as you're told." He was unwilling to admit to himself that his own emotional state was chiefly responsible for his generosity. Her new clothing might be shocking by civilization's standards but was less provocative than her flimsy costume of woven reeds, and he hoped that, when she wore the attire of skins, the braves of the town would stop ogling her.

The strain of dwelling with Elizabeth under the same roof was beginning to tell on Jonathan. He realized she felt the tension, too, but believed that she, far more than he, was responsible. Certainly the approach she had taken after he had joined several other sachems for a swim in the icy waters of the lake was her own fault.

When he had returned to their hut, chilled, he had found her waiting with a vial of oil, and she had been prepared to anoint him with it. "It's the duty of a slave woman," she had said. "A sachem who wears an eagle feather isn't supposed to do things like that for himself. You'd be disgraced if anyone found out."

"I'm capable of smearing oil on myself," Jonathan had told her, "and no one else will know." It was difficult for him to believe she could be so innocent that she would not realize the complications that her performance of the duty would cause.

At times her common sense predominated. At first it caused him discomfort to use the bed of pine boughs while she slept on the hard ground at the opposite side of the fire. But he had to agree when she said the Seneca would be indignant if they learned that a supposed slave woman used the bed of pines while her alleged master slept on the ground.

Each day Jonathan found it more difficult to resist the temptation to suggest to her that they use the bed together, just as he found it a torment not to approach her. But he forced himself to maintain correct relations with her, two compelling reasons ever present in his mind.

He could not forget she had been quick to reject his advances at Presque Isle, and his pride would not permit him to take advantage of her, now that he was in a position to force her to accept his love-making. Equally important, he was gaining an understanding of Elizabeth and realized that her modesty, her virtue were integral parts of her nature. Unlike the uncounted girls he had known in the past, she would not treat an affair lightly and forget him when it was ended. If and when they returned to civilization, her life, he believed, would be blighted for all time by the knowledge that she had been his mistress.

There had been a time, he knew, when he would not have allowed his concern for her attitude to deter him. But his own misfortunes since coming to the colonies had given him a new and surprising sense of humility. It was preferable to be considerate of Elizabeth than to be troubled by his own conscience, even though he wanted her.

They succeeded in maintaining the delicate equilibrium for a week, but one day an unexpected incident upset the balance. Jonathan had selected a site for his firearms instruction, and although gunpowder was short, he had obtained the promise of Mi-la-ine that an adequate supply would be obtained in the immediate future from the neighboring Cayuga, who had stolen a large quantity in a daring raid on Fort Albany, the prominent New York trading post on the Hudson River.

All that remained in the way of advance preparation was the selection of an assistant, so Jonathan staged a competition, which was won by Ni-jo, a senior warrior endowed with a natural talent for handling firearms. Jonathan returned from the forest site with the burly warrior and soon discovered that the Seneca's disposition was not as faultless as his skill.

Two of Ni-jo's small children came running to greet him when they reached the town, but he angrily cuffed them, knocking one down and sending the other tumbling into a snowbank. They had failed to show him sufficient respect, he said, and was enlarging on the theme when they encountered his squaw, who was carrying a heavy pail of water from a well to their hut. The woman was slow to put the pail on the ground and make her obeisance to him, which further enraged Ni-jo, who struck her a stunning blow on the side of the head that sent her careening against the wall of the nearest hut.

A number of braves witnessed the incident but remained unruffled by it, and Jonathan had to pretend indifference, too. The savages, as he well knew by now, lived according to their own sense of values in their relations with those they considered their inferiors. There was little the Englishman could do to help the unfortunate squaw, but he had the presence of mind to ask Ni-jo to accompany him to his own house, which saved the woman a more severe beating.

Only a few visitors had come to the hut since Jonathan had taken possession of it, but Elizabeth, whose experiences in the Seneca town had made her alert to the nuances of every situation, played the role of servant to perfection. Unobtrusive, discreet, and nimble, she brought her master and his guests chunks of cold venison left from breakfast and, prostrating herself in the approved manner, first offered the tidbits to the guest. Then, without waiting to be bidden, she went off to the house of a neighboring sachem to borrow a quantity of the bitter root brew that was the favorite beverage of Seneca braves.

Jonathan made an attempt to bear down on the subject of firearms training, and although Ni-jo was interested, he began to glower when Elizabeth returned. Behaving as was expected of her, she went to the far corner of the room and sat on the ground, cross-legged, available to respond at once to her master's summons. Ni-jo continued to eye her sourly, and it occurred to Jonathan that he might be wise to send her off on a time-consuming errand before an unpleasant incident developed.

But he thought of the idea too late.

"The servant of Jo-na-tan," Ni-jo said, "is as slow as the creature-with-hard-shell that crawls on land and swims in water. The servant of Jo-na-tan is as lazy as the bird-with-long-beak that lets others kill its food."

The startled Jonathan searched for an adequate reply.

But Ni-jo, unsated in his encounter with his own family, was not to be denied. "The servant of Jo-na-tan," he continued, "sits when the fire dies!" He pointed accusingly at the small pit in the center of the room.

Elizabeth jumped to her feet and hastily collected dried wood from a pile that stood against the wall.

The accusation was unjust, Jonathan thought. It was true that the fire had dwindled, but it had not died and could be renewed with ease. Besides, he and Elizabeth did not like too warm a room in midday. "The house of Jo-na-tan is warm," he said.

Ni-jo's shrug indicated that the relative heat was irrelevant. "Jo-na-tan," he said, "has the eye of the eagle when he makes fire with his fire stick. Jo-na-tan helps Ni-jo. But only Ni-jo knows how to make a squaw bend her back. Ni-jo will help Jo-na-tan." He added something in a sharp undertone to Elizabeth

She paled beneath her dark skin stain but obediently went to the far side of the hut, returning with the two-foot length of rawhide that the Seneca used as a lash.

Jonathan immediately recognized the complex delicacy of the situation. A direct clash with Ni-jo would not only jeopardize the firearms-training program but, as the quarrel would take place under Jonathan's own roof, would violate every canon of Seneca hospitality. The feud that would grow out of the situation could be settled only by a fight, literally to the death. And, regardless of the outcome, the attention of the entire community once again would be called, unduly, to Elizabeth.

There seemed only one way to handle the explosive problem. "The servant of a warrior," Jonathan said, "must learn to bend her back to her own master." He reached out and took the lash.

For a moment Elizabeth's eyes met his, and both realized the situation offered them no choice. The brave who behaved squeamishly, unable or unwilling to exercise authority, suffered immediate disgrace, and it was possible that Jonathan, the outsider whose rapid rise undoubtedly had caused jealousies, might be deprived of his new rank if he failed to demonstrate severity.

There was calm acceptance as well as fear in Elizabeth's expression.

The whole business was so distasteful to Jonathan that it was he who first averted his gaze.

Ni-jo, unaware of the subtle interplay, chuckled and wiped the palms of his hands on his rawhide shirt.

Jonathan realized that the savage was not only unaware of the feelings of the others but would not have understood them had they been explained to him. Ni-jo had created this predicamant, and it was difficult to refrain from striking him across the face with the lash.

Winding one end of the lash around his hand, Jonathan hesitated. The very thought of beating Elizabeth was abhorrent to him, and he continued to search his mind, frantically, for some way to escape the dilemma.

The girl herself reminded him there was no alternative. Knowing what the Seneca expected of her, she folded her hands over her breasts in a gesture of submission, then slowly lowered herself to the dirt floor where she stretched out, her face downward, pressing into the cold earth.

Jonathan could wait no longer and, raising the lash, brought it down on her buttocks. The leather of the heavy thong made a sharp report as it struck the leather of Elizabeth's rawhide skirt, but it inflicted no real pain.

Ni-jo was not fooled, and a fleeting expression of disappointment crossed his face.

Jonathan realized it was too dangerous to indulge in subterfuge and struck again. This time the whip cut into the bare flesh of the girl's shoulders, leaving an ugly, red welt.

Elizabeth made no sound and did not move.

Ni-jo was elated, and his eyes were becoming glazed.

Jonathan knew that a prolongation of the agony was the worst torture he could inflict. So he quickened the pace of the beating, repeatedly raising his arm and slashing at the girl's bare back.

Still Elizabeth neither cried out nor flinched.

Bubbles of foam covered Ni-jo's mouth, and he was breathing heavily.

Jonathan could not let himself dwell on what he was doing. Emptying his mind, he heard nothing but the faint, whistling sound of the lash each time it descended and saw nothing but the blur of bruised skin that was his target.

Suddenly it occurred to him that Elizabeth might have lost consciousness and he wanted to retch. He had administered a sufficiently thorough beating to satisfy a jury of his Seneca peers that he had not shirked, so it did not matter if Ni-jo's lust was sated. Lowering his arm, Jonathan brought the cruel farce to an end. But his mind was functioning again, and he kept a tight hold of the lash, afraid that the savage would want to wield it if he cast it aside.

Ni-jo, who looked like a man in a trance, continued to peer at the inert body of the girl. Then he shook his head, and gradually his eyes lost their unnaturally bright look. Wiping the spittle from his mouth with the back of his hand, he straightened and grinned. "Jo-na-tan," he said, "is a true sachem of the Seneca." Grasping the Englishman's upper arm in a formal gesture of friendship, he turned and left the hut, still chuckling softly.

Jonathan stared down at Elizabeth, heartsick and numb. Suddenly he dropped to his knees beside her. "My God," he muttered, "I'm so sorry."

Her eyes were open, so he knew she heard him, but she made no reply.

It occurred to him that her pain might be too intense for her to speak. Knowing he had to do what little lay within his power to alleviate her distress, he hauled himself to his feet and ran to the far side of the hut, where their few supplies were kept. After a brief, frantic search he found what he was seeking, a gourd containing a malodorous unguent made of herbs, roots, and other ingredients which were boiled by the squaws.

He had seen the unguent used in the Algonkin campaign and knew that warriors who had suffered deep spear or knife wounds had felt relieved of pain after using the substance. At the time he had been skeptical of the unguent's medicinal properties, attributing its effectiveness to the imaginations of the braves. But the nearest apothecary was hundreds of miles from this remote barbarian community, and, lacking anything better, he would have to try the unguent.

Returning to Elizabeth, he spread a layer of the ointment on the welts that crisscrossed her back. Soon, to his surprise, her skin became less inflamed and the puffiness was reduced.

At last she stirred.

Still kneeling beside her, Jonathan reached out to help her.

But she needed no assistance as she raised herself to a sitting position.

He saw she was smiling faintly. "I don't know what I can possibly say to you."

She silenced him with a gesture. "There's no need to apologize. That beast forced you to do it."

"But I needn't have struck you so hard!" Never had he felt such remorse.

Elizabeth surprised him by laughing. "I'm sure you wouldn't want your fellow Seneca to hear this, but you're positively gentle. The squaws who are in charge of the prisoners do far worse to their captives with a whip."

He didn't know whether she meant it but suspected she was merely trying to ease his overwhelming burden of guilt. "I won't forget Ni-jo for this, and I promise you I'll find a time and way to repay him."

"You can't really blame a savage for the cruelty he isn't capable of understanding." She picked up the gourd of unguent and examined it. "My father told me the tribes of the Iroquois used a potent ointment that could heal even a serious wound, but I always thought that was just another foolish frontier legend. In the ways that the Indians are wise, they know so much more than we do." She put the gourd on the ground and started to rise.

"No," Jonathan said. "You can't walk around. You need to rest." Giving her no opportunity to disagree, he picked her up and carried her across the hut to the pine bed.

Elizabeth made no protest and curled her arms around his neck.

Her face was close to his, and all at once he found himself kissing her.

For an instant he expected her to fight him off, but she tightened her hold and her lips parted.

They continued to kiss as he lowered her to the pine bed, and their embrace became more fervent. In some mysterious manner that neither understood the beating had torn away the invisible barriers that had kept them apart, and Elizabeth had been the first to recognize the changed atmosphere.

All that they had suffered, separately and together, since their capture at Presque Isle, strengthened the bonds that drew them to each other now. Jonathan, however, recognized only vaguely that more than desire for an attractive woman was involved in his relationship with Elizabeth. He wanted her, to be sure, but he knew when he began to caress her breasts that he felt a tenderness toward her, a desire to protect her, that was unique.

Then, as he took her, everything but the intimacy they shared was blotted from his consciousness.

Later, when they stretched out on the bed of pines, he tried to explain his feelings to her.

He bumbled, becoming almost inarticulate, but Elizabeth did not seem to mind. "I was afraid," she murmured, "that you'd think I was like all your other women."

"There are no others."

"Not right now, but I'm sure there have been many."

His past seemed very remote. "Is that why you rejected me at Presque Isle?"

"It was one reason."

He propped himself on an elbow. "What were the others?"

She made no reply and smiled at him.

His curiosity became overwhelming, and he was seized by a desire to know everything that went on in her mind. "Tell me!"

"You ask too many questions," Elizabeth said, and ended the conversation by drawing him to her.

13

The Great Conspiracy

The day began like many that had preceded it. Slivers of early morning light slanted into the hut through cracks in the skins that covered the windows, awakening the couple. As always before arising they made love, quietly yet with a sense of urgency, and as always they were conscious of the present, putting the past behind them, not allowing themselves to dwell on the uncertain future. Then they assumed the roles the Seneca had given them, with Jonathan donning the mantle of a sachem, while Elizabeth acted the part of his servant.

While she prepared his breakfast in the outdoor pit, he anointed his body with oil and applied streaks of paint to his face and torso. They took care to maintain appearances and under no circumstances ate together; as far as the Seneca were concerned, they were still master and slave.

Then, when Elizabeth went off to obtain fresh provisions, Jonathan wandered from hut to hut in the area arranging an afternoon's hunting expedition with a sachem or a fishing trip with a senior warrior. Eventually the throbbing beat of a drum summoned the sachems and elders to the long house of Olu-a-su for the regular morning meeting of the community's leaders. According to custom these braves comprised a ruling council and served the function of advising the sachem of three eagle feathers in all matters ranging from intertribal diplomacy to local discipline.

In practice, however, Olu-a-su made his own decisions, and neither knew nor cared what his subordinates thought. When he was in a talkative mood he told them a little about problems that had arisen and his disposition of them. Sometimes, too, Mi-la-ine had something to report. But even on these occasions the news these senior leaders imparted consisted of trivia. Certainly Jonathan had no interest in a squabble between two squaws over a fish that both claimed or in the punishment meted out to a young brave who had tried to enter the quarters of the unmarried maidens late at night.

Today, however, there was a change in the routine. As the unproductive meeting was drawing to an end, Li-solu arrived from his own town, accompanied by a band of his warriors. They had brought the kegs of gunpowder and cases of ammunition that Jonathan had requested for his firearms classes, and everyone brightened at the prospect of using rifles and muskets.

Jonathan and his friend exchanged warm greetings, then went together to inspect the munitions. Their quantity surprised the Englishman, who counted fourteen barrels and six boxes, or enough to supply a brigade of trained infantry for a major battle. Jonathan started to examine the munitions, and something he saw caused him to draw Li-solu aside.

Disturbed by the implications of his discovery, yet not wanting to create unnecessary turmoil in the event he was mistaken, Jonathan took care to speak in English. "There are some things I need to know," he said, "for all our sakes."

Li-solu looked at him anxiously. "Powder not good? Bullets too soft?"

"You needn't worry about that. The powder is fine-grained and sifted, and I doubt if you'll find a single lump in a keg. The bullets are perfect, too. They're a little heavier than the kind I prefer, but they'll do what's expected of them."

Li-solu was relieved.

"Now, where did you get these munitions?"

"Brothers of Oneida give to Seneca. Seneca ask, Oneida share."

"Where was it the Oneida got them?"

Li-solu obviously thought his friend was bothered by scruples concerning stolen goods. "Jo-na-tan Seneca now. No care any more about English."

"Where, Li-solu?"

"Oneida raid Fort Albany." The sachem of two eagle feathers grinned.

Jonathan did not share his amusement. "Neither the powder nor the bullets came from a British colonial fort," he said solemnly. "Look here."

Li-solu followed him to a keg, then a box, and on each saw an identical symbol which meant nothing to him. Unable to understand his friend's sudden gravity, he shrugged. "No care where come," he said. "Seneca use."

"You'll care, all right, and so will all the rest of the world, civilized or barbarian. This is the crest of King Louis XV!"

The name meant nothing to the savage.

"Louis," Jonathan said slowly, "is the king—the chief sachem—of the French."

"English and French have new war?"

"The French say they don't want a war," Jonathan replied, remembering what he had learned of Major Washington's conference with Legardeur de St. Pierre, the commandant of the French wilderness fort. "But they refuse to give up their claims to territory that belongs to England."

"Land belong to Seneca," Li-solu said.

Jonathan was in no position to debate the matter with him. "If the French are bringing in major supplies of munitions, the Seneca and all the other Iroquois will be caught between two giants. I'm not sure which of them will win, but I can guarantee you'll lose everything—your towns, your fields, your hunting grounds. When England and France fight a full-scale war, everybody else in the area is certain to be badly hurt."

Li-solu pondered the remark and, although he made no reply, seemed to agree.

"I'd like, very much, to talk to the Oneida who got these supplies. If they told you they came from Fort Albany, they're lying. And I'd like to know why."

The question intrigued Li-solu, too. Much to the disappointment of the younger sachems and senior warriors who were eager to start rifle and musket practice, the pair went off to discuss the matter with Olu-a-su and Mi-la-ine. The nations that made up the Iroquois confederation long had adhered to the unvarying policy of maintaining strict neutrality in the continuing quarrels of England and France, but now it appeared that the Oneida might be guilty of a departure that could cause serious consequences for all of the Iroquois tribes.

Olu-a-su immediately grasped the significance of the problem, as did his deputy, and within a few moments the largest of the message drums boomed. The signal they sent would be repeated by others, just within hearing range, and would be relayed to the leaders of the other four towns, summoning them to a national council. Such meetings were called only when the security of the Seneca was at stake, so the others were expected to appear without delay, and it was possible that some might even arrive that night.

Li-solu elected to sleep in Jonathan's hut and share his friend's meals, a gesture that could not be turned aside or ignored. So Elizabeth was forced to retreat to a far corner and, even in private, play the part of the slave woman. Although Li-solu had been in large part responsible for her presence in Jonathan's quarters, he carefully refrained from recognizing her proximity, much less her identity. It would have been beneath his dignity as a leader of the nation to address another man's slave, so he did not glance in the girl's direction when she served him a meal or retired meekly to the corner where she awaited her master's command.

The following morning the leaders from the other towns began to arrive, and not until noon, when their formal meeting began, was there an opportunity for Jonathan to spend a few minutes alone with Elizabeth in order to tell her what was happening. She promptly forgot her own precarious situation.

"If there's a full war," she said, "the French will take my Presque Isle properties away from Andrews and confiscate them in the name of the French crown. It won't be the first time they've done that sort of thing."

"I wouldn't put it past Andrews," Jonathan replied, "to make a deal of some sort with the French. If he could deliver your whole village to them without a fight, for instance, they might agree to let him keep an interest in both the estates. Yours and mine." This was hardly the moment for either to press a claim, but he couldn't resist the opportunity to restate his rights.

The girl's wry smile indicated her appreciation of his quick defense. But she, too, was far more concerned over the basic situation. "Once the French take possession of the area," she said, "it wouldn't help either of us, even if we were able to escape from the Seneca."

"That's a very personal reason for stopping the French before it's too late. But there are far more urgent reasons. As a loyal subject of King George, I must do what I can to fend off a possible conspiracy that threatens to destroy the heart of our empire. I had been thinking of ways we might leave here—logical ways that wouldn't send the Seneca in pursuit of us. But all that will have to wait now, until we learn whether the French are really planning to launch a major campaign."

Knowing that the senior leaders would want to hear his views, Jonathan went off to the long house of Olu-a-su and waited outside for the summons. It came only a short time before the session began, and he was admitted to the meeting of sachems who wore either two or three eagle feathers.

No one interrupted him when he explained his finding of the French royal crest on the containers of gunpowder and ammunition, nor did anyone question him when he offered his theory that the French were seeking native allies for a large-scale attack on Great Britain's New World colonies. He was not in a position to judge, he said, whether the French were offering bribes to the Oneida, but he found it inconceivable that French munitions would be stored at Fort Albany. Therefore he could not help wondering why the Oneida were concealing the truth.

"There is more," he said, "that Jo-na-tan does not know. The mighty Seneca were at peace with the nation of the north, the Algonkin. Why did the Algonkin come to take the scalps of the mighty Seneca? Are the Algonkin the friends of the French? Do the French seek the scalps of the Seneca?"

He had no idea whether there was any basis for the strongly

hinted accusation and realized, too, that he was on delicate ground. If the leaders of the Seneca suspected that he, an Englishman, was making a deliberate effort to enroll them on the side of the English in a forthcoming war, he would be certain to lose their trust and with it the rank he had won.

But his gamble paid off. There was a stir of interest, and two of the sachems of three eagle feathers, tall, middle-aged warriors with shrewd eyes and scarred faces, nodded as they muttered to each other.

Olu-a-su was anxious to discuss the suggestion with his peers, and dismissed Jonathan with a quick, impatient gesture.

Returning to his own hut, where he and Elizabeth could only speculate on the possible outcome of the council, Jonathan settled down for what proved to be an interminable wait. The afternoon dragged, Elizabeth went to the outdoor fire to begin her preparation of the evening meal, and not until dusk approached did Li-solu return to the hut.

The Seneca sat down to eat, his friend joined him, and neither spoke. Jonathan knew better than to ask questions; he would be told all he needed to know, perhaps more, if he exercised patience.

Li-solu took his time eating a fish, a dripping chunk of venison, and a gourd of dried berries, bark, and a chopped, sweet root. Then, after belching politely and wiping his mouth with the back of his hand, he asked, "Does Jo-na-tan speak the tongue of the French?"

"He speaks it in the same way that Li-solu speaks the tongue of the English. He knows what is said when others speak. He speaks so the French know his meaning. But he does not speak it with the ease of a son of France."

"Then he will not go to the land of the French and say to the people there that he is a son of France."

The idea of pretending to be French was so absurd that Jonathan laughed.

"He will stain his skin and scalp lock, as the skin and hair of his slave woman are stained. He will go with Li-solu, and both will be sons of the Seneca."

176

Plans were being made too rapidly for Jonathan's comfort. "The eyes of Jo-na-tan are not the color of the eyes of Seneca!"

Li-solu shrugged. "Only Jo-na-tan knows the signs that show when men from across the sea make ready for war." They would go to New France, he said, on a mission with a double aim. First, they would learn what they could about the war plans of the French and at the same time would see what they could discover about French intentions toward the Seneca.

In order to provide themselves with a seemingly logical reason for their visit, they would carry with them several valuable bales of beaver pelts and would explain they were coming to the French because the prices offered them by the English colonists were too low. "When Li-solu took skins to the English, they put him in their prison," the Seneca said. "He swore he would not trade again. But he does not break his oath when he goes to the French. He will not trade his furs for cheap beads, like the Tuscarora, who have the minds of squaws. But he will not care if they make no trade with him. He goes as the warrior, not as the trader."

"Let's make certain," Jonathan said, impatiently speaking in English, "that we don't find ourselves in a French gaol. Philadelphia was enough for me. But I don't understand what all this has to do with the bribing of the Oneida by the French. I don't mind taking risks if we stand a chance of accomplishing something positive. On the other hand—"

"Chief sachems," his friend replied, also in English, "go to land of Oneida. Make big visit. Can't accuse in open. Oneida allies of Seneca. If chief sachems learn Oneida work with French, call council of all Iroquois sachems. What Jo-na-tan and Li-solu learn in land of French more important. Find out whole truth."

His logic did not impress Jonathan, who thought it absurd that an Englishman, even though familiar with Seneca ways, should go to New France disguised as a Seneca warrior. Apparently he was being given no real choice, however, and he knew that if he refused, the savages would accuse him of cowardice. They measured a man far more by his courage than by his common sense, and in this instance the stakes were so high it would be extremely difficult to present a strong case in favor of caution.

Elizabeth, who had been listening to the talk from her corner of the hut, was disturbed, too. But she knew better than to intervene and tried to conceal her feelings by keeping her head lowered.

"How soon are we to leave on this expedition?" Jonathan wanted to know.

"Leave when Gu-goe-ro-no come," Li-solu replied calmly.

It was startling to learn they were expected to set out at sunrise the following day, and Jonathan's uneasiness increased.

Elizabeth could no longer hide her alarm. Jonathan had become her protector and stood between her and the Seneca. But, if he should be killed or taken prisoner for a long period, the sachems of the town would feel free to dispose of her as they pleased. Inevitably, then, she would become the property of some other warrior and not only would be forced to endure a life in which she was passed from one to another but would have to abandon virtually all hope of returning to civilization.

Jonathan knew how she felt but could not offer her any consolation. He had been given an assignment that was important not only to the Indians but to England and her colonies, and he could do no more than promise himself he would return to Elizabeth, no matter what obstacles might be placed in his path.

14

The French

It was obvious that Quebec, the capital of New France, had been founded and built by men who appreciated a military site when they saw one. High on a bluff above the St. Lawrence River, at a spot that dominated the entire countryside, stood the most modern and best-equipped fortress in the New World, the Citadel. Its outer walls, ramparts, and turrets made of stone, cannon of various sizes protruding from gun ports, it was a mighty symbol of the power and majesty of France in North America. The cannon were sentinels that could halt the shipping of a hostile nation on the great river below, and the problems involved in reducing the fortress in a siege were too numerous and complicated for Jonathan to contemplate.

Even the city, which nestled in the shadow of the Citadel and was protected by its own stone walls as well, could not be taken in a surprise attack and undoubtedly would give a good account of itself in a siege. Although surrounded by wilderness, with only a scattering of farms in the immediate vicinity, Quebec was secure and self-confident.

The differences between it and the English colonial towns Jonathan had seen were astonishing. At first glance Quebec looked like a community that had been moved, intact, from France to the New World. Although vast, uninhabited territory stretched out toward the horizon in every direction, the streets were narrow and the cramped buildings had been constructed so close together that overhanging balconies almost touched in the middle of cobbled roads.

If the French had refused to utilize the greater space offered them in the wilderness, in other ways they accommodated to the frontier far more freely than did the English. Virtually everyone, even the wealthiest fur traders and merchants, dressed in buckskins, although some of the nobles appeared in coats and cloaks of thick silk thrown over their leather shirts and trousers. There seemed to be relatively few French women in the community, other than in the brothels that flourished openly and unashamed. So, many of the men lived with Indian women and, showing none of the Puritanical restraints that kept the races separate in the English colonies, were accompanied by their native mistresses—and in some instances, wives—to the many taverns, inns, and other eating places in the crowded town.

Certainly the wilderness spirit was rampant in Quebec. Fur traders who had spent months in the interior drank, brawled, and spent their hard-earned money with an almost ferocious abandon. Soldiers returning from duty at isolated forest outposts in the interior entered and left the brothels at all hours of day and night. And fishermen who had braved the worst of the weather and the sea off the Newfoundland Banks in search of the lucrative cod were equally boisterous and reckless.

The Quebec constabulary, of necessity, was lenient, its members endowed with both wisdom and humor. When two men began to fight, they were ignored by the law-enforcement officials, and no one interfered if they beat each other unconscious. Only if they used firearms, knives, or other lethal weapons did the constables intervene. Theoretically, fighting was forbidden in the taverns, but men who had been drinking to excess inevitably quarreled, particularly when they had seen no women for long periods and found themselves in the presence of many attractive wenches.

There was no need for the constables to patrol the drinking, gaming, and eating establishments of the town, however, thanks to a farsighted policy initiated by the tavern owners themselves. Anyone who halted a genuine brawl by throwing the offenders out into the street before they could damage the tavern was rewarded with rounds of free drinks. Therefore volunteers were always ready to spring into action. And the proprietors had become adept at distinguishing real fights from simulated disturbances staged for the purpose of winning the supposed peacemakers a ration of liquor free of charge.

From a purely military point of view, Jonathan found it ridiculously easy to fulfill his mission. Within a few hours of his arrival in Quebec he was able to ascertain, to his own satisfaction, that the French were increasing the size of their armed forces in the New World at a rapid rate. Two frigates and three sloops of war had arrived recently from their home port, Brest, in spite of the winter weather, and rode at anchor in the river below the Citadel. Several troop transports had put into port in recent weeks, too, bringing an additional brigade of veteran French troops, and a quick walk through the upper part of town was enough to establish the fact that this was just the beginning. Since the quarters in the fortress itself were filled to overflowing, new barracks were being constructed, outside the walls, for still more regiments expected in the spring.

Although all of these signs pointed toward a possible major war with England on New World soil, Jonathan was inclined to believe that London officialdom and the colonial governors already knew of these activities. If he discovered them with ease on his first day in Quebec, qualified agents in the pay of the Crown or of the colonies undoubtedly had alerted the Royal Army and Navy as well as the colonial militia.

It soon proved far more difficult to determine the extent to which the Indian tribes of the continent might be involved in the French preparations, however. There were warriors everywhere, and Jonathan estimated that at least one thousand could be found in the city on any given day. Those who had funds, thanks to successful fur trades and other ventures, made themselves at home in the taverns, where they drank heavily. Few bothered to eat in the inns, however, and preferred their own supplies of smoked meats, fish, and corn, which they usually consumed in the open. Nearly all slept outdoors, too, by choice, and rolled up in their blankets in the entrances and beside the sheltering walls of every available building. Late revelers paid no attention to them and picked their way past the still bodies.

Li-solu identified the members of several important tribes. The Ottawa, who were among the most numerous, were tall warriors with a proud, almost regal bearing, and the Seneca spoke of them with respect, a rare tribute. Even huskier were the Huron, whom Li-solu described as belligerent but lacking courage in large-scale intertribal conflicts. There were many Algonkin, too, and it was necessary to restrain the Seneca when he saw them; obviously the recent campaign still rankled. Prominent, also, were braves belonging to a far-flung northern nation, the Abnaki, a breed of small, wiry men who, in spite of the heavy snow and bitter cold, were lightly clad.

What impressed Jonathan, above all, was the casual warmth, on both sides, that marked the relationship of the French and the Indians of all tribes. The English colonists held the savages at arm's length and, at most, sometimes entered into uneasy, temporary alliances with them. But the French treated the Indians with open-handed generosity, regarded them as equals in every sense, and showed no fear of them. It was impossible to imagine the authorities in Philadelphia or any other English colonial city permitting one thousand braves, all armed, to sleep where they pleased in the community's streets.

As nearly as Jonathan could judge, he and Li-solu attracted no special attention from their French hosts. They were just two more warriors who had come to Quebec to sell furs, and the merchants whom they visited concentrated only on the bales they offered. But they created an immediate and lasting stir in the ranks of the other Indians, however, and wherever they went they found warriors staring at them.

This interest was natural, Li-solu said, and left him undisturbed. Few Seneca came to Quebec, so the members of other tribes found their presence unusual. Also, since the Seneca had acquired a widespread and lasting reputation as the most warlike of tribes, the least emotion they aroused in the others was curiosity. It amused Li-solu that the Algonkin, although obviously resentful, took pains to avoid the pair.

Jonathan was unable to share his friend's phlegmatic attitude. Always conscious of his hazel eyes and consequently afraid his real identity would be discovered, he felt an unyielding tension. As a former officer he knew how the French would react if they learned, at a time they were building their forces, that he was an Englishman with a military background. He had been stupid, he thought repeatedly, to allow himself to be persuaded to take part in such a clumsy espionage effort. He was jeopardizing not only his own immediate liberty, but Elizabeth's lifelong freedom, and would never be able to forgive himself if the French captured and imprisoned him.

The frequency with which he found himself thinking of Elizabeth alarmed and confused him. Extraordinary circumstances had made her his mistress, but he could not allow himself to forget that, regardless of their intimacy, she stood in his path, blocking his inheritance. Yet it was difficult to see her in that light, since she was completely dependent on him in her present unfortunate situation. If she were free to come and go as she pleased, their relationship might be far different. In fact, it wouldn't surprise him if she refused to have anything to do with him. On the other hand, he could not put the ardor of her love-making out of his consciousness, either.

It was absurd that a man who had known so many women should find himself able to conjure up images of only one. And it made him doubly uneasy to discover he had no desire, regardless of his Indian disguise, to visit one of Quebec's brothels, even though some of the girls he saw in the taverns and on the streets were as attractive as the London doxies on whom he had squandered a small fortune.

On the fourth day of his visit to Quebec he found himself thinking more than ever of Elizabeth. He and Li-solu had shown their furs to every prominent merchant in the city, and the time had come to make a choice, sell their wares, and depart, even though they had learned nothing specific about the extent to which the

French might want to involve the Indian nations in their military enterprises. So, with luck, the pair would be returning to the land of the Seneca before nightfall, and within a week Jonathan would be reunited with the waiting Elizabeth. Although he hadn't realized it before setting out on his journey, her safety was as important to him as the information he and Li-solu could glean in Quebec.

The merchants who paid the highest prices for furs, timber, and other New World merchandise were the brothers Martin, third-generation residents of New France whose grandfather had founded the business and, after taking an Indian wife, the family. His son, who had been educated in France, had expanded the trading empire, a relatively easy task because the Indians of all tribes had preferred dealing with a half-breed. His own sons, Jean and Paul, had been beneficiaries of the same legacy, and newly arrived warriors usually headed straight for their ramshackle offices and warehouses of unpainted clapboard.

Jean Martin, whose high cheekbones, slanted eyes, and swarthy skin made it unnecessary for him to demonstrate his kinship with the savages who came to his offices, was one of the few men in Quebec to wear clothes cut in the latest Paris fashion. His yellow coat and scarlet waistcoat were made of the finest French velvet, and his silk shirt was the product of tailoring that could not be duplicated in the New World.

In spite of his finery, however, the slender, hawk-faced merchant felt completely at ease with the pair in buckskins and Seneca war paint who perched awkwardly on the edges of their chairs in his office. Finding they could not understand the language of the Ottawa, he had to fall back on French, which he spoke slowly and distinctly. "So, my friends, you decided the brothers Martin offered you the best prices after all!" He examined the beaver pelts with care. "What did my brother agree to pay you?"

Li-solu knew no French, so Jonathan had to act as spokesman. He had learned enough of Indian ways to exaggerate blandly and replied without hesitation, "Frenchman say he pay forty *écu* for all skins." Pitching his voice in a low guttural, he did his best to imitate the singsong cadence of the savages.

"Quite right, my friend, thirty *écu*," Martin replied, his manner indicating they were in complete agreement.

Jonathan admired his poise and had to stifle a grin. "Want forty," he said and, folding his arms, stared out of the window at the snow piled high on the ground. "Want gold."

"These pelts aren't worth a sou more than thirty." Martin was pleasant but firm. "I can't blame you, though. Everyone wants gold. And perhaps I can help you. I may be able to arrange it so you'll get another thirty. You'd like that, eh?"

Jonathan shrugged. "Have no more skins."

"You won't need them. Wait here." Martin left the room.

Li-solu listened as his friend told him, in Seneca, the gist of the conversation.

Jonathan saw an apprentice who, pulling on his stocking cap, ran out of the offices across the snow-littered yard.

Martin returned with a leather pouch and counted out twenty-nine small gold pieces, which he laid out side by side on his battered desk.

Jonathan's ability to play-act was strained to the limit as he laboriously counted aloud.

The merchant, pretending he had made an error, added another gold coin.

Li-solu, at a nod from his companion, swept up the money and dropped it into the pouch at his belt.

Then the pair were alone again and waited for more than a half-hour until, finally, the breathless apprentice raced back across the yard. They could hear him speaking to Martin in an outer office, his tone too low to make out what he was saying, and Jonathan's sense of uneasiness returned.

Before he could express his fears, however, Martin came back into the room. "Go with the young one, my friends, and he will lead you to more gold. And when you have more pelts to sell, remember the brothers Martin, who pay the highest prices in New France."

Jonathan and Li-solu accompanied the apprentice through the winding streets of the city, and the Englishman realized they were climbing the hill at the back of the Citadel. At last they came to the gates of the fortress, where the youth spoke to a sentry in an immaculate white and gold uniform, and the soldier, lowering his musket, waved them in.

His misgivings mounting rapidly, Jonathan wondered if they were entering a trap. But Li-solu continued to follow the apprentice, so there was no opportunity to hesitate, much less discuss the situation. Jonathan knew only that if his true identity had been discovered or was suspected, he was moving straight into the arms of his jailers.

They walked across a courtyard lined with barracks of stone and wood, then headed into the Citadel itself. For some minutes they made their way through corridors of stone with thick walls and, coming at last to a stone staircase, climbed part of the way toward the top of a turret. Another sentry was stationed at the landing and appeared to be expecting them, which aggravated Jonathan's fears.

The soldier opened a door of oak, vanished for a moment, and then reappeared, beckoning. The apprentice stayed behind, and when the door closed again, Jonathan and Li-solu found themselves in the office of an elegantly uniformed, bewigged officer who wore the epaulette of a lieutenant colonel of infantry on his left shoulder.

Rising from his desk, the officer said a few words in the language of the Ottawa, then tried another Indian tongue before speaking in French. "His Christian Majesty, Louis, extends his greetings to the illustrious warriors of the Seneca and welcomes them to the capital of New France," he declared.

His wording was clever, Jonathan thought. An ignorant savage might actually believe himself in the presence of King Louis.

"Sons of Seneca," he replied briefly, "greet son of France."

The colonel, smiling broadly, waved them to seats and offered them pewter mugs of liquor the color of pale tea.

Both refused.

"Very few warriors of your great nation come to Quebec," the officer said, "so we're particularly delighted to welcome you. What brings you here?"

186

"French," Jonathan replied, "pay more for skins than English."

The delighted colonel laughed as heartily as though he had heard an amusing story. Then, sobering, he reached for their rifles and examined them. "You carry excellent weapons, although I see they're of English make. We prefer our own, of course."

Jonathan translated into Seneca for Li-solu's benefit but made no direct reply.

Standing abruptly, the officer went to a cabinet on the far side of the room and removed a box, which he brought back to his desk and opened.

Li-solu's eyes gleamed, and Jonathan couldn't blame him for becoming excited. Two superb dueling pistols reposed in the box, and no one could equal the French manufacturers in making this type of firearm.

"His Christian Majesty makes a gift to each of you," the colonel said, and handed them the pistols.

Li-solu greedily snatched the weapon that was extended to him.

Jonathan pretended avarice, too, and was privately elated when the officer presented each of them with a small powder-and-ammunition case bearing the royal French seal. This was a moment, he decided, to pretend stupidity. "Have no more skins to trade for fire sticks," he said.

The colonel gestured reassuringly. "These are free gifts to you from His Majesty. He neither wants nor expects furs in return."

Jonathan translated for his friend, and both knew they had acquired the evidence they had sought in Quebec.

The colonel made the final, necessary move. "If you are grateful, you might want to make a small offering to His Majesty in return."

"What King want?" Jonathan simulated the sudden, hostile suspicion of the savage.

"Only this. When you go home, tell the warriors of your people that the King of France is the most generous of all men. Tell them he will give every warrior of your tribe fire sticks and ammunition."

"Give rifle?" Jonathan asked innocently, knowing the new weapon was made only in England.

"Your warriors," the officer replied hurriedly, "will be given the finest of muskets. Thousands of blankets await those who want them. Yes, and we have cooking pots for you, and knives. And gold." With the air of a conjurer he reached into a desk drawer and withdrew a fist filled with gold *écus*.

Li-solu promptly reached for the money, and Jonathan, imitating him, did the same.

The officer, still clutching the money, slowly withdrew his hand. "King Louis gladly gives you fire sticks and supplies of all kinds. But he will give you gold only when the people of the Seneca become the brothers of the people of France."

The evidence was complete. A brother nation was expected to form a firm alliance with those who were related, and this meant fighting beside the French in the event of war.

"French have battle soon?" Jonathan realized he might be pushing too hard but was anxious to learn every detail he could.

The colonel, however, had no intention of revealing too much. "Every nation wants peace," he replied vaguely, "but there are times when one must fight."

"Who French fight?" Jonathan persisted.

The officer let the coins dribble out of his hand onto the desk, where he rearranged them in a neat pile. "The enemies of the French," he said, "are the enemies of the Seneca."

Obviously it was against French policy to reveal to their Indian allies that they were preparing for a campaign against the English colonies. Jonathan found it easy to feign disappointment.

The colonel knew the stakes were high: if the fierce Seneca could be persuaded to form an alliance with France, the other nations of the Iroquois Confederation probably would follow. Certainly the Seneca were more influential than the Oneida, a smaller and less warlike Iroquois tribe. "Together we will banish all our foes," the officer said, "and the Seneca will again occupy all the land they owned before their old hunting grounds were stolen from them."

Jonathan had to admire the colonel for doing thorough work; his hint was masterful and was calculated to whet the appetite of any savage tribe that had been dispossessed by the English colonials.

"The doors of this great city and fort are always open to the friends of France. Tell that to the people of the Seneca, too." The colonel escorted his guests to the door.

When the pair were alone again, in the streets of Quebec outside the Citadel, Li-solu lovingly fingered the pistol, which he wore in his belt. "The work of Li-solu and Jo-na-tan in this place is done," he said, speaking in his own tongue. "They have learned all they came to find out. They have been given fine fire sticks as well, and they carry much gold of the French."

Jonathan was as relieved as he was pleased and suggested they purchase additonal provisions for their long homeward journey through the wilderness. If they hurried, they could be well on their way by nightfall.

But Li-solu demurred, saying he wanted to celebrate their success with a feast before they departed.

Jonathan, afraid he would drink too much, insisted there would be ample opportunities for celebration after they reached safety.

The Seneca stubbornly refused to listen to reason. They had accomplished what they had set out to achieve, and his attitude was like that of a child; he would feel cheated if they departed from the scene of their triumph without toasting their success in wine and food.

He was so adamant that Jonathan had difficulty in persuading him to stop at the shop of a retail merchant for jerked venison and beef, parched corn and smoked bacon. Once their supply pouches were filled, the Seneca headed for the nearest tavern, where he demanded a tankard of rum.

Jonathan, hoping to keep him relatively sober, ordered them bowls of French soup, venison steaks, and a specialty of the city, turnips boiled in white wine.

Li-solu grinned at his friend over the rim of the tankard, from which he was happily sipping. "Jo-na-tan knows," he said, "that his brother does not have the weak head of a squaw. He will not drink too much of the French fire-wine."

He kept his word, and, although he drained his tankard, he took care to eat all of the huge meal that a half-breed barmaid set before him.

All the same, complications developed. The tavern was located only a short distance from the Citadel, and most of the patrons were soldiers who had gone off duty for the day. Most were non-commissioned officers, hard-bitten French regulars whose shrewdness and devotion to their monarch through the years had won their promotions to the ranks of sergeant and corporal. White and gold uniforms were everywhere in the taproom, and Jonathan was glad they were seated some distance from the hearth, where it was fairly dark.

Even though they were inconspicuous, the pair were the center of considerable attention, and it dawned on Jonathan that they were the only Indians in the place. Inadvertently he and Li-solu had come to a tavern frequented exclusively by off-duty troops, and a number of soldiers openly resented the intrusion. Speaking in low tones, he called his companion's attention to the situation.

Li-solu became aware of the hostility, too, and, apologizing for causing the predicament, hastily finished his meal.

They paid with a gold *écu*, which caused another stir, and Jonathan grew tense as they waited for their change. When it came he rose at once, starting toward the exit, but cursed himself for his impetuosity when he saw that three sergeants and a corporal had risen from their table to block his path. He should have allowed Li-solu to precede him, but now it was too late.

A burly sergeant, his face drink-flushed, acted as self-appointed spokesman for the group. "Where did you get the money to pay for that food and drink, eh? And where did you steal those pistols?"

Jonathan resisted the urge to drive a fist into the thick face that confronted him, and forced himself to weigh the situation coolly. At least a score of other soldiers were watching and listening and would come to the aid of their comrades if given the opportunity. So it was best to tread lightly, causing no offense, and he decided the troops might become still more aroused if he pretended not to understand French.

"Sell furs," he replied. "Get gold."

The sergeant was not satisfied. "The pistols! What about the pistols?"

"Colonel give." Jonathan hoped he was succeeding in simulating the calm of a Seneca warrior at bay.

The sergeant spat an obscenity.

Another noncommissioned officer, sitting at a nearby table, unexpectedly came to the aid of the beleaguered pair. "That's probably true, Pierre," he called. "These swine are Mohawk—something like that—and you know the general's staff. They'd give their own wives to the swine if it would win them more allies."

The sergeant turned to dispute the matter with his colleague.

Moving swiftly but delicately, Jonathan slid past the man, with Li-solu at his heels. A moment later they stepped into the open, where the cold air of early evening struck them like an icy blow. Neither wanted to loiter in the vicinity, and when Jonathan suggested that they start on their journey at once, even though night had fallen, Li-solu agreed.

The quickest route to a thoroughfare that would take them to one of the few city gates remaining open after dark lay through a long, narrow alleyway adjacent to the tavern, and they started down it. But they had gone only a short distance before a side door opened and four figures in white and gold uniforms emerged. The quartet who had started the row were still intent on making mischief.

Retreat would be the worst of tactical errors, Jonathan realized. No self-respecting brave would retire without proving his courage, as Li-solu's attitude indicated. Although their situation dictated supreme caution, the Seneca continued to advance.

Jonathan, who had slowed his pace, fell in beside him, and they moved shoulder to shoulder down the alleyway toward the spot where the four French soldiers awaited them. A loud brawl would empty the tavern, Jonathan knew, and when troops became involved in a fight, their own provost would take charge rather than leave the matter to the local constabulary. Inevitably, that would lead to the imprisonment of those who had "caused" the trouble— the Indian pair.

So, he told himself, he and Li-solu would have to act silently as well as swiftly.

"Trying to run away from us, were you?" the burly sergeant demanded, laughing. "That won't do you any good. We've decided to relieve you of those pistols. I've never yet seen an Indian who can shoot straight, and good pistols are wasted on you!"

Jonathan stood so close to him that he could smell the brandy-wine on the man's breath, and it was evident that the Frenchmen intended to manhandle the pair they thought were savages. The odds were two to one, and, with the need for quiet complicating the problem, Jonathan realized he and Li-solu could get away without causing a riot only by striking swiftly in a surprise attack. Unable to warn his friend, he could only hope the Seneca would respond immediately when he took the initiative.

"My God!" the sergeant cried. "This one is no Indian! Look at his eyes—they're pale!"

Jonathan struck him full force in the pit of the stomach with the butt of his rifle and, when the sergeant bent double, brought the heavy wood stock up sharply, hitting him under the chin and sending him sprawling.

Not hesitating for an instant, the Englishman used the rifle like a club. Grasping it by the barrel, he swung hard at the corporal, who stood a few feet behind the fallen sergeant, and so sudden was the attack that the soldier had no opportunity to protect himself. The butt caught him on the side of the head before he could even raise a hand to ward off the blow, and he, too, crumpled to the snow-strewn cobblestones.

Jonathan turned to find Li-solu struggling in the grasp of the other two soldiers, who had caught hold of him before he could emulate his friend. Both were so intent upon subduing him that they did not realize their comrades had been knocked out of action, so this gave Jonathan a moment's advantage.

He could not use the rifle as a club again for fear of hitting Li-solu. But the situation was even more dangerous now that the quartet knew he was merely disguised as an Indian, and desperation forced him to resort to desperate measures.

Drawing the knife from his belt, he threw it with all of his might, and, although the alleyway was dark, his target was only a short distance away. He heard the Frenchman gasp before slumping to the ground, blood spurting from a deep wound.

Jonathan hastily withdrew the knife and wiped it dry on the soldier's clothing.

Meanwhile Li-solu, facing only one opponent, made short work of the man, catching him from behind and, with a forearm around his throat to stifle his cries, striking him on the back of the head with his pistol butt until the Frenchman slumped to the cobblestones.

The entire fight had lasted no more than a minute or two, but there was no time to lose. The defeated soldiers were stirring, and a single cry for help would send the whole garrison in pursuit of the victors. Above all, the issue was no longer a mere tavern dispute. A French noncommissioned officer had been seriously wounded, an act which neither the military nor civilian authorities could tolerate. Jonathan knew from his own experience as an officer stationed in a garrison far from home that, if captured, he would be given the most severe punishment provided under French law. At the very least he would be subjected to long imprisonment, but it was possible he might be sentenced to death.

Li-solu needed no urging to leave the scene of the fight quickly. He and Jonathan sprinted to the far end of the alleyway, then slowed to a rapid walk as they emerged onto a street where other pedestrians, ignoring the cold, were strolling.

Listening for the cry they expected to be raised at any moment, the pair made their way to the Marie de Medici Gate, named in honor of a French queen, which remained open until midnight. This gate was used, in the main, by fishermen returning to Quebec after a long day. It was unusual for anyone to leave after dark, and certainly the Indians who came to the city knew better than to go off into the wilderness at night.

So the two sentries stationed at the portal stared curiously at the pair who were departing. Jonathan felt certain that he and

Li-solu would be remembered when the alarm was given and the man hunt began.

Once the walled city had been left behind, Li-solu took command and Jonathan was satisfied to let the Seneca assume the lead. No word was exchanged, and none was necessary. It was obvious to both men that their chance of escape and survival was improved under the Indian's direction.

Although there had been no opportunity to plan their departure they had left the city on the southwestern side, and Li-solu started across the open fields toward the shelter of the beckoning forest. Once they reached the thick woods, he immediately changed course and started due south toward the St. Lawrence.

Jonathan wanted to protest. They would be in the open again once they reached the river and would be far easier to find when the search for them began. But he kept quiet, aware that the Seneca knew what he was doing and realizing, too, that circumstances forced him to put his complete trust in another.

In a short time they reached the shore of the broad St. Lawrence. Now and then they came to clearings, where farmers had built their cabins, and it seemed to Jonathan that they were taking unnecessary risks. A property owner who happened to glance out his windows and saw two Indians heading across his fields toward the west would remember the pair when questioned by searching troops.

But it soon developed that the risk Li-solu was taking was calculated. He was looking for something, and when he found it he indicated his triumph with a soft grunt of satisfaction.

Jonathan looked down at a narrow boat made of a long, hollowed log, the type of craft that fur traders and hunters used when they traveled on the great river. Hand-fashioned oars rested in the boat, and lashed to a crude mast was a furled sail of heavy canvas. The boat provided a perfect mode of transportation for a rapid departure from the area, and with luck, the owner of the boat would not discover his loss until morning.

Untroubled by the knowledge that he was stealing someone's property, Jonathan bent down and picked up one end of the boat. He and Li-solu carried it to the water's edge, and, as they launched

, the Englishman felt increased respect for his companion's knowledge of the wilderness. Off to the east they could hear the boiling, churning sounds of vicious rapids they had noted on their approach to Quebec; the Seneca had waited until they had cleared the dangerous rapids before beginning his search for the craft that would take them westward.

Li-solu raised the sail and secured it, then took his place in the stern, where he could steer the craft with an oar. He stationed Jonathan in the prow, armed with another oar, and instructed him to keep a watch for floating objects and partly submerged rocks that might cause them to founder.

Under the Seneca's expert guidance the boat nosed out a short distance from the north bank of the St. Lawrence into the main channel, then quickly picked up speed as the sail filled. The forest closed in on both banks, and Jonathan could hear no sound but the lapping of water on the near shore. The cold was numbing, forcing him to drape his blanket around his shoulders, and after a time tears streamed from his eyes as he maintained his watch.

But he maintained his vigil through the long, seemingly endless night, and not until Li-solu beached the boat on the north bank shortly before dawn did he become conscious of his exhaustion. They ate the usual wilderness rations of cold meat and parched corn, and Jonathan, who was ravenous, smiled to himself when it occurred to him that he no longer objected to the crude fare he had loathed on his first travels in the North American interior.

They would spend the day sleeping and resting, Li-solu said, and would resume their voyage at dusk. Without further ado both stretched out in their blankets, their rifles near at hand, and Jonathan promptly emptied his mind, as he had taught himself to do as a cavalry officer. Sleep was essential, so he could not permit the ever-present danger, the physical discomfort, or disturbing thoughts of Elizabeth to keep him awake.

A light tap on his shoulder aroused him instantly around noon, and he sat up, clutching his rifle. But Li-solu's grin reassured him. "Fre-is-to, the god of winter, protects the Seneca," the Indian said. Jonathan saw that a heavy, wet snow was falling.

195

They would resume their journey at once, Li-solu told him, since visibility was restricted to a few feet and searching parties would find their task complicated by the weather.

In spite of the continuing snow the wind was gentle and remained steady, and they covered a considerable distance before making a halt at nightfall for another meal and brief nap. Again they started out, and it seemed to Jonathan that the thick snowfall dulled the sharp edge of the cold.

That night they passed the little village of Three Rivers, without knowing it, and kept up their unrelenting pace. By dawn Jonathan estimated they had traveled more than one hundred miles from Quebec, and his body ached for a rest. But Li-solu was determined to take advantage of every break in the weather and would not halt again. The snow would not stop coming down for several more hours, he declared, and they would be womanly if they gave in to weakness. Furthermore the gods of the Seneca, who were helping them, would become disgusted and would turn on them.

Driving his companion and himself to the limit of their endurance, Li-solu did not head for the shore until late morning. Jonathan was so weary that he craved only sleep, but the Indian insisted he eat first, so he did as he was bidden.

He could have slept until the following morning, but at nightfall Li-solu's insistent tap on the shoulder awakened him, and the tortured journey was resumed. Jonathan knew only that they were somewhere east of the little fur-trading town of Montreal, the only community of consequence other than Quebec in New France. But the Seneca seemed to carry a map inside his head, even though the area was strange to him. Soon after midnight he steered to the south bank of the river, and at his direction they concealed the boat deep in the forest.

From this point, the Seneca announced, they would head almost due south, through forests dotted with occasional French villages and farms. In two or three days they would reach the land of the Iroquois.

From his description Jonathan guessed they were entering that portion of French Canada that lay directly north of New York, and wo- to three-day journey meant they were about fifty miles from relative safety. Nodding cheerfully as they ate a larger meal than usual, even though their supplies were dwindling, he knew he would be warmer on an overland march than in the log boat on the St. Lawrence.

They slept for a few hours, starting out again soon after daybreak, skirting several small lakes and crossing a number of frozen rivers. Occasionally they made out a clearing in the distance and avoided it, but most of the time they sacrificed silence for speed. Jonathan knew that only his many months of wilderness living had given him the endurance to keep up the grueling pace, and this recognition of his stamina made it easier for him to overcome the creeping weariness that numbed his legs and back.

Suddenly, at noon, Li-solu halted, dropped to his knees, and put an ear to the ground.

Jonathan needed no instructions to do the same and heard a thudding sound, faint but distinct. "Horsemen?" he asked.

Li-solu continued to listen for a moment. "There are more than the fingers on the hand of Li-solu. They seek him and Jo-na-tan."

They had made no great effort to conceal their trail on the overland march, so it would not be difficult for men who knew the wilderness to follow them. It was useless to speculate, Jonathan knew, on what he once would have considered miraculous. It seemed almost impossible that the French and their Indian allies knew how far they had traveled on the river and then had picked up their trail only a short time after they had started south through the forest. Perhaps the enemy had enjoyed extraordinarily good fortune, but it was more likely that the search was being conducted by a network of patrols, each assigned to a specific region.

One fact stood out above all others. "We need horses, too," Jonathan said.

Li-solu had already regained his feet and started off toward the west at a rapid clip, not bothering to hide his trail through the forest. Apparently he knew where he was headed and had a goal in mind. Certainly Jonathan had no intention of wasting time and breath questioning him.

After they had made steady progress for the better part of an hour the Seneca paused long enough to listen to the ground again. "Come much closer," he said in the impassive tone the savages used in moments of great stress.

A quarter of an hour later they saw clear sunlight, and halted at the edge of a clearing. Directly ahead was a farmhouse, which consisted of two connected log cabins and several smaller outbuildings. It seemed insane to Jonathan to seek refuge with a French farmer, but the neigh of an unseen horse on the far side of the house told him what Li-solu had in mind.

They could not hesitate, and, as Jonathan well realized, only bold action might save them. If the French authorities in Quebec had sent cavalry patrols to capture him, they plainly considered it a matter of importance that he be apprehended. But it was far more important to him that he not be caught.

With one accord he and Li-solu moved out into the open and made a swing around the farmhouse. They could see horses now in the field beyond the buildings, two bay geldings and a mare, all nibbling at the stubble of grass on the ground from which snow had been removed.

Someone shouted, and Jonathan saw a man in a heavy wool shirt and buckskin trousers standing in the entrance to the house.

Every moment of delay was precious, so the Englishman raised a hand in a friendly, cheerful wave.

As he had hoped, the unexpected gesture momentarily perplexed the farmer, causing him to wonder why these warriors had suddenly appeared on his property.

By now the horses were only a few yards away. Jonathan broke into a run and leaped onto the bare back of a gelding. Li-solu tried to do the same but was less at home with horses and, slipping to the ground, had to repeat the effort.

The farmer, realizing that an attempt was being made to steal his animals, dashed inside the house and reappeared a moment later a musket in his hands. Behind him was a teen-aged boy, similarly armed, and both shouted loudly as they raised their firearms.

Jonathan, bending low on the bare back of his mount, dug his cels into the animal's flanks. The horse responded with a leap, and Jonathan headed him toward the south at a canter that quickly eveloped into a full gallop.

Li-solu, he was relieved to note, was following his example but was not finding it easy to keep his seat. It suddenly occurred to onathan that he had seen no horses in the land of the Seneca and hat, consequently, his friend was not an experienced rider.

A musket roared and a shot passed far overhead. Then the second nusket sounded, its bullet whining off to the right.

By the time the man and boy managed to reload and fire again, he retreating thieves had gained the sanctuary of the forest.

Then another sound intruded itself on Jonathan's consciousness, nd he heard approaching hoofbeats. His pursuers had been gaining ground, but he had been too preoccupied to realize it. Now a ew dilemma presented itself. Had he been alone, he thought, it would have been no problem for him to outstrip the patrol. He was superb horseman, able to handle any mount, and his years of xperience in the cavalry gave him unbounded self-confidence. But e could not leave Li-solu behind and had to devise new tactics. Meanwhile the pursuers were steadily drawing closer.

"Take the lead!" Jonathan called in English. "You set the pace and ll match it!" In this moment of crisis he could not be distracted y translating his thoughts into Seneca.

Li-solu was puzzled, but Jonathan's gestures indicated what was xpected of him and he moved ahead.

Jonathan checked his rifle, then loaded his pistol. The French ould not take him before he gave them the fight of their lives.

They came to the bank of a river, where there were fewer trees nd bushes, and the relatively open spaces gave them the opportunity to ride more rapidly. They could hear the pursuing horsemen alling back, but Jonathan realized that the advantage was temporary. When the French came to the river, they would more than hake up what they had lost.

There had to be some way to overcome this seeming handicap, owever, and when the idea occurred to him he was able to complete is plan of action. Its simplicity appealed to him, and his feeling of discouragement was washed away by a new surge of hope. Cocking his rifle, he held it ready for immediate use.

When the pursuers appeared on the riverbank, Jonathan was ready for them. He counted six white uniforms and saw one figure in buckskins, so he knew that a patrol of professional French cavalry was being led by an Indian guide. Reducing the situation to the laws of military probability, he had to assume that the Frenchmen were his equals as riders. Therefore the only elements in his favor were the factor of surprise, combined with the range of his rifle, which no French weapon could match.

The moment the buckskin-clad leader came within range, Jonathan raised his rifle to his shoulder and fired.

The Indian grasped his shoulder and faltered.

Jonathan immediately conquered his feeling of self-disgust. He had hoped to kill the man but instead had merely wounded him. An injury, however, served almost the same purpose: the rider slowed his pace, forcing those behind him to do the same.

Reloading, Jonathan fired again, aiming this time at the savage's horse. The animal stumbled, throwing its rider, and the fleeing pair continued to gain ground.

By the time the French cavalrymen made their way past their fallen guide and resumed their gallop, the fugitives were far ahead. But it was impossible for Li-solu to match the pace of professional horsemen, and soon the pursuers began to gain again.

Jonathan realized that luck as well as skill had been at least partly responsible for the temporary advantage he had won. His rifle was not the easiest of weapons to fire accurately, and shooting from the bare back of a galloping horse compounded the difficulty. Next time he might be less fortunate and miss. If that happened and they came within range of the French muskets, the odds against him and Li-solu would soar.

A sudden inspiration made him realize he had overlooked the greatest advantage he had gained. "Turn into the forest!" he shouted. "Quickly! Go as deep as you can!"

Li-solu obeyed as rapidly as he could control his mount.

Jonathan, close behind him, explained the abrupt change in tactics. "I wounded one of them. Their guide. In the open, along the riverbank, they'll be certain to catch us. But I think we can do better here. Without a guide they won't find it easy to stay on our trail."

The Seneca immediately understood the situation and grinned. "Make more harder," he called, and deliberately led them on an erratic course.

They made their way through a stand of pines, rode close to the edge of a long, meandering nest of brambles, and, whenever they came to a small river, crossed and recrossed it several times. Even a savage experienced in following a wilderness trail would have found it difficult to follow the pair, and the French were suffering from the loss of their guide. They fell farther and farther back, until it was no longer possible to hear the hoofbeats of their mounts crashing through the forest's winter debris.

Jonathan promptly suggested they abandon their subterfuge and head due south again.

But Li-solu, instinctively more cunning, demurred. That was what the enemy would expect, he said, and if the French had gained even a partial knowledge of the forest, they might be waiting in ambush. It would be better, he believed, to work their way southward gradually, on an indirect course, in order to increase the probability that they could avoid the French. It might be necessary, he declared, to spend as long as an extra day and night in the forest, but the increased margin of safety they would enjoy would make the time well spent.

Jonathan could not dispute the matter with someone who knew so much more about the wilderness.

The days that followed were unexpectedly harrowing. Viciously cold winds blew down from the north, making it necessary for both men to rub snow on their hands and faces at frequent intervals to ward off frostbite. They spent much of the time in a portion of the forest that winter had stripped of all foliage and grass, so they had to feed their horses all of their supplies of parched corn. The animals suffered from the icy blasts, too, and it proved better for the horses as well as the men to keep moving, no matter how great their exhaustion.

The lack of adequate food, shelter, and rest wore down Li-solu, who previously had appeared indestructible, and, although his resolution did not falter, he became glum and uncommunicative. There was no sign of the French cavalry patrol anywhere, but the elements created hazards just as menacing. Unable to light a fire for fear of giving themselves away, Jonathan and the Seneca ate their bacon uncooked, and when it was gone they went without food. The cold spell drove away all game, and such a thick shield of ice appeared on the rivers and lakes that the pair could not afford time to cut through it in order to fish.

Birds and small animals had stripped bushes of their berries, and Li-solu made no attempt to find edible roots. It would have been difficult to take them from the hard ground, and, lacking a fire to thaw them, they would have been unpalatable.

Snow drifts in open places were so high that neither the men nor their reluctant mounts could plod through them, and long, unplanned detours slowed the march. Li-solu's extra day stretched into the better part of a week, and Jonathan gradually lost count of time.

Then, late one afternoon, Li-solu roused himself. A Mohawk town was nearby, he said; without knowing it the pair had traveled far beyond the border that separated French Canada from New York and were deep in the land of the Mohawk, the closest friends of the Seneca in the Iroquois Confederation. Using their last reserves of strength, they pushed on to the sentry outposts and were escorted in triumph into the town.

That night a feast was held in their honor, but they were so tired they dozed through the better part of the long, ceremonial meal. But Jonathan did not care. It was enough that he had accomplished his mission and was safe.

15

The Iroquois

The geldings created a sensation when Jonathan and Li-solu rode into the Seneca town of Olu-a-su. Many of the women and children had never seen horses, and, forgetting their usual phlegmatic poise, they stared in open wonder at the mounts. It was immediately evident that ownership of the stolen animal gave Jonathan a new standing in the community.

He and Li-solu went straight to Olu-a-su and Mi-la-ine, who listened without comment to the story of all they had learned and of their adventures.

It was galling that neither volunteered any information concerning their own aspects of the problem, but Jonathan felt he had earned the right to be told what had been happening here. "Did the sachems of the Seneca visit the Oneida?" he demanded, indifferent to the fact that his question violated custom.

Olu-a-su was mildly indignant but knew it would be wrong to rebuke someone who successfully completed a difficult assignment. "It is true," he said, "that the brothers of the Seneca took the firestick bullets and powder of the sachem Louis. But they gave no promises to the warriors of the sachem Louis."

Mi-la-ine reached for the pistol the French lieutenant colonel in Quebec had given to Jonathan and turned it over in his hand, his expression thoughtful.

He handed it to the sachem of three eagle feathers, who was equally covetous. "The great sachem Louis gives fine gifts to the friends of his people."

Jonathan wanted to retort that the French would demand a return in the form of an alliance, a point he thought he had already made clear. But this, he decided, was not the moment to argue the matter.

"The Oneida have been given great wealth," Olu-a-su continued. "The Seneca can become wealthy, too. All the sachems of the Iroquois will hold a council. Jo-na-tan and Li-solu will come. They will tell the sachems of all the Iroquois what they did in the city of the sachem Louis. They will show the sachems of the Iroquois the gifts they were given."

The indignant Jonathan realized that the tribulations he and Li-solu had been forced to endure because of the French attitude were being ignored. The Seneca leader was impressed only by the firearms they had been given and, presumably, by the promise of gold if the nations of the Iroquois entered into a formal alliance. The officials of New France, it appeared, truly understood the mind of the North American savage.

The audience ended abruptly, and Jonathan was dismissed. He obtained a pledge from several young braves who were loitering outside the long house to build him a stable for his horse, promising to let them ride the mount in return. Then, his business completed, he hurried off to his own hut, relieved that Li-solu had not accompanied him.

Elizabeth sat in a corner, patiently waiting for him.

Jonathan surprised himself by going to her and, without saying a word, drawing her to her feet.

Her response to his kiss told him all he wanted to know; she had missed him, too, and had been worried about his safety.

Both started to speak simultaneously, but Elizabeth said she had no news of importance and wanted to know what had befallen him.

Jonathan told her everything, including the disturbing meeting with Olu-a-su.

The girl immediately grasped the significance of the situation. "Instead of regarding the Oneida as traitors to the Iroquois, the Seneca are jealous. And the gifts to you and Li-solu make them even greedier."

"They won't or can't realize the full implications of an alliance with the French," Jonathan said. "But I can tell you this—if the Iroquois nations join the other tribes in going to the side of the French, the English colonies can't win. The French will take possession of all our territory."

"And my property," the girl said.

"All through the terrible journey back here," Jonathan said, "I was comforted by the knowledge that you and I have acquired a horse and that I have a pistol you can use to protect yourself. But what good will it do us to escape now? It simply didn't occur to me that the Seneca might succumb to the French offers!"

"If the French had realized how much your visit in Quebec would help their cause, they'd have given you an escort to the Canadian border to insure your safety." Elizabeth smiled sourly. "And the worst of all this is that the American authorities may not even know what's happening."

"If I could," Jonathan said, "I'd send a letter to Dr. Franklin. But that's impossible. I have no writing materials, and I wouldn't trust a Seneca messenger to deliver a letter to him, even if I could write one."

"I'm not sure which would be worse," the girl murmured, "becoming French subjects or staying here with the Seneca."

"We'll do neither," Jonathan told her firmly. "I've delayed in making any attempt to leave the Seneca because I haven't wanted to put you in jeopardy. But now the English colonies themselves are in the gravest danger they've ever known. I'm going to insist that I be given the right to go off to Philadelphia to see Dr. Franklin, and I'll demand that you be allowed to come with me. Everything else will have to wait—including the estates at Presque Isle!"

Elizabeth looked dubious but kept her thoughts to herself as Jonathan, too impatient to wait, hastily returned to the long house of the town's principal sachem.

There he found Mi-la-ine and Li-solu still in council with Olu-a-su but did not hesitate to interrupt them. "It is right," he said, "that the men who live in the colonies on the sea know what the sachem of France offers to the people of the Iroquois nations."

To his surprise Olu-a-su nodded in solemn agreement. "It may be," he replied, "that the sachems of the English will give greater gifts to the Iroquois than the sachem Louis will give them."

His greed might make it easier to expedite the matter, and Jonathan found it easy to lie. "The sachems of the English," he said, "give many gifts to their friends. Jo-na-tan will go to the chief town of the English colonies and will tell the sachems all that has happened."

Li-solu immediately supported the suggestion. "It is good that Jo-na-tan take the message," he said. "Jo-na-tan will speak to the sachems of the English in their own words."

Pressing his luck, Jonathan said, "The slave woman of Jo-na-tan also speaks the language of the people of the English. She will come with him."

There was a long silence, and everyone waited for Olu-a-su to speak. His expression had become guarded, and he stared off into space for what seemed like an interminable time. "It is true," he said at last, "that Jo-na-tan is a sachem of the Seneca. Once Jo-na-tan was a son of the English. If the slave woman goes with him, he might want to stay in the town of the English. The English might send their warriors with fire sticks to the land of the Seneca." His voice rose slightly. "The slave woman will stay in the town of the Seneca. Then Jo-na-tan will return and the warriors of the English will not come."

The final decision had been made, and there was no appeal to a higher authority, so Jonathan had to be content that Elizabeth would not be harmed pending his return.

She had felt certain she would not be released, and the news didn't surprise her.

It made Jonathan feel slightly better when he gave her the French dueling pistol and ammunition box. "Hide these in the hut," he said, "and if anything untoward happens to me on my journey, you'll have at least a chance to protect yourself."

The Seneca wanted to send a large escort with him, but he knew he could make far better time traveling alone, on horseback, so he declined the offer. He set out on his journey early the next morning, his saddlebags filled with supplies for himself and fodder for his gelding, his head freshly shaved on either side of his scalp lock, and his skin stained anew and oiled.

He would make a long journey by himself through a savage-infested wilderness in winter, but the forest neither mystified nor frightened him, and he knew he could master it. He had only one regret: Li-solu had returned to his hut for the night, so there had been no opportunity for further conversation with Elizabeth, much less the chance to make love to her.

Li-solu had given his friend a rough verbal sketch of the countryside he would cross, and Jonathan, using the burned end of a stick, had drawn himself a map on the inside of a piece of birch bark. When he had come to the New World he would have considered himself insane to be so ill-prepared for a long trek through the wilderness, but now he believed he had all the equipment and knowledge he needed.

His self-confidence was not ill-placed. Traveling eastward through the lands of the Oneida, Tuscarora, Cayuga, and Mohawk, he accepted the hospitality of the Iroquois allies of the Seneca, eating their food so he could save his own provisions and spending his nights in their towns. Reaching the Hudson River he followed its west bank southward, and although there had been a time when he had wanted to visit New York Town, he avoided it now, when the presence of a warrior with hazel eyes might cause complications.

Traveling through New Jersey, he used roads when he could but again avoided centers of population by making detours through woodlands. At last he reached Pennsylvania without incident and, arriving in Philadelphia, rode straight to the house of Dr. Benjamin Franklin. Indians were no novelty in the metropolis, although few owned horses, so a number of citizens stared at the tall, paint-smeared warrior. But no one halted him to accuse him of stealing the mount, and he reached Franklin's brick house without incident.

Leaving the gelding tied to a hitching post, Jonathan threw his blanket over his shoulder, and, his rifle in one hand, he tapped at the door with the shining brass knocker.

A serving woman in a trim black uniform answered his summons. Although people from every walk of life came to see Benjamin

Franklin, the woman's eyes bulged slightly and her fingers plucked with quiet nervousness at her starched white apron.

The humor of the situation struck Jonathan, and he couldn't resist speaking in his most formal manner. "Be good enough to inform Dr. Franklin," he said, "that Captain Jonathan Lewis desires to see him on a matter of the most urgent business."

The serving woman screamed, turned, and fled, leaving him on the stoop.

After a few moments Franklin himself appeared, warmly bundled in a quilted jacket, a quill pen in one hand. "What's this?" he asked brusquely.

Jonathan identified himself.

Franklin peered at him through the upper part of his bifocal spectacles, then through the lower, but showed no other sign of surprise. "I advise you to come in, young man," he said. "You're letting all the cold in Pennsylvania into the house."

Jonathan followed him into the familiar library he recalled so vividly and, as he took a leather chair, realized that for the first time in months he was being treated like a civilized man.

"You didn't strike me as one who enjoys a masquerade," Franklin said.

Succinctly, omitting only his affair with Elizabeth, Jonathan told him all that had happened.

"Extraordinary," Franklin murmured several times as he listened, but did not appear surprised.

"I've come to you, sir, because I don't know the Crown authorities in New York, and I thought you'd know what to do."

"Most men in your situation would have been fortunate to survive, but you've actually prospered. Extraordinary." Franklin removed his spectacles, shaking his head as he cleaned them, and then his manner became brisk. "As it happens, I'm delighted you came to me. I've recently been given a commission in the Pennsylvania militia, due to the threatening situation. Of course we've known the French are planning to open a campaign against us, Lewis."

A feeling of relief flooded Jonathan.

"All the colonies except Georgia, which was founded too recently to be of much help, have been mobilizing, training and expanding their militia, and we've requested as large a contingent of redcoats from London as the War Office will give us. A number of regiments are being sent under a general named Braddock."

"I know him." This was not the moment to express the opinion that the general, although courageous, was too stubborn and narrow-minded to adapt himself to the informal type of warfare the American wilderness demanded.

"We've also been certain the French would obtain help from some of the Indian tribes in their territory, particularly the Huron, Ottawa, and Abnaki. We had hoped the Algonkin might be sensible enough to stay out, but I can't say I'm shocked by the news that they've entered the French fold. What does disturb me is the possibility that the Iroquois might join the French. That alliance could be disastrous for us."

"That's why I'm here, Dr. Franklin."

"It would be helpful if you could meet some of my colleagues and tell them your story. I trust you'll be free for dinner this afternoon?"

Jonathan had almost forgotten the polite codes of conduct observed by civilized people. "I'm at your service, sir."

"Good. I'll send word around town at once, and we can begin our discussions as soon as they get here."

Eleven men were seated at the table in the Franklin dining room, and although the meal had been arranged on short notice, it was excellent and Jonathan relished every bite. The soup, a local pepper-pot concoction, was delicious. The roast was tender, and the Midlands pudding served with it was a delight to someone who had been eating only basic frontier foods. Crisply brown on the outside and soft in the center, it deserved to be featured as a special course. The Italian salad greens were tender, a far cry from the roots and herbs of the wilderness, and the fruit tart that followed was so good that Jonathan felt no shame in asking for another.

His dinner companions, grave Pennsylvanians in dark suits and waistcoats trimmed with pewter buttons, took their food for granted and throughout the meal bombarded Jonathan with questions. One in particular was asked repeatedly: "In all, how many warriors can the Iroquois nations put into the field?"

It was astonishing, Jonathan thought, that someone who had spent only a short time in the New World should have gained a better understanding of the Indians than native-born colonists had obtained. "The savages," he replied patiently, "can't be judged by our standards. If their towns were attacked, their elders, squaws, and even their small children would fight. When they go off on an expedition, every warrior who takes part is a volunteer. If the tribes of the Iroquois were to join the French, they might send ten thousand men against us. But, if the Miami of the Ohio Valley attacked them, they might be able to send twenty-five thousand into combat."

"Suppose they joined us to fight the French," asked Robert Morris, a shrewd and energetic young merchant who, although considerably younger than his colleagues, displayed an ability to grapple with fundamentals. "How many would they send?"

"To an extent," Jonathan replied, aware that the oil smearing his body was causing those who sat near him to feel uncomfortable, "that depends on the offer."

Morris gave him no chance to continue. "Name a conservative figure."

Jonathan shrugged. "Ten thousand."

"What would we have to offer to persuade more of them to join us?"

"The Indian," Jonathan said, conscious of the eagle feather bobbing in his scalp lock, "is ruled by his feelings, not by reason or his purse. I'm not suggesting you match the French, powder keg for powder keg, and then offer more. How you make your offer will mark the difference."

Several of the gentlemen started to speak at the same time, but Benjamin Franklin tapped on a wineglass. "There have been exchanges of opinions between colonies of late," he said, "and virtually all of us agree there's a need for a meeting with the chiefs of the Iroquois. Everything Captain Lewis has said confirms this conviction."

"If you want to hold a council with the Iroquois, it will have to be soon," Jonathan told him, "before they accept the bribes of the French."

"Commissioner William Johnson, the New York superintendent of Iroquois affairs, holds the same view," Franklin said. "Do you know him, Captain Lewis?"

"I've met no one civilized since I was abducted by the Seneca," Jonathan replied, "but I've heard the Mohawk speak of a friend at Fort Albany. They place great faith in him."

"I shall write to Johnson today," Franklin said to the entire group, "and if he agrees, I shall propose that every colony send delegates to a meeting with the Iroquois. Would you come to the meeting with the Seneca, Captain Lewis?"

"Rely on it, sir, I'll find a way," Jonathan said.

"Then we'll be in good hands," Franklin declared. "Between Johnson and Captain Lewis, we'll find ways to treat generously but firmly with the Iroquois."

The others agreed, but Morris was not satisfied. "In all of our planning for a war that hasn't yet started, gentlemen, we've neglected a serious problem that already exists. From what Captain Lewis has indicated to us, a young lady who is a citizen of Pennsylvania is being held in permanent bondage by the Seneca. It seems to me that our first duty is to win her freedom."

"I propose," another gentleman declared, "that we send an expedition into Seneca territory to win her freedom. Not only does her liberty depend on us, but the Indians won't treat us with respect unless we deal with them as they deserve."

Several others agreed.

"I forbid it," Jonathan said, unconsciously folding his arms over his chest in the Seneca manner. "You'd not only antagonize the Seneca and drive all of the Iroquois into the camp of the French. You'd guarantee Elizabeth's murder. The savages have their own ideas of what's fair in their treatment of a hostage."

"What alternative do you propose?" Morris wanted to know.

"I make no proposals." Jonathan was uncompromising. "The girl

211

is my responsibility. I'll see to it, in my own way, that no harm comes to her!"

The meeting at Dr. Franklin's house lasted through the better part of the afternoon and was devoted to a discussion of the offers that would be made to the Iroquois and the methods that might be used to prevent the savages from biting the hands of those who fed them. It was agreed that Commissioner Johnson of New York would invite the Iroquois tribes to such an intercolonial conference, as he had long wanted to do, and that Jonathan would use every means at his disposal to win the endorsement of the powerful Seneca.

Everyone present thanked Jonathan for the effort he had exerted on behalf of the English colonies, and Dr. Franklin invited him to spend the night at his house before starting off on his return to the land of the Seneca. Jonathan was grateful for the distinguished American's offer of hospitality but had ideas of his own and crossed the city to the waterfront tavern where his adventures in the New World had begun.

He arrived during a late afternoon lull, and at first glance it appeared that the cheerful taproom was deserted. But, suddenly, a young, very attractive blond woman in a green velvet gown materialized from the kitchen, brandishing a broom. "Your kind aren't wanted here!" she called. "Get out!"

Abel French, who had put on weight since Jonathan had last seen him, followed her, wiping his hands on his leather apron. "We want no fuss, my dear," he murmured.

Jonathan grinned at his old friend. "When I first knew you, Abel," he said, "you were happy to serve any patron who'd spend a sixpence here."

French stared hard at the warrior, recognized him, and embraced him.

Jonathan, laughing, pounded him on the back before turning to the astonished woman. "We meet again, Mistress Patience," he said to the girl who had betrayed him on the night of his arrival in Philadelphia from England.

Abel French's embarrassment was excruciating. "This is Captain

Lewis, my dear. The man we've discussed so frequently. Jonathan, Patience became my wife a few weeks ago. She came to me, destitute, and—well, it's a long story."

Jonathan's months with the Seneca stood him in good stead, and his face was wooden. "Accept my felicitations, Mistress French," he said dryly. "I hope you realize you've married an honorable man and treat him accordingly."

Patience managed to look at him without flinching. "You'll never know how much I've regretted the harm I've done you, sir," she said.

"I bear you no malice," Jonathan told her candidly. "Much that has happened to me has been for the good."

French, anxious to change the subject, insisted they go to the kitchen for a drink of spiced punch and a joint of beef.

Accompanying the couple, Jonathan was surprised and pleased to note that a large staff was at work, preparing meat at the hearths, baking bread, and stirring kettles of soup. "You've prospered, Abel."

"The Almighty has been good to me. In more ways than one." French put an arm around his wife's shoulders and hugged her. "But I'm eager to learn how you, of all people on this earth, have been transformed into a barbarian."

Again Jonathan told his story but gave them a sharply censored version, omitting all mention of Andrews and his daughter, Elizabeth, and the significance of the meeting the Pennsylvania and New York authorities were planning to hold with the nations of the Iroquois.

Patience was not stupid, however, and knew he was concealing something. "I had a letter from Felicity not long ago," she said, "and she told me she had seen you. She and her father bought some property from you and a girl who also owned an estate in western Pennsylvania, she said."

The bald lie outraged Jonathan, but again he concealed his feelings. "It interests me that you correspond with your old associates," he said.

"I hate them, and I've never answered one of her letters!" Color rose in Patience's cheeks.

French's solemn nod confirmed the truth of his wife's claim.

"I'd do anything to repay them for their treachery!" she continued.

"If you mean that," Jonathan said slowly, "I'll give you an opportunity. Tell them the nations of the Iroquois are being invited to a great council at Fort Albany. Once the details are settled, the date will be no secret. Tell them that, for reasons you can't explain, all the property they've acquired is in jeopardy, and if they don't want to become paupers, they'll come to Fort Albany while the meeting is being held."

"Tell me what to write, and I'll put it down as you direct, word for word," Patience declared.

Jonathan allowed himself the luxury of a broad, anticipatory smile. Perhaps, he thought, divine justice sometimes did intervene in the shabby affairs of men.

16

The Great Council

Signs of coming spring, faint but distinct, were everywhere in the forest as Jonathan returned to the land of the Seneca from Philadelphia. Snows were melting and rivers rising, buds were starting to appear on trees and bushes, and a man whose ear was attuned to the sounds of the wilderness knew the small animals were returning in large numbers.

Acting on the suggestion of Dr. Franklin, Jonathan made a slight detour in order to visit William Johnson at his home on the Mohawk River, about thirty miles west of Fort Albany. Knowing only that Johnson was an English immigrant who had prospered in the New World through his operation of trading posts, acquisition of land, and friendship with the Mohawk, Jonathan was unprepared for what he saw.

Working under a vaguely worded warrant from New York as Commissioner to the Iroquois, Johnson had built himself a magnificent manor house, far more impressive than the disputed properties at Presque Isle. There he lived with the Indian woman, Molly, whom he called his housekeeper, and their large brood of children. A full staff of servants was in attendance, and every luxury of English country living was at hand, but the New World had left its indelible stamp on Johnson. A high-spirited man who enjoyed an early morning ride in polished boots and a brocade coat, he changed to buckskins after breakfast for a tour of his fur-trading posts in the vicinity. Two cooks were employed in his kitchens, one to prepare delicacies that were the equal of the finest that London and Paris could offer, the other to cook in Indian style for the many warriors he entertained.

Johnson gave Jonathan a boisterous welcome and assigned him to a place of honor at the dinner table, where eighteen persons, including two sachems of the Mohawk, one of the Oneida, and several warriors from regions as far distant as the Mississippi River were served a bewildering variety of dishes. These included a beef, veal, and kidney pie in wine sauce, raw fish marinated in forest herbs, a rich custard and fruit tart, and salted strips of venison.

The strange meal finished, the burly host led Jonathan to his book-lined study on the second floor and, after listening to his story, questioned him closely. "Are the French placing any limits on the firearms they're giving our friends?"

"None that I can see. Their generosity with ammunition and powder, as well as with muskets and pistols, is staggering. All they're holding back is money."

"The council at Fort Albany must be convened as soon as possible," Johnson said after pondering briefly. "I won't wait for the colonies to settle the dates and make arrangements. I'll make my own plans and force them to conform. That'll save at least a month." He chuckled as he scribbled some notes on a sheet of paper.

Returning his grin, Jonathan found himself in complete rapport with this energetic former Englishman who had made himself wealthy and powerful by gaining a thorough understanding of the New World.

"I can control the Mohawk, and through them the Cayuga and Tuscarora. But the Oneida will follow the lead of your people, and I've had little luck trying to influence the Seneca. Can you handle them, Lewis?"

"To an extent," Jonathan said, "I think I might persuade them to listen to me."

"You'll have to do better than that. We'll need the unanimous agreement of all the Iroquois to join a formal alliance with Great Britain. If one hesitates—particularly one as potent as the Seneca —all of them will back off. And if that happens, they'll surely end in the French camp. If they waver, we'll have to rely on you to bring them into line, Lewis. There's no one else. Not that we'll need anyone. You've done remarkably well since you've joined the Seneca."

Jonathan doubted that he could sway the savages if they were indecisive or balked, but Johnson spoke to him earnestly, the younger man found it was his turn to ask questions, and they talked for another hour. By the time Jonathan went off to bed he realized he did not dare allow himself to think in terms of failure.

The next morning he resumed his journey at dawn, and three days later he arrived in the Seneca town of Olu-a-su. The English, he told the sachem of three eagle feathers, were summoning all of the Iroquois to a meeting in the immediate future, and he felt certain the Seneca would want to throw in their lot with the New Yorkers and Pennsylvanians and Virginians rather than with the French. There were reasons that would be revealed in due time, he hinted, but, acting on William Johnson's advice, he spoke mysteriously and refused to elaborate.

His duty finished for the moment, Jonathan went off to his own hut, where Elizabeth waited for him. Her greeting was subdued, and she seemed only vaguely interested when he brought her up to date on what he had done. She roused herself briefly when he told her of the letter that Patience French had promised to send to Andrews and Felicity, but she soon lapsed again into lethargic state.

Jonathan was concerned and eyed her carefully. "Are you ill?"

"Not really. It's just that I don't much care any more. Alliances are being formed and broken, but what's that to me? I don't even feel very strongly about my estates. Why should I, when I seem doomed to spend the rest of my life as a servant and concubine in the wilderness?"

"Let me finish bringing you up to date before you give in to despair. The Pennsylvanians wanted to send an expedition out here to rescue you—"

"That's absurd. I'd be killed and scalped before they came within a hundred miles of this town."

"So I told them. But I've had a most instructive talk with William Johnson about you— He doesn't happen to be related?"

"The Mohawk sometimes thought he was Papa's brother or cousin, but there's no blood relationship, and we've never met."

"Well, he's acquired an enormous knowledge of Indian ways, and he's explained there's a solution of your problem that can be arranged very simply. If you're still a servant when I go off to the council meeting at Fort Albany, you won't be allowed to come with me. The Seneca will insist you stay here."

"I'm not surprised. They'll hold me as a hostage for the rest of my life!"

"I dare say. But we can arrange matters so that I alone will have the authority to say where you can go and what you can do. If I make you my squaw, they'll have to let me take you along!"

The girl stared at him, her eyes huge.

"At the end of the council meeting, I can dispose of you as I see fit. I can make a—a gift of you to William Johnson, for instance, or to Benjamin Franklin. And then you'll be free."

She raised a hand to her bare throat, then asked in a tremulous voice, "Will the Seneca give their permission?"

"It's customary, Johnson says, for a warrior to make a gift to his principal sachem when he wants to marry a slave. So that will be the easiest of all. I'll present Olu-a-su with my horse. He's wanted it from the moment I brought it here."

"You're—very kind."

"Since the animal was stolen," Jonathan replied dryly, "he didn't cost me anything."

"Then, if you're willing, there's nothing to lose."

"You understand," he added quickly, "this isn't like a real marriage. It won't be binding on either of us, and the first chance we get at Fort Albany, I'll hand you over to the colonial authorities so you'll be free."

"Oh, I understand. And I certainly wouldn't want to hamper your own freedom."

The ironic bite in her voice surprised him, but he had learned it was impossible to make sense out of her reactions to any situation. "You won't cause me any inconvenience, I assure you, and it's the least I can do for you. And when everything else is settled, you might even become more reasonable and work out some sort of agreement in our property dispute."

Three days later a brief ceremony took place in the long house of Olu-a-su. Jonathan, his face streaked with blue paint for the occasion, entered the presence of the sachem of three eagle feathers and raised his hand in greeting to the elders who were grouped on the opposite side of the room. Then Elizabeth came in, her hands folded over her breasts, her head lowered.

She was required to cast herself at the feet of the warrior who would become her husband and remain prostrate while the elders chanted an incantation. They used an archaic form of the Seneca language, so only a portion of what they said was intelligible. As nearly as Jonathan could make out, they were asking the gods of the tribe to keep watch on the marriage and make certain the squaw was obedient to her husband at all times and in all matters.

Finally, Olu-a-su's senior squaw entered the long house and draped Elizabeth in a loose-fitting, fringed dress of cured skins, a symbol of her new status. The new squaw, no longer a slave, was permitted to rise and return to her husband's hut, where she was expected to begin the preparation of their usual evening meal.

Jonathan presented his gelding to Olu-a-su, and the principal sachem's attitude indicated his obvious belief that this was the most important part of the ceremony.

Mi-la-ine wanted Jonathan to go fishing with him, so they spent the afternoon on the far side of the lake, paddling back shortly before nightfall. Jonathan, carrying his catch of seven fish, went through the town to his hut, where Elizabeth had built a fire in the outdoor pit and was waiting for it to grow before roasting their venison. He noted that she seemed slightly constrained and discovered that he, too, felt somewhat ill at ease.

"These are for your wedding supper," he said, showing her the string of fish.

Her laugh was forced. "Very nice."

He boned and scaled the fish, taking care to perform the task inside the hut, where a warrior couldn't be seen doing what was considered a squaw's work.

Elizabeth watched him. "Every girl thinks about marriage and

219

wonders about her future. I never thought mine—would be like this."

"You'll soon be rid of me," Jonathan told her. "A messenger from the Mohawk arrived this noon with word that the council will meet in nine days."

Elizabeth took the fish from him without comment and went out to the fire to cook them. Jonathan waited inside the hut, knowing the Seneca would have thought it unseemly for a warrior to loiter in the vicinity when his meal was being prepared.

Eventually she brought the food into the hut, and he was conscious of the increased tension, although unable to recognize its cause, and they ate in a deepening silence. Then the girl threw a few logs of slow-burning hard maple onto the indoor fire and went to the corner to which she had been consigned as a servant. She stretched out on the ground, turning her back to him, and a few moments later he heard the sounds of soft weeping.

He was uncertain whether he had offended her or whether the mockery of an Indian wedding was responsible for her tears. All he knew, or thought he knew, was that she wanted to be alone.

Scores of houses had been built on the banks of the Hudson River, and others, behind them, perched on the sides of the gentle, rolling hills of the town that stood at the gateway of the Iroquois country. Dominating the community, situated on the highest hill in the vicinity, was the citadel from which the town took its name, Fort Albany. Its buildings made of heavy logs and its high palisade fashioned of sharpened poles, it was an enlargement of Fort Orange, the original defense bastion erected by the Dutch soon after they had founded the community in 1614.

Many meetings of consequence, including several intercolonial conferences, had taken place in the town during its one hundred and forty years of existence, but none had been so important as the gathering in the early spring of 1754. New York, the host colony, had assigned seven officials as its delegates, and the Pennsylvania commission was headed by her most distinguished citizen, Benjamin Franklin. New Hampshire and Rhode Island sent both civilians and militia officers, as did Virginia and Maryland. Never before had so many colonies sent official delegates to a meeting, which eased the disappointment of the representatives over the absence of Massachusetts Bay and Connecticut, New Jersey and Delaware. The Carolinas and Georgia were so far away that no one had expected them to attend.

Three all-day sessions were held before the sachems of the Iroquois arrived. At the instigation of Franklin, a resolution was passed urging the formation of a single, unified military command to take charge of the coming war with France. The vote in favor of the resolution was enthusiastically unanimous, even though everyone present knew he was indulging in a dream. London, afraid the colonies might become too strong, would be certain to veto the plan, and Massachusetts Bay, always jealous of Virginia and Pennsylvania, undoubtedly would refuse to cooperate.

The delegates were realists and also adopted a somewhat less ambitious plan, which was suggested in a memorandum written by George Washington of Virginia, recently promoted to the rank of colonel in his colony's militia. His assumption of command in Virginia prevented him from attending the meeting, but he was vitally interested in the deliberations and suggested that each colony set up a liaison office for the purpose of keeping the others informed of all military activities within its borders.

William Johnson of New York explained his plan for winning the support of the Iroquois, and his success in the past won him the unqualified support of his colleagues. He was granted the power to deal with the savages as he saw fit. The others understood that the Indians would become suspicious if Johnson had to submit a proposed treaty to each of the colonies represented at the meeting, so the delegates agreed, in advance, to accept any treaty terms that Johnson arranged. This exraordinary right was unique in American colonial history, and Johnson promised he would not abuse the trust placed in him.

The Mohawk and the Onondaga, whom many of the Iroquois regarded as a subnation, were the first to arrive, pitching their tents on Indian Hill at the outskirts of Albany, where warriors who came to the town for the purpose of trading furs usually lived. The Mohawk established themselves near the summit on the west and north sides of the slope, the Onondaga contenting themselves with a lower place. The Cayuga and Tuscarora arrived simultaneously, the former satisfying themselves with a low place on the slope, while the latter, although a large and powerful nation, did not push for a high position because they were newcomers to the Confederation.

The Oneida took places on the southern and eastern sides of the hill, but were careful to leave space open above them. The Seneca were the last to appear, their delegation including several sachems of one eagle feather as well as all who wore three or two. These proud warriors, some accompanied by their squaws, automatically occupied the heights on the southern and eastern slopes, where they would enjoy the most sunlight, and took possession of the crest as well. This gesture was enough to convince the colonials unfamiliar with the Iroquois that they were the dominant nation in the Confederation.

Jonathan wanted to make no move that might jeopardize his standing with the Seneca at a time when Johnson and the other American representatives were relying on his support. So he did not go down into the town to call on Dr. Franklin and the other delegates but contented himself with remaining close to the tent of skins that Elizabeth, aided by two or three other squaws, had raised for him.

The Iroquois, all in full ceremonial paint, paraded to Fort Albany on the morning of their critical conference, and most of the four thousand residents of the town gathered to watch them in silence. The Mohawk, who lived closest to the community and long had dealt with William Johnson, felt that they should lead the procession, but the Seneca had no intention of giving up the place of honor, and their brothers, who had known them to make war for lesser insults, stepped aside for them.

The delegates awaited the savages in the log building that long had been used as the garrison's officer mess hall, and Johnson astonished some of his colleagues when he greeted each of the Indians by name. The colonials unfamiliar with Jonathan's story had been warned that an Englishman would be masquerading as a Seneca, so no one commented on his presence, although some stared hard at him.

Pipes of friendship were passed, and even though the meeting convened early in the morning, William Johnson saw to it that a hearty, hot meal was served. Most of the Indians were fond of a Scottish dish, oatmeal, so large bowls of it were served, along with grilled fish, roasted beef and venison, broiled chunks of bacon, and a very sweet pudding made with rice that Johnson had taken care to order from South Carolina for the occasion.

The better part of the morning was spent in feasting and the exchange of speeches in which each side proclaimed its undying friendship for the other. Then, the formalities having been completed, Johnson got down to business.

"France, the enemy of England," he said, speaking in the Mohawk patois which all of the warriors understood, "has promised many things to the Iroquois if they will become the brothers of France. They will give the Iroquois many fire sticks, much fire, and many bullets. They will give the Iroquois blankets and iron pots to cook their food. They will give the Iroquois fine knives. They will give the Iroquois much gold.

"Will the English give to the Iroquois, their brothers, these gifts? The English promise their brothers as many fire sticks as they can spare. They will give their brothers as much fire and as many bullets as they can spare. They have already given their brothers blankets and knives and iron cooking pots.

"George, the chief sachem of the English, has more wealth than Louis, the chief sachem of the French. But he does not promise his brothers, the Iroquois, that he will give them much gold. George is an honest man, but Louis is not. George has no gold to give, so he does not promise. Louis has no gold to give, but he promises. He cannot keep his promise. He will give only a little gold. Then the stream will become dry, like the beds of the little rivers when the gods of rain and thunder do not come.

"But George, the chief sachem of the English, will give a far more precious gift to his brothers, the Iroquois. He will make a sacred promise to the Iroquois, and he will put that promise on the writing bark of the English, so the sons of the Iroquois, and their sons, for all time, will see the promise and will know that the sons of George, and their sons, will keep the promise. The English will not try to steal the lands and hunting grounds of the Iroquois. As long as the gods of the sun and the moon, the gods of night and of day shall live, those lands will belong only to the Iroquois.

"The Iroquois know Johnson, their brother. He promises that the English will keep their word forever. This promise the English will make, if their brothers will go to war with them against the French."

He sat down, and in the long, eerie silence that followed, additional pipes of friendship were smoked. Then the Indians withdrew, the leaders of each nation adjourning to its own meeting place within the Fort Albany compound to consider the proposal.

The Seneca elected to hold their council in the open and sat cross-legged on the infantry parade ground. They spoke in order of seniority, the eldest of the sachems of three eagle feathers speaking first. No one wasted words, and the tenor of each address was roughly the same.

All foreigners, the principal sachems declared, made many promises, but, as the Indians had learned to their sorrow, promises were broken as readily as they were made. The Seneca knew little about the French, slightly more about the English. They had enjoyed good trade relations with the English, but now they were learning that the French paid higher prices for furs. Above all, since the French intended to give them gold in the immediate future, they believed that gift should be accepted in preference to an English promise that might become meaningless in the years ahead.

The sachems of two eagle feathers, who were younger and more aggressive, questioned the reasoning of their elders. The lands in Canada, where the French lived, were sparsely occupied. The French had established only one large city, Quebec, and their towns could be counted on the fingers of two hands. It was true they had built a great fort, Louisburg, on an island far to the north, in the land of the Abnaki, but they had fewer ships of war than the English, who might take the island from them. The English were more numerous. Philadelphia, Boston, and New York Town were great cities. It was said that distant Charleston also was a great city. In addition the English had many smaller towns, which were larger than the towns of the Iroquois.

Therefore, if they became the allies of France, they would be the enemies of the English. Johnson would not forgive them and, if the English won, might drive them from their homes and hunting grounds. In that event French gold and weapons would prove useless, so they would be wise to consider carefully before making a final decision.

One by one the sachems of one eagle feather asked to be excused from making their opinions known to the council. If their superiors could not agree, they preferred to remain silent. Jonathan, the last to be asked his views, did not share their reluctance. "The men-from-across-the-sea have two faces," he said. "Jo-na-tan knows this."

The Seneca, challenged by his candor, gave him their undivided attention.

"The French," he declared, "will be the brothers of the Iroquois for a few winters and summers. When all of the Indian nations of the New World trade their furs for the gold and fire sticks of the French, the French will pay only what they would give to a beggar. The Indians will have no choice, so the French will abuse them."

Several of the sachems of three eagle feathers saw the validity of his argument and, making no attempt to remain impassive within the circle of their own council, nodded in agreement.

"If the French drive the English out of the New World, they will not need the friendship of the Iroquois. But they will keep the friendship of those who long have been their brothers. They will keep the friendship of the Huron, of the Ottawa, of the Algonkin, of the Abnaki. They will become greedy for land. They will seek the land of the Iroquois. That land the Ottawa, the Huron, the Algonkin, and the Abnaki long have wanted. The Indian nations of the north lack the strength and courage to take those lands from the Iroquois. But the French, who have many fire sticks, will help them.

"The French lack the courage of the Iroquois. But they have

225

many warriors who have the skill of Jo-na-tan when they shoot their fire sticks."

This revelation made an impression on all of the Seneca, who had not expected to hear an admission that his marksmanship could be equaled by anyone.

"The French and their brothers will win. The Iroquois will lose their lands, their hunting grounds, and their honor." Jonathan paused dramatically.

His words were having an effect, and a number of the sachems, including the principal leaders, stirred uncomfortably.

"The English also have two faces," he said gravely.

Aware of his own background, the Seneca leaned forward, listening avidly.

"The English also want more land. The English also want more furs. They, too, are greedy, but their greed is not like the greed of the French. Always they will want more furs, so they will pay for skins. Always." Daring to depart from the Indian style of oratory, which precluded broad gestures, Jonathan pointed in turn at each of the sachems of three eagle feathers. "The fathers of the Seneca will keep their lands and hunting grounds if they become the brothers of the English. The sons of the Seneca, and their sons, will keep their lands and hunting grounds.

"The English will not steal from their brothers, the Iroquois. They will take the lands of other tribes. They will take the lands of tribes that lack the strength and courage of the Iroquois. Always the nations of the Iroquois will remain strong. That is why the English will remain their brothers."

His argument was identical to that which William Johnson had used for years in his dealings with the Mohawk, and the Seneca knew it. In Jonathan they saw a foreigner like Johnson, two members of the same, unique breed, willing to criticize their own people for the benefit of Indians who had become their brothers.

Li-solu was overwhelmed by his friend's oratory. Snatching a knife from his belt and brandishing it over his head, he shouted, "Death to the French! Let the Seneca become the brothers of the English!"

A number of other junior leaders picked up the cry, and soon all were clamoring. Only the sachems of three eagle feathers remained silent.

Jonathan had intended to make a somewhat longer speech but thought it wise to let the savages conclude it for him on the emphatically positive note. So, without further ado, he resumed his seat in the circle.

Soon the sachems of two and one eagle feathers were dismissed, the principal leaders remaining for a private conference before joining the other senior leaders of the Iroquois for the purpose of making a final decision.

Jonathan had done everything within his power to influence the Seneca in favor of the English alliance, and the time had come for him to turn to personal matters. Returning to Indian Hill, he found Elizabeth seated at a fire near the crest, where a number of squaws were warming themselves.

She came to him at once, as Seneca custom required.

"We're going into town now," Jonathan told her. "Are there any belongings in the tent that you want to take with you?"

Elizabeth's eyes widened as she grasped the significance of his words. "None," she said.

A strange, constricted feeling in his chest made it difficult for him to speak, so he turned away and started in the direction of Fort Albany.

The girl, playing the role of an Indian squaw for the last time, meekly fell in behind him.

They had walked only a short distance when Li-solu appeared, hailing his friend. "Li-solu and Jo-na-tan," he said, "will go tavern in town and eat food of English." His grin indicated embarrassment in acknowledging a liking for the dishes of civilization.

Jonathan hesitated for only a moment. He had wanted to hand Elizabeth to the English colonial authorities in private, so any possible protest on the part of the Seneca would be muted. But he was acting within his rights when he disposed of a squaw and could only hope that Li-solu, who was seemingly unaware of the girl's presence, would not protest.

"Come along," he said calmly, and the warrior fell in beside him, with Elizabeth still trailing behind.

King James Street, named after the town's first English benefactor when he had been Duke of York and Earl of Albany, was the only cobbled road in the frontier community. Most of the leading shops, trading posts, and inns were situated on it, and it was crowded, as usual, with local citizens and men from New York Town. No one paid any attention to the Indian trio, and Jonathan wryly congratulated himself on the authenticity of Elizabeth's appearance and his own.

Suddenly the girl gasped.

Jonathan turned to her, as did Li-solu, who was startled by the unusual gesture of a squaw calling attention to herself.

"Andrews and his daughter," she murmured. "Straight ahead."

All three stared at the couple who had been responsible for so much of their difficulty. Apparently they had been on a buying spree since coming to Fort Albany. Andrews was dressed in a new suit and matching cloak of maroon velvet, his knee-high frontier boots the only concession to the wilderness. Felicity, dark curls cascading down her back, was exceptionally attractive in a gown of yellow satin, over which she had thrown a cape of green brocade with a beaver collar.

Li-solu reacted before Jonathan could stop him. Moving forward swiftly, the Seneca said, "You Andrews."

At Jonathan's quiet signal Elizabeth lowered her face to avoid recognition.

But she could have saved herself the trouble. Neither Andrews nor his daughter looked in her direction. Barely glancing at Li-solu, they did not recall him. "What do you want?"

The Seneca shrugged, his eyes cold, but made no reply.

Andrews laughed. "How do you like that, my dear? We've become such prominent landowners that even these savage scum know us." Still laughing, he offered her his arm and they moved on.

The trio continued to walk down King James Street, each busy with private thoughts. Without explanation Jonathan pointed toward the fort and started up the hill toward it, the others accompanying him.

Two sentries were stationed outside the main gate, and Jonathan approached one of them. "Is Dr. Franklin inside, do you know?"

The young militiaman blinked in astonishment at the warrior who had addressed him in an upper-class English drawl. "Yes, he's at headquarters," the soldier said, recovering. "But he's meeting with the other delegates and can't be disturbed."

"Take the lady to him," Jonathan said, "and you'll be surprised to see how quickly he leaves that meeting!"

Elizabeth's eyes met Jonathan's for a long moment, and she started to speak but changed her mind and followed the dumfounded militiaman into the grounds of the fort.

Jonathan watched her, his heart suddenly heavy, and when she looked back at him over her shoulder he had to struggle to prevent himself from calling out to her, from begging her to halt. Then she disappeared from sight, and he took a deep breath, steadying himself before turning to Li-solu.

The Seneca had vanished.

Assuming he had gone ahead to a tavern, Jonathan headed back toward King James Street. The realization that he had actually parted with Elizabeth and that he might not see her again filled him with a sense of despair unlike any feeling he had ever known. He had been right to terminate the relationship abruptly, he believed, since farewells would have been painful as well as pointless. But he couldn't help wishing there had been some other solution, some other way to work out their relationship.

Anxious to keep busy, he searched in every tavern and inn on King James Street and elsewhere in Fort Albany but could find no sign of Li-solu. Conscious of the fact that he had no money to buy a meal or drink for himself, he finally went for a long walk down the bank of the Hudson River before the approach of night sent him back to Indian Hill.

There, with no squaw to prepare his meal, he had to join the other warriors who were forced to cook their own food. But he had little appetite and became impatient for the others to depart with him for the fort, where the principal sachems of the Seneca and the senior leaders of the other Iroquois tribes, who were still in council, would make known their final decision.

Everyone smeared more paint on his face and torso, and at last the sachems of two and one eagle feathers were ready to leave. As they made their way down the hill in a body someone fell in beside Jonathan, who felt a surge of anger when he saw Li-solu.

On the verge of demanding to know where his friend had gone, Jonathan said nothing. Dangling from Li-solu's belt was a fresh scalp, and a glance at the balding patch of skin and wiry hair identified the Seneca's victim. Never again would Andrews cheat anyone.

But there were complications. The authorities at Fort Albany would intervene if they learned that a Pennsylvanian had been murdered and scalped. Li-solu was sufficiently familiar with the laws of civilized people to have disposed of Andrews' body and was clever enough to have hidden it so it wouldn't be found. But there was one aspect of the situation he might have overlooked.

Jonathan addressed him in English, so the other warriors wouldn't understand what was being said. "I hope Andrews' daughter won't complain to the authorities that her father is missing. Felicity is the sort who can cause trouble anywhere, for anyone."

His friend's shrug indicated complete lack of concern.

"Do you have any idea where she is?"

"For long time Li-solu want slave woman," the Seneca said. "Not to make squaw. Not to give back to English. Keep for all time a slave woman."

Jonathan chuckled and felt that, although the punishment might be drastic according to the standards of the society he had known, he had become enough of a barbarian to approve. Certainly he couldn't feel sorry for Felicity, but he found himself sympathizing with Li-solu. The fortitude and patience of the Seneca would be tested to the utmost, repeatedly, in the years ahead.

The lesser chieftains of the other Iroquois nations were filing into the fort and making their way to the officers' mess hall, and the junior Seneca sachems joined their colleagues. The older leaders were already in their places, as were the colonial delegates, and the new arrivals moved silently to their seats.

When all were in their places, William Johnson rose, his face reflecting none of the apprehension he was feeling. "Have the mighty Iroquois decided their future?" he asked. "Will they become the brothers of the English or the brothers of the French?"

The oldest of the principal sachems, an Oneida with a scarred face, pushed himself to his feet.

Only his peers, who already knew the decision, looked complacent. The colonial delegates were unable to conceal their tension, and the younger sachems, although outwardly phlegmatic, stared straight ahead, a sure sign they, too, were concerned.

"The nations of the Iroquois Confederation," the elderly Oneida declared, "are the brothers of the English. Death to the French!"

The spontaneous cheer that greeted the announcement made the thick log walls tremble.

A victory in the coming war was assured, Jonathan thought. The campaign might be long, and undoubtedly would be viciously fought, but the English colonials, supported by London and actively assisted by the most powerful group of Indians in the New World, could not be defeated. The French were resourceful and their savage allies cunning, but they would be outnumbered by men equally courageous and ingenious, and eventually would be forced to their knees.

William Johnson had already prepared the text of a treaty of alliance, a simple document that placed emphasis on the pledge of the British government and the separate governments of the colonies to recognize the property rights of the Iroquois in perpetuity.

The senior chieftains needed little discussion, and within a short time the treaty was approved.

Only one immediate item of business remained. Johnson asked each of the tribes to appoint three leaders who would perform military liaison duties, coordinating the activities of the tribes with those of the militia of each colony, who would appoint a similar body. It was obvious that this point had been discussed at some time during the afternoon: Johnson named the colonial representatives,

231

and then a senior chieftain of each Indian nation announced his tribe's appointments.

The first to stand was Olu-a-su of the Seneca. All representatives of the greatest of warrior nations were themselves great warriors, he said. All were leaders of standing, sachems of two eagle feathers. The first he named was Jo-na-tan.

The appointment of the Iroquois liaison officers was the last business of the night, and at Johnson's signal a hearty feast was served. In addition to the usual roasted meats and grilled fish there were many delicacies, the ladies of Fort Albany having spent the past few days cooking and baking in preparation for just such an occasion.

Jonathan still had no appetite, however, and, his head whirling, went out into the open for a breath of air to help clear his mind. But he had no opportunity to ponder. Someone followed him from the mess hall, and he turned to see Dr. Franklin.

"Let me offer you my congratulations on your promotion, Lewis. Or should I refer to you as Jo-na-tan?"

It was difficult to return his smile. "I'm pleased that the Seneca have so much faith in me," Jonathan replied, "but I'm not sure I can accept. I've been thinking of returning to England, and I imagine I can find some ship's master who'll give me my passage if I'll work my way. Now that the Iroquois have joined us, there's no doubt in my mind that we'll win the war."

"In due time, and unless something extraordinary happens, I'm certain we will." Franklin's gaze was steady. "Earlier this evening we had some preliminary talks with the Iroquois about the war. Our militia will have to cross colonial borders, and our allies will do the same. We've just learned, for example, that the French are building a citadel at the forks of the Ohio and calling it Fort Duquesne. We'll have to drive them out, and it's been tentatively decided to give the task to General Braddock and his regulars. Colonel Washington's Virginians are the strongest colonials, so they'll help, even though the French, technically, are invading Pennsylvania. Of course we'll have work of our own—are you interested, Lewis?"

"Please go on, sir."

"Our primary concern is western Pennsylvania, the Presque Isle

erritory, and western New York, which is the land of the Seneca.
The Pennsylvania commissioners have proposed a joint campaign,
and the Seneca chiefs approve."

"That makes sense."

"Great sense. Our principal need is for leaders, men who understand both the French and their Indian allies. That's why we
thought of offering you command of a mixed regiment, Lewis, with
the rank of lieutenant colonel. A battalion of Pennsylvania militia
and another of Seneca warriors. I know of no one else qualified for
the post, so we'll have to change our plans if you really want to go
back to England."

The opportunity was dazzling, and Jonathan stammered his
thanks but was still upset. "There's one thing holding me back, Dr.
Franklin, so I'd like to think about this for a little while. Meanwhile, I wonder if you could deliver a message for me. It concerns a
property dispute that you know all about—"

Franklin cut him off, took his arm, and walked rapidly across the
compound with him. Several sentries stared at them curiously, surprised that the most distinguished of Americans should be on such
friendly terms with a savage. Halting at the door of a cabin that
ordinarily served as the residence of a senior officer, Franklin rapped
hard on the door.

"Some messages should be delivered in person," he said, and
headed back to the mess hall.

The door opened and Elizabeth stood in the frame. For a moment Jonathan did not recognize her: she was wearing a dress and
other clothing provided by the Fort Albany ladies, her hair was its
own color again, and the stain had been scrubbed from her skin.
She seemed more delicate yet more austere than he remembered
her as a civilized woman, and he felt distinctly uncomfortable.

"I didn't mean to disturb you, but Dr. Franklin brought me
here—"

"Come in, please," she interrupted, and led him into a small parlor in which several oil lamps were burning. "Won't you sit down?"

"I'd smear Seneca paint and oil on the furniture," he said, more
conscious than ever of his savage appearance. "I just wanted to tell

you that you'll have no problem taking possession of your prop‐
erties. Andrews is—gone. And so is his daughter."

Elizabeth understood it would be undiplomatic to question him
Offering her thanks, she changed the subject. "Dr. Franklin tol‐
me this evening that the Seneca were promoting you. And tha‐
Pennsylvania is offering you a command of a kind that will make i‐
possible for you to accept both."

Jonathan nodded, unable to find the words he wanted.

"I think that's wonderful for you! You've certainly earned every‐
thing you've won."

"I may—go back to England."

"Oh." For a moment she looked crushed. "Is that what you want?"

"No!" Jonathan didn't realize he was shouting. "This has become
my land, and I want to fight for her! I've won my own battle with
the wilderness, and I can't go back to another kind of world. Thi‐
has become home!"

"I'm so glad. For you," she amended hastily.

He calmed himself with an effort. "I'd advise you not to go back
to Presque Isle just yet. That area is part of my command, and I wan‐
to make certain we drive out the French and their friends before
you settle on your estates again."

"Dr. Franklin," she said after a slight pause, "suggests there's ‐
way to settle our property dispute amicably."

"Keep both estates," he told her. "I'll earn others for myself afte‐
the war is over."

"There's no need for you to give up your rights."

"This afternoon, after I left you here, I spent hours wandering
through the town. I wonder if you know there are eight churche‐
in Fort Albany. Think of it, in a town this small." He took a ste‐
closer, and his voice gained confidence. "So you'll have quite a choice
selecting the one you'll want for your wedding."

"I've already chosen it, but I couldn't tell you until you asked m‐
to marry you," Elizabeth said, her words muffled as Jonathan em‐
braced her.

There are a lot more
where this one came from!

ORDER your FREE catalog of ACE paperbacks here. We have hundreds of inexpensive
books where this one came from priced from
75¢ to $2.50. Now you can read all the books
you have always wanted to at tremendous
savings. Order your *free* catalog of ACE
paperbacks now.

ACE BOOKS • P.O. Box 690, Rockville Centre, N.Y. 11570

76b

More Fiction Bestsellers From Ace Books!

Sharp Shooting and Rugged Adventure from America's Favorite Western Writers